# Winter of the

# Metal People

*Dennis Herrick*
*april 12, 2014*

## DENNIS HERRICK

# Winter of the Metal People

For information about special discounts for bulk purchases, please contact Sunbury Press, Inc. Wholesale Department at (855) 338-8359 or orders@sunburypress.com.

To request one of our authors for speaking engagements or book signings, please contact Sunbury Press, Inc. Publicity Department at publicity@sunburypress.com.

FIRST SUNBURY PRESS EDITION
*Printed in the United States of America*
June 2013

Trade Paperback ISBN: 978-1-62006-237-1
Mobipocket format (Kindle) ISBN: 978-1- 62006-238-8
ePub format (Nook) ISBN: 978-1-62006-239-5

Published by:
**Sunbury Press**
Mechanicsburg, PA
www.sunburypress.com

Mechanicsburg, Pennsylvania   USA

# Praise for *Winter of the Metal People* and author Dennis Herrick

"A riveting historical novel of immense scholarship and insight. Dennis Herrick makes the story of the first American Indians in the West to face the military might of European forces as vivid and real as if Coronado's expedition had ridden out of Mexico yesterday. *Winter of the Metal People* will forever influence your perception of the stunning landscapes and rich cultures of the Southwest."

—Margaret Coel, author of *Killing Custer*

"In *Winter of the Metal People* Dennis Herrick, journalist and award-winning writer of fiction, offers us a consummately humane novel of the first encounters between Pueblo peoples of the Southwest and a European, African, and Native American expedition led by Francisco Vázquez de Coronado in the early 1540s. Herrick skillfully brings the Native side of those encounters into vivid focus. We are brought to imagine the complexity and variety of Pueblo reactions as they struggle to come to grips with the foreign presence and how it violently impacts their lives and traditions."

—Richard Flint, Historian
Author of *No Settlement, No Conquest:
A History of the Coronado Entrada*

*Fiction reveals truths that reality obscures.*
—Ralph Waldo Emerson

# To Evelyn and Hiram Herrick

Grateful acknowledgment is made to authors Richard Flint and Shirley Cushing Flint, as well as to University of New Mexico Press, for permission to reprint excerpts from *Great Cruelties Have Been Reported: The 1544 Investigation of the Coronado Expedition,* © 2013, containing testimonies from members of the Coronado expedition; from *Documents of the Coronado Expedition, 1539-1542,* © 2012, which contains Flint translations of several key documents from the period; from *No Settlement No Conquest: A History of the Coronado Entrada* © 2008; and from the anthologies titled *The Coronado Expedition: From the Distance of 460 years,* © 2003, and *The Latest Word from 1540: People, Places, and Portrayals of the Coronado Expedition,* © 2011. Thanks also to University of New Mexico Press for permission to reprint excerpts from *Narratives of the Coronado Expedition, 1540-42,* ©1940.

Grateful acknowledgment is made to the Indian Pueblo Cultural Center of Albuquerque for permission to quote from and refer to its museum narratives; to Duke University Press for permission to reprint excerpts from A. Grove Day's 1940 article, "Mota Padilla on the Coronado Expedition" in *Hispanic American Historical Review*; and to the many other sources cited in the bibliography and historical notes on the book's complementary website at http://tinyurl.com/d7wfb69.

*One of the great shortcomings in the early history of the western hemisphere is our lack of a record of what the Indians thought ... If we only knew what he said and thought about our ancestors.*

— Historian Herbert E. Bolton

# CONTENTS

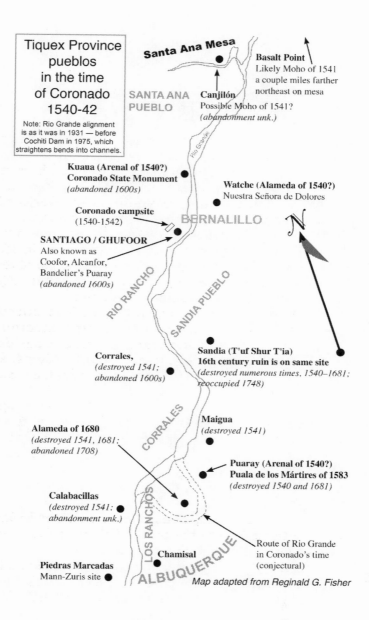

**Tiquex Province pueblos in the time of Coronado 1540-42**

Note: Rio Grande alignment is as it was in 1931 — before Cochiti Dam in 1975, which straightens bends into channels.

Santa Ana Mesa

**Basalt Point**
Likely Moho of 1541
a couple miles farther
northeast on mesa

SANTA ANA PUEBLO

**Canjilón**
Possible Moho of 1541?
*(abandonment unk.)*

Rio Grande

**Kuaua (Arenal of 1540?)**
**Coronado State Monument**
*(abandoned 1600s)*

**Watche (Alameda of 1540?)**
Nuestra Señora de Dolores

**Coronado campsite**
(1540-1542)

BERNALILLO

N

**SANTIAGO / GHUFOOR**
Also known as
Coofor, Alcanfor,
Bandelier's Puaray
*(abandoned 1600s)*

RIO RANCHO

SANDIA PUEBLO

**Corrales,**
*(destroyed 1541;
abandoned 1600s)*

**Sandia (T'uf Shur T'ia)**
**16th century ruin is on same site**
*(destroyed numerous times, 1540–1681;
reoccupied 1748)*

CORRALES

**Maigua**
*(destroyed 1541)*

**Alameda of 1680**
*(destroyed 1541, 1681;
abandoned 1708)*

**Puaray (Arenal of 1540?)**
**Puala de los Mártires of 1583**
*(destroyed 1540 and 1681)*

**Calabacillas**
*(destroyed 1541;
abandonment unk.)*

LOS RANCHOS

Route of Rio Grande
in Coronado's time
(conjectural)

**Chamisal**

**Piedras Marcadas**
Mann-Zuris site

ALBUQUERQUE

Map adapted from Reginald G. Fisher

This drawing is adapted from topographical maps in Reginald G. Fisher's 1931 survey. Shaded text designates locations of today's cities and pueblos. A second Bernalillo area pueblo washed away in an 1800s flood. The map covers about 16 miles from the top to the bottom.

# PROLOGUE

In the first four decades after Columbus landed in the Caribbean, Europeans took military control of several great native civilizations in Mexico, Central America, and South America.

Genocidal war, murder, and unintentional disease decimated Indian populations. Other major causes of fatalities were the mines and tribute-paying Spanish jurisdictions known as *encomiendas*. Colonists used Indians for slave-like forced labor in both. The tribute payments on the encomiendas impoverished the Indians and made some Spanish owners fabulously wealthy.

In that short time, the Spaniards all but wiped out the Caribbean's tribes, replacing them with African slaves. In Mexico the Spaniards—with the generally uncredited assistance of tens of thousands of Tlaxcalan Indian allies—defeated the Triple Alliance Indian empire of the Mexicas, now known as Aztecs.

Even the *conquistadores*, the conquerors, had described the Mexica/Aztec capital of Tenochtitlán as the most wonderful and busiest city in the world. They immediately began demolishing it. With the rubble, they built churches, government buildings, and a crowded European-style streetscape that they renamed Mexico City.

Using that conquered city as a base, the Spaniards spread outward, plundering and killing Indians to the west and south, eventually reaching the Inca empire in Peru. Again with vast numbers of Indian allies, they began a war there in 1532 that would last forty years.

Then rumors began floating that there were wealthy Indian cities to the north as well.

Viceroy Antonio de Mendoza, Spain's administrator in Mexico City, won the right to explore to the north. This time, however, he decided Spanish conquest would be more restrained.

Despite his opulent lifestyle, Mendoza was more enlightened than most Spaniards in the "New Spain" of the Americas. He also was coming under pressure to be less rapacious for the following reasons:

- Citizens of Spain, gradually being made aware of the atrocities being committed by colonists and conquistadors across the ocean, were appalled at the deaths of millions of Indians in such a short period.

- Spain's king, Carlos I, who also ruled as Holy Roman Emperor Carlos V, still wanted the New World's gold but wanted it taken with less brutality.
- Pope Paul III declared in 1537 that the Indians were humans who had souls. He declared as a point of Catholic doctrine that they should not be enslaved or dealt with violently.
- Bartolomé de las Casas, a Dominican friar, had worked tirelessly in defense of Indian rights and for their peaceful conversion to Catholicism. By the 1530s, he had become a man to be reckoned with because of friends in the king's court in Seville and in the Vatican. Spain's citizenry, king, and the pope were all coming around to his way of thinking.

In this context, Mendoza set out to determine the truth of rumors that great wealth could be found to the north, where Friar Marcos de Niza reported discovering the Seven Cities of Cíbola. Colonists began referring to them as the fabled and wealthy Seven Cities of Antilia, said to have been set up in an unknown land centuries before by seven Portuguese bishops.

In 1540 Viceroy Mendoza launched a two-pronged invasion into the unknown land north of Mexico. He sent enough force to conquer if necessary. For the first time, however, he also issued orders that Indians were to be treated humanely.

By water went Hernando de Alarcón. He would sail a fleet of ships up the Sea of Cortés to the turbulent mouth of the Colorado River, which Spaniards would call the *Río de Tizon*. Alarcón then proceeded up the river in boats against the current, passing between what would become the states of Arizona and California.

By land, Mendoza sent a twenty-nine-year-old conquistador named Francisco Vázquez de Coronado with more than three-hundred-fifty European men-at-arms and about two thousand Mexican Indian allies, including a large contingent of Aztec and Tarascan Indians. The expedition took thousands of horses, mules, cattle, and sheep. They would travel up the Mexican coast, cross the Sierra Madre Mountains, and head up the valley of the San Pedro River.

With an advance group so he could travel faster, Coronado entered today's southeast Arizona near present-day Bisbee. The Spaniards would arrive in what is now the U.S. almost half a century before the first English colonists would land at Roanoke, Virginia, and eighty years before the Pilgrims reached Plymouth Rock.

Alarcón's intent was to ferry goods to resupply Coronado. But as Alarcón moved north and Coronado moved northeast, both came to realize the distance had become too large for resupply by ships.

Encountering hundreds of Indians on his second day on the river, Alarcón refused to panic. "Looking at them, I began to make signs of peace ... trying to make them understand by this and other signs that I did not seek war with them," Alarcón reported. He threw down his sword and shield, lowered his flag, and told his men to sit in their boats. "Taking some of the things I carried for trading, I called to the natives and offered to give these articles to them."

As he passed out glass beads, mirrors, strips of colored cloth, and other trade items, the Indians returned the favor by giving him corn, beans, and bread.

Later he encountered a thousand warriors armed and painted for war, but he won them over peacefully as well. Repeatedly, he told the Indians he met that he wished to be their brother, not their master. His interpreters learned how to communicate with them so they could understand each other.

Alarcón soon learned that Coronado's destination of Cíbola was forty days travel away across a forbidding desert landscape.

Although Alarcón wouldn't find out until later, less than seven weeks earlier Coronado had attacked the first town of Cíbolans, who are known today as Zunis.

Indians brought the first news about Coronado to Alarcón near present-day Yuma, Arizona. Alarcón said they reported that at Cíbola "there were bearded men like us who said they were Christians." Excitedly, they told him the Christians rode swift beasts and killed many natives there with swords and "things that shot fire."

The Indians asked Alarcón if the Christians who attacked Cíbola might join him. If they did, he promised, they "would show everyone the same courtesy and kindness that I showed."

It astonished Alarcón that Indians knew about Coronado's attack from so far away. Alarcón returned to his ships upon "seeing that there was no way to go to Cíbola, and that if I remained longer among those people they might find me out."

Alarcón had greeted and left the Colorado River Indians in peace. Coronado would embroil the Indians near and along the Rio Grande in a merciless war.

No one could know that Coronado would do nothing of note for the rest of his short life. But he would win fame with this single armed reconnaissance into the unknown vastness north of

Mexico. History has forgotten the names of all but one of the natives he would wage war against. History would remember him. Today his name is on public spaces from schools and parks to university dormitories, most in Arizona and New Mexico. He is a heroic figure to many present-day Americans who know almost nothing about the man—and what they do know is more myth than fact.

# PART I – INVASION
## June to September 1540

An excerpt from the orders of January 6, 1540, by Spanish Viceroy Antonio de Mendoza appointing Francisco Vázquez de Coronado to lead the first expedition north of Mexico:

"God, our Lord, had been pleased that there be discovered in our times such great lands [to the north], where His Holy Name might be known and worshipped and His Holy Faith and Catholic Church enlarged and our royal patrimony increased ... [The viceroy] would send ecclesiastics ... to go to the aforesaid lands to preach and proclaim the Holy Gospel and to attract and convert the natives to the brotherhood of the Catholic Church. And then they would recognize and take us as their king and natural lord ... We name you once again as captain general of the company which is now on its way ... to reconnoiter and pacify lands and new provinces ... to attract its natives to the knowledge of our Holy Catholic Faith and to place it under our royal crown ... You may protect and defend those [lands] in our royal name, and their natives so that harm is not done to them nor any other abuse."

1

Two months before Alarcón's ships reached the *Río de Tizon*, Coronado was already plodding up a desert river valley with his advance force of seventy-five lancers on horseback, thirty men on foot with arquebus muskets, crossbows, and swords, and hundreds of Mexican Indian warriors.

The advance force's first men emerged from a cloud of sand. A strong desert wind shifted from behind and blew from the side, clearing the air so they could come into view. A fifteen-year-old boy was riding a borrowed brown horse and carrying the staff from which fluttered a large banner. Beardless, unlike most, he wore a thick elk-hide jacket and striped brown pants puffed out on his thighs. He couldn't stop coughing.

The banner pictured Viceroy Mendoza's coat of arms on one side and an image of the Virgin Mary and Christ child on the other.

Francisco Vázquez de Coronado turned his gray horse toward the boy and pulled alongside. His metal helmet glowed yellow with a patina of gold, which proclaimed his wealth and influence in being named captain general of this first foray into the unknown lands north of Mexico in 1540.

"Are you well, Alonso?" Coronado's brow wrinkled with his concern. The boy had been his page in Mexico, where Coronado had ruled as governor of the Province of New Galacia. Alonso Álvarez had become like a much younger brother to him—at least as much as a peasant boy could be. Coronado had appointed Alonso the expedition's standard-bearer.

The boy hacked some more before he could catch his breath to reply in Castilian Spanish. "Yes, my lord. The sand is out of my lungs now." He swept his hand to his mouth and coughed six more times.

Coronado laughed and batted dust out of his long and pointed black goatee.

Alonso shifted in his saddle and raised his banner a little higher. He looked forward across the desert that rolled on as far as he could see toward mountains blue in the distance. "How much farther must we go?"

"We are at the edge of the wilderness," Coronado said. "Captains Melchior Díaz and Juan de Zaldívar spent last winter at an Indian ruin our Aztec friends call Chichilticale. The captains said it is two or three days travel from here. No man knows how much farther it is to the Seven Cities of Cíbola. Not even Friar Marcos is sure, even though he said he was there last year."

"How many times has he gotten us lost already, my lord, guiding us this far? I am starting to wonder if he ever saw the Seven Cities as he says."

Coronado wiped the sweat from his forehead with a cloth he carried for that purpose in the summer heat. "We will see," he said, as he pulled his horse's reins to the side to return more to the vanguard's center. He looked back at Alonso. "I have been wondering the same thing," he said, before riding off.

Coronado had pushed this advance force ahead of the main expedition because he was eager to find the Seven Cities of Cíbola. The expeditionaries' imagination had already elevated the reported Indian towns to being the fabled Seven Cities of Antilia sprung from centuries of Spanish legend, which would be rich in China's silks, spices, and dyes.

He and many others had staked their families' fortunes on the reports Friar Marcos had brought back a year earlier. The friar had said there were Indian cities shining with gold in the sunlight, just like Coronado's armor. Windows were made of silver. There were natives with riches beyond belief, so plentiful that they could, as forced laborers, serve the encomiendas and estates that could make their Spanish owners even richer than those who brought back gold and silver.

Such incredible riches had already been found in conquering the Aztecs at Mexico City and in the war still going on against Incas in Peru. Why not to the north as well?

Spain's King Carlos I offered no support for the expedition. All the money had been raised by the expeditionaries—from nobles with vast holdings in mines or encomiendas, to the rank-and-file who had mortgaged or sold all they owned to earn a place in the expedition.

Coronado's advance force had forged weeks ahead of the bulk of the expedition. They kicked up clouds of dust in their trek that summer across the desert of bushes and bunch grasses. As dirty, hot, and sand-blown as the men in the front of the vanguard were, it was worse farther back.

"I cannot breathe," said one swordsman on foot with a shield. Another Spaniard with him carried a crossbow as they walked through the choking dust cloud that the horses churned up.

Others around them grumbled in agreement. Their faces were brown-streaked from sand and sweat, both of which burned their eyes.

"All I can taste is sand," said another man, using his sword and scabbard as a walking stick. "And I have no water left to wash even that down with."

"Stop your complaining," said a man with a smooth-bored arquebus musket across his right shoulder walking beside the crossbowman. "We are on a mission for God and the king."

"And gold," said the first man. "That will be a gift from God if I can scoop some of that gold before the nobles grab it all. I know a common man like me will never get his hands on the silk or spices. These nobles and hidalgos refuse to work or even own a shop, but they'll travel around the world for a handful of gold or spices—or a rich widow."

"There will be all the riches you can carry once we get to the Seven Cities," said another swordsman, joining their group. "That is the promise Friar Marcos gave. His word has gone across New Spain as fast as men on horses could gallop."

"I don't care anymore," said the man poking his sword and scabbard ahead of him as he walked. "For almost seven months I have been walking up river valleys, over mountains, and now into this devil-cursed desert where there is no food or villages. Thank God the natives showed us this river to walk along or we would all be dead by now."

"You have walked from Culiacán," the man with the arquebus said with a sneer. "How would you like to carry your wife from Mexico City? That is where I started. This gun seems to weigh about as much. And I swear it gets heavier with every month of walking."

"I will carry your wife if you will carry mine," the sword-and-scabbard man said. "Mine weighs as much as a cow, while I have seen yours and she is skinny as sticks and better suited to scare birds out of a field."

"No thanks," the arquebus man said. "I have carried your wife to my bed too many times already." All the men around laughed, most ending by choking on the sand they inhaled. After he'd coughed and spit, the man with the arquebus pointed to one of the officers riding ahead of them. "See that dandy," he said. "I have walked all the way every day, month after month. I have never seen him walk farther than to squat behind a bush to relieve himself."

The bitter and weary grumbling of all foot soldiers through time continued as they trudged forward. What choice did they have? They knew the nobles and officers would claim any wealth ahead in the Seven Cities of Cíbola. They'd be lucky to get a little land to settle on. Their hope was that they could build a little land into something. If the country didn't get any better, they wouldn't even get that.

Once they emerged from the mountain-lined Sonora River valley, a land renowned for its abundant cultivated and irrigated Indian tracts of corn, they turned northward along the San Pedro River through a flat, dry country. Then they were in the desert, and it seemed to go on forever under a scorching sun.

"I should have done what our captain general Coronado did," said a man with a crossbow who joined them. "He married Beatríz de Estrada four years ago, when she was only twelve. Why marry a girl so young, you ask? Because she is probably the richest young lady in all of New Spain. And now he is rich too."

"He will be richer when we reach the Seven Cities," the arquebus man said. He took off his cloth hat and beat it against his bloused, striped pants, from which puffs of sand came off to be carried away with the wind. He glanced through the haze around them at a dozen Aztec warriors walking by at a faster pace. The Aztecs carried their shields, clubs, and obsidian spears and never looked at the Spaniards. The leader wore the skin of a jaguar.

"Look at those savages," one Spaniard said. "I do not trust them."

They could see Coronado on his horse dimly through the sand storm. He stood out because of the red feather plume that festooned his helmet. A nearby rider led a mule loaded with Coronado's gold-gilded armor and some possessions.

Coronado was a man of his time. He was a rising young governor. Like many sixteenth-century Europeans, he also conducted warfare with terror tactics, torture, stake burnings, summary executions, and the slaughter or enslavement of combatants and civilians alike. His actions were in the name of God and on behalf of the Holy Roman Emperor Carlos V, who as Carlos I was king of Spain. The world's superpower in the 1500s.

"We are led by rich men like the captain general who can afford metal armor," the crossbowman said. "When any fighting starts, we must make do with quilted coats stuffed with cotton. And we walk while they ride."

"Say what you will," said another swordsman on foot who linked up with them, "but he is a governor who knows how to fight Indians. Look how he handled those rebels who killed our first field master several weeks ago. After one of the barbaric

Indians fired an arrow into the eye of Lopez de Samaniego, Coronado had us hang every Indian man and woman we could catch to teach them to fear us."

"Yes," said the crossbowman. "Last year he also put down an uprising by capturing the leader named Ayapín. He tortured the savage and then executed him by having him quartered. I was there. I saw the four horses tear off the arms and legs of Ayapín."

"We are certain to find more savages just like that at Cíbola now that we know what they did to Esteban," the swordsman said.

They knew about the Cíbolans because two other men from their world had preceded them the previous year. At that time, Mexican Indians had accompanied the gray-robed Friar Marcos de Niza, who now was guiding them back to the Seven Cities. The priest, a French Franciscan, had himself been guided then by the African slave Esteban, dressed in the finery of several Indian tribes he'd met in his travels with feathers and copper bells tied to his legs.

Coronado's goal was the first of the Seven Cities, an Indian town Friar Marcos had described as prosperous and rich in jewels and trade goods. It was the town where the Franciscan said Esteban had been killed. Friar Marcos said the town was the first of the Seven Cities of Cíbola.

The Zunis who lived there knew it as Hawikku.

# 2

Hundreds of miles from the approaching invasion and even many days travel east from Hawikku, a young warrior named Poquis relaxed on a high ridge overlooking the valley of the desert river. He knew it in his Tiwa language as Big River.

From his vantage point, black boulders lay jumbled down a long ridge overlooking Big River, which flowed in curves between its cottonwood-lined banks through the desert.

Poquis wore a cotton loincloth he had woven, tied at each hip with tassels. A short deerskin shirt covered his torso. His mate, Panpahlu, had made his deerskin moccasins with leggings that reached to the knees to protect against cactus spines and shrubs. He had wound a dark blue cotton band around his head. It held two eagle feathers in his shoulder-length black hair.

Father Sun warmed Poquis with its life force as he listened to the prayers of the old Katsina priest, Turshán, chanting in a soft voice among the rocks below. Poquis lay halfway down the ridge's east slope. On the other side, an expanse of bunch-grass prairie extended west as far as a man could walk in two days before fragmenting among cliffs and mesas. He turned his face to the east toward forested peaks of mountains beyond the river.

Poquis, four other young warriors and the Katsina priest had walked for a day to reach this sacred place. Here, religious images were pecked with pointed stones into the black boulders. Along the top of the ridge were six cones of burned rock opening into the inner world from which the ancestors had emerged. The sacred cones rose high above the river valley.

Turshán's cry of alarm snapped Poquis's reverie. Even as Poquis leaped to his feet, he heard a club thud against the priest's head. Poquis had not realized four men from the wandering tribes of the desert and mountains had crept forward. Now he could see them below where they gathered around the prostrate Tiwa priest. Poquis snatched his stone-headed club from his cotton-sash belt. He bounded down the boulders and dropped into their midst with a shout. He struck one man in the head with his club. As that man fell, the others swarmed around him. One gave a shocking blow with his club to Poquis's back. Poquis grabbed the nearest enemy and pulled him down. Each of them fought for advantage as they rolled down the desert slope in puffs of dust. The other two ran after them in a rage. Poquis leaped to his feet still clinging to his club and faced the three enemies.

They began circling him. One brandished a wood club and the other a black obsidian knife. The third man, who had lost his weapon in the tumble down the slope, looked for a chance to grab Poquis. The enemies shouted threats at Poquis as they maneuvered around him. Poquis turned, nowhere to go, parrying the thrusts of their weapons with his club.

The unarmed warrior managed to grab Poquis from behind. Poquis spun out of the man's grasp as another enemy leaped forward and swung a club, missing him. Poquis dodged his three circling opponents, keeping them at a distance with swings of his club. Knife-Wielder reached in, quick as a rattlesnake's strike, and slashed Poquis's left side below his shirt. Poquis felt warm blood running down his side and leg. As he turned to swing his club, the unarmed warrior grabbed him again from behind. Head-Pounder jumped toward him with his club raised. But the attacker jerked to a stop at the sound of arrows whizzing past the group. Poquis wrested himself free. All three enemy warriors jumped apart as more arrows flew toward them like diving hawks.

Poquis looked up to see his friend Ishpanyan and the other three in the priest's guard shooting arrows as they scrambled down the rocky hillside toward them. The enemies fled toward the river and rock-cliff mountains in the distance, zigzagging to avoid the arrows. Poquis watched them go, clutching at his side to stop the knife wound's bleeding.

Ishpanyan ran to Poquis. He pulled off Poquis's headband to stop the flow of blood. He pressed it onto the cut, which was shallow but longer than a man's hand.

The others stayed higher by the unconscious priest, yelling taunts as the enemy ran out of arrow range. They would wait before striking their bows against the enemy warrior Poquis had slain. They would let Poquis strike first, forming their brotherhood for an honor dance upon return to their village of Ghufoor in the Tiguex homeland.

# 3

For centuries, the Ashiwi, now known as the Zuni, had lived in the country of dry grasslands, mountains, and flat-topped mesas rising like pedestals of red and white sandstone. Above them spread the dome of the sky, a luminescent blue and often cloudless. Theirs was a land of little rain. Every summer they held days of ceremonies around the solstice with prayers asking the Creator to drop rain on their crops of corn, beans, and squash. They called their country with its six towns Shíwana. Their town of Hawikku was the farthest to the southwest.

The first Zuni scouts to see the invaders were a middle-aged man and a teenage boy. They hid behind a boulder atop a mesa. Looking down toward the desert plain, the younger of the two gasped at the sight. Coming up the trade route were a mass of bearded men, riding on the backs of beasts as large as elk, and carrying long lances. Colorful cloths fluttered among them in the wind. Thirty men walked with them. Most of them were bearded too. They carried weapons never seen before

The older scout raised himself higher, leaning on his stone-pointed spear for support. He grabbed the boy's arm. "Look at that," he said.

In the dust kicked up by the beasts, the boy could make out hundreds of foreign warriors. He turned to the older Zuni with wide eyes. "Who are they?"

"I have seen men like that among the Nahuatl-speaking traders," the man said, crouching back below the rim of the boulder. "They are Aztecs from the land of forests and wild rivers far to the south. They carry painted leather shields. Those they sometimes trade, but they never trade those club-like paddles, which are edged with sharp chips of obsidian. They love war."

The Zuni watchers talked to each other in whispers. They watched the invaders' dust cloud move forward, like a drifting fog, toward their Shíwana homeland.

"Since I was a child," the older Zuni said, "I have heard there were pale and black people also in the world. I saw the black man who came to us last year. But I have never seen these pale, bearded people until now. Traders said these strangers would come here some day, but I did not believe it."

Travelers along the trade route between Shíwana and the

south brought live parrots, brilliant macaw feathers, copper bells, and seashells. The Zunis sent them back with buffalo hides, turquoises, painted pottery, and cotton blankets, much of which they had obtained in trade from the people of the flat-roofed houses along the Big River to the east. For years the traders had also brought news of powerful bearded invaders who conquered everyone. In a long walk to the land that had come to be known as Mexico, all Zunis knew that the invading strangers conducted slave-hunting raids.

"I have heard the strangers work people of the southern tribes to death digging into mountains for rocks," the boy said. "These savage people kill others just for rocks. I do not know why."

"I have heard the same stories. Now the strangers are using our trade route to come after us." The older scout bit his lower lip and eased his head over the boulder again. "Those beasts they are riding." He paused to think about what he was seeing. "Those beasts must be the ones the traders call horses. It is the horses that make these strangers so invincible in warfare. With the horses, traders have told me these strangers they call Christians can travel much faster than any man afoot. And with their lances, the Christians on horses will be able to kill our warriors as fast as a man can count."

He ducked back down and they thought of the stories they'd heard from traders about the warlike strangers. *They'll come to Shiwana some day*, the traders always warned. *Beware of the horses.*

"They already have more fighters than our whole country can muster," the boy said, shifting his position and looking into the valley below.

"Yes, and there are even many more following many suns behind. An elder told me he had heard the second force contained at least a thousand more fighting men and thousands of animals we have never seen before. Some look like the sheep of the mountains, but smaller, and others look like the buffalo of the plains, but with short hair. He said there also are hundreds more of these horses, if that is what they are."

They both peered over the boulder now. "That man with the yellow shiny cover on his head," the older scout said. "He must be their leader. The elders told me he is coming because of the death of the dark-skinned man named Esteban."

"How do you know all this?" It surprised the boy how little he had been told before being sent out.

"Runners came from Chichilticale across the mountains. I heard them tell the bow chief that the strangers are coming. Our elders suspected the strangers would come to seek revenge against us, and they had asked the desert people who live near Chichilticale to warn us so we could prepare. That is what our bow chief Nayuchi was doing when we left. Did you see the women, children, and many elders leaving Hawikku for sanctuary atop Dowa Yalanne?"

"I had just returned from hunting for meat for the summer solstice ceremonies," the boy said. "As soon as I returned, they told me to go with you. I did not know anything until you told me."

"Now it is certain the strangers will arrive at the time of our rain ceremonies. No matter how crucial the ceremonies are for our crops, they will need to be stopped. Keep low and follow me. We must report what we have seen to the elders."

# 4

Poquis leaned on his bow at the edge of the bluff beside Ghufoor overlooking Big River. Ishpanyan stepped beside him without saying a word. The summer night's warm air had eased the long day's heat. To reach the terraces and rooftop entrances to their apartments, the others in their group climbed the ladders leaning against Ghufoor's doorless adobe walls.

This early part of the evening relaxed Poquis after the long walk back with the injured priest from the cones of burned rock.

Crickets chirped in the bunchgrasses and bushes along the stony and dry land of the bluff on which Ghufoor stood. Poquis watched a bat fly back and forth above him. Its wings fluttered in the dim light of Corn Moon. The moon sparkled the river's water below. Ripples and small shadows revealed three ducks swimming.

Poquis and Ishpanyan were twenty. They had been friends since boyhood and looked like brothers although they were from different clans. Both were slender and muscled. Mountain lion-skin quivers holding their arrows and unstrung bows hung across their backs. War clubs were thrust into the cotton belts of their loincloths—a stone-headed club in Poquis's belt and a wooden club with a heavy knob on its end in Ishpanyan's belt.

Ishpanyan clapped his hand onto Poquis's right shoulder and held it there.

Together, they looked at the shining river water. The Night People scattered overhead, sparkling like quartz chips.

"I will speak to the elders of your battle," Ishpanyan said, looking out over the river. "I will tell them how the wild raiders knocked the priest down. I will tell how you leaped from a high boulder with your war club. How you fought all of them alone until we could come to help."

Poquis nodded. He'd been determined to give his life if necessary to protect the unconscious priest. It was good that his battle should be remembered in the tribe's oral history. However, he was not popular with some leaders. He worried that some might accuse him of negligence for leaving the priest open to attack.

Ishpanyan interrupted Poquis's thoughts with a low laugh. "You and the priest are lucky you were not killed," Ishpanyan said, slapping his hand twice against Poquis' shoulder. Ishpanyan had stitched Poquis's knife wound shut with a cactus spine and strands of hair plucked from his own head. He looked down at the wound. "Does it hurt?"

"No. It feels like a mother's caress."

Ishpanyan laughed again. "You are a brave fighter, Poquis. You bring honor to our people. The priest is being cared for inside the kiva. Already the elders wait to hear from you."

Poquis felt a bit breathless. "I am weary. I have lost so much blood. I need to rest, not speak with the elders all night. Tell them I will come at dawn."

His hand still on Poquis's shoulder, Ishpanyan looked toward Ghufoor as a ladder rubbed against the wall from a person descending.

"It is Panpahlu. The women hear as soon as the elders. I will go and tell the elders you have returned safely. I will speak to them for you." He squeezed Poquis's arm and turned to leave as the woman ran toward them. She was wrapped in two cotton blankets sewn together that Poquis had woven for her when he asked her to be his mate. The cloth bared her left shoulder and was tied around her waist with a white cotton sash. Her black hair was in a round whorl on each side and tied inward in the middle. Around her neck hung a large scallop seashell, brought at great effort from the endless salt water to the west and accented with sky stones of blue turquoise.

Poquis grimaced from a sharp pain as Panpahlu hugged him. Her body shook with soundless crying. She pulled back and looked up at his face in the shadow-light. He had washed most of the blood out of his headband in the river, where he and the others had bathed upon arrival to purify their bodies and their minds. But even in the moonlight she could see pinkness in the cloth.

"Poquis, are you all right?"

"I am home, Panpahlu. So now I will be all right."

She examined him as well as she could, gasping as she turned him and saw the sutures and seeping blood on his side. He felt her hand caress the swollen bruise on his back. She smiled in relief that the wounds were not worse. She pulled his head down, pressing her cheek to his face for a long time, whispering her fears for him.

"You must talk to the elders tonight," she said as she led him by the hand to the ladder.

"I feel weak. I have asked the elders to wait."

They climbed a ladder to the roof of the first terrace. From there, people could walk around the entire rectangular block of the village. He pulled the ladder up the wall so no one else could climb up and enter the doorless village. They stood next to the rooftop opening into their apartment, where another ladder descended. He had one duty to perform first. All day he had been rehearsing his honor song in his mind. As a warrior who'd slain an enemy, he was to sing it each night and each morning for the sacred number of four days, singing his song atop each of Ghufoor's four sides.

Moon Mother cast a shadow against the wall of a tower rising behind Poquis. His voice split the nighttime silence like the call of an eagle as he sang:

*He has returned, Poquis, who killed the enemy.*
*He draws his strength from the ancestors*
*And the Warrior Twins, Maseway and Oyoyeway.*
*The noise of the enemy falls quiet.*
*The people are protected.*
—

Fire lit their room from the cobblestone-lined hearth in its middle. The mud walls scented the room with an earthy smell. Panpahlu listened, sitting on the floor facing him. He told her first of the wall of black boulders, which wound in lazy turns at the base of the ridge where the six cones of burned rock rose in a line, one after the other. He told her how he and the others had watched as the priest pecked an image of a shield-carrying warrior on the living surface of a black boulder facing the rising sun. They spent three days at the sacred rocks, plus most of a day walking there and another day walking back. Each morning and evening the priest and warriors climbed to the summit of a different cone along the ridge. Poquis told how he'd felt close to the Creator while peering into the ragged holes of burned rock, honoring the inner world with prayers and ceremonies. The people had emerged in a time past remembrance from such holes in the earth or out of a sacred lake. Poquis tried to describe his sense of wonder as he had gazed into the darkened depths.

It was not until he finished telling her about his religious experience that he told her of the fight with the enemy warriors.

"Poquis!" She tilted her head and her eyes widened. "You were relaxing on the rocks when you were supposed to be guarding the priest. What were you thinking?"

He tried to protest. But he knew he should have been at the priest's side.

He was spared from further explanation by the footsteps of a Medicine Society member walking across their roof. The man descended the ladder into their room. He wore a kilt with a blanket across his back, carrying healing herbs and fats for the wound Ishpanyan had described. The room's shadows hid details of his dark face.

Poquis and Panpahlu greeted him. Panpahlu stood aside as the healer examined Poquis's cut, turning the young warrior's side to be brightened by the room's fire. He sang a prayer and placed a potion of herbs and fats on Poquis's sutured gash.

He gave Panpahlu directions for treatment. Then the healer paused at the ladder and turned to face them. "I can see the wound and long walk has made you feel dizzy, Poquis. Ishpanyan told me he worried about you. You need to rest. I will explain and speak on your behalf in the kiva tomorrow. Even so, the elders still might be upset that you did not visit them tonight."

The man nodded to Poquis, a pleasant look on his unsmiling face, before he ascended the ladder.

After the healer had gone, Panpahlu spoke softly to Poquis. "Tonight you must sleep," she said, her hands warm against his wound as she applied more herbs and fats. "When you are recovered from this day of your heroism, perhaps then we will give life to a child."

He eased her face toward him, feeling her softness next to his cheek. She whispered, "I wish you had gone to the kiva and made your report to the elders tonight. The elders have not left yet. Perhaps you should still go. Then come back."

He walked to the ladder rising toward the roof's opening into their room. He pulled the ladder down from the opening and leaned it against a wall.

As he had told her, the elders could wait.

She smiled at him from where she was sitting. "We must begin planning for your honor ceremony and feast," she said. "Other women will help me cook the corn, beans, and squash we have stored. We will keep only enough for us until the harvest. We have some dried meat, and hunters are sure to bring more so we can feed the entire village."

He sat on the floor beside her. "I will give the warriors who came to my aid the four buffalo robes I traded for last spring. Ishpanyan has one, but it is in poor condition. The other three are young and do not have robes for this winter."

His excitement built as he thought about the expected ceremony and feast. "I will give Turshán the blanket I just finished weaving," he said as he watched Panpahlu's smile grow more expressive. "And I will give my new mountain lion quiver to Xauían. I can use my old one."

She leaned up against him. "The bow priest's mate admired my heishe necklace once and praised me for how I ground the shells down so small and drilled the holes. I will give him the necklace, and he can give it to her."

"That will be wonderful, Panpahlu. I also have saved some macaw and turkey feathers. I must think of who could use them the best."

She hugged him, being careful to avoid his stitched side and bruised back. "Your courage and generosity are making you a leader of our people."

—

Toward morning the pain in his side awoke him, and he lay for a few minutes beside Panpahlu on a soft buffalo hide, enjoying the warmth of her right arm slung over his waist and her body next to him. He listened to her sleep-heavy breathing.

Loyal Panpahlu, he thought, to support him in the community. He knew it was not easy for her.

Panpahlu had not been able to become pregnant. For the past year, the elders had said Poquis should find another mate. Any other man would have listened to the priests and elders. But not Poquis. The man with the title of Eye-Black Leader, who led the village in organizing the fall-winter ceremonials, had told Panpahlu to pile Poquis's belongings outside the kiva because Poquis would not leave her. When she'd tried to obey, Poquis had stopped her. He'd held her and told her, "Do not leave me, Panpahlu, and I will never leave you. Do not pay any attention to those who would separate us. You are my loved one. You know I never care what others say."

His stubbornness had cost them both. There were harsh punishments for tribal members who did not obey priests and elders. As a boy, Poquis had been flogged while living at nearby Puaray. He'd even been flogged once at Ghufoor after he took Panpahlu for his mate. He was eighteen then and she was seventeen.

After Poquis saved the battle against warriors from Pecos, however, there had never been another flogging. Instead, because he'd conquered two Pecos warriors in hand-to-hand combat, Poquis had been accepted into the Warrior Society. Other battle exploits followed, and now some warriors already considered him their leader.

Even so, Panpahlu often expressed her worries. She said other women scolded her when he defied Tiwa customs. Living in the close quarters of the Tiwa apartment homes, everyone had to cooperate and follow rules. Individuality was condemned. Poquis often did things against the established order—such as his walks into the mountains for days at a time and his defiance of Eye-Black Leader's order of a new mate.

Perhaps he should have reported to the elders in the kiva. He worried Panpahlu would be criticized because he had not gone to the kiva. Women were cherished for childbearing. In Ghufoor's matrilineal society, they even owned the homes. However, they were not to interfere in men's affairs. He hoped she would stay strong. He would advise her to go see the matriarch, the aged woman who passed secrets and duties on to young women as their confessor and adviser. The matriarch did not approve of Poquis's attitudes, but he knew she would not blame Panpahlu.

He closed his eyes as the pain in his side throbbed. He fell asleep thinking of the one time his individualism had been accepted. Although his occasional improvisations in the religious dances often drew disapproval, who could forget the buffalo dance two years ago? Poquis surprised everyone when he paused at one point and, to the beat of the drum, stomped his feet and shook the huge animal's head he wore like an angry bull. The other dancers had adopted that action since, making Ghufoor's buffalo dance distinct among other villages.

—

Poquis awoke to pre-dawn's melody of chirping birds all around outside. Panpahlu already had gone out. It surprised Poquis he had not heard her rise. The pain in his side had awakened him.

He ate the cornbread breakfast Panpahlu had left for him near the flat-rock griddle beside the fire. He considered his meeting with the elders. Ishpanyan would have alerted them to his exhaustion and wound, but they might still be upset with him for not reporting immediately. He did not care much. His concern, rather, was with actions. He should have been more vigilant in guarding the priest. As he sent the other warriors to hunt rabbits for the evening's meal, Poquis had promised to stay close to the priest until they returned. Instead, he had lain—like a child, he admitted—half-asleep on the boulders.

The enemies might not have attacked if they'd realized Poquis was nearby. In the long desert walk back to Ghufoor, Ishpanyan had not criticized him. The others also did not speak about their leader's lapse in diligence. But Poquis sensed their disapproval hanging in the air like smoke.

Poquis knew his neglect had almost cost the priest's life. If Poquis was to rise in the Warrior Society, he must become more single-minded about his responsibilities. He must act the part of a man. He vowed to never allow himself to be so careless again.

# 5

Alonso Álvarez carried Coronado's standard and pennons on a tall staff. He and his friend, sixteen-year-old Juan Pastor, sat astride their horses walking along the trail near the river. It was Alonso's sharp eyes that detected movement on top of the mesa.

"Look," Alonso said, pointing up to their left.

"I don't see anything," Juan said.

"Are you blind? There. By that rock. Two men are running in a low crouch."

Juan reigned his horse to a stop. "Indians!" he shouted as he turned toward other expeditionaries to one side.

Others used short gallops to bring their horses alongside. Other men on foot and several Aztecs broke into a run to catch up to them.

"They're gone now," a horseman said. "Down the other side. We'll never be able to catch them." Everyone else agreed. The mesa was too long and the country was too rough.

Another horseman, Pedro de Castañeda, would write years later about the incident, saying the expedition saw no Indians until they were about eight leagues from Hawikku, which would have been about twenty-one miles. "The first Indians from that country were seen here—two of them, who ran away to give the news [about the expedition]," he wrote.

The expedition kept moving forward. Everyone went on greater alert knowing they were approaching the people who had killed Esteban the previous year. Men put on chain-mail vests, and some, despite the heat, put on their armor.

Field Master García López de Cárdenas led eight horsemen a day's journey ahead of the rest of the expedition to look for any trouble. After about four leagues, he saw seven Indians standing on a low hill watching him.

He suppressed his trained reflex to charge the Indians with lances. He knew Coronado was under the viceroy's orders to show restraint toward natives he found in the new country.

"Wait here," he told the other horsemen. "We will all put on our armor. Stay mounted and ready if I call for you or you see that I need help. I will try to meet these Cíbolans in peace."

Cárdenas kept his horse at a walk as he climbed the long, grassy hill. He loosened his sword and kept a tight grip on his lance's pole. He thought the Indians would run away as he approached, but they stood their ground. They wore loincloths and moccasins. He noticed they had notched arrows into the strings of the bows they carried. He tried to calm himself, not wanting to show any fear toward the Indians—and certainly not in front of his own men. He rubbed his metal breastplate, reassuring himself of its protection. Stopping before the Cíbolans, he stayed in his saddle as they stared at him. They'd never moved during his ride up the hill.

He reached into a saddlebag and pulled out some glass beads. As one Indian taller and older than the rest stepped forward, Cárdenas held out his hand. The Indian reached forward with his free left hand, his right hand still gripping his bow and an arrow. Cárdenas dropped beads of many colors into the Indian's palm. The Indian looked and gave an expression of delight. He turned and showed the beads to the others, who walked closer. Each took one, while the leader kept the rest.

"See these," Cárdenas said. He reached in his bag and pulled out two small mirrors, more beads, combs, and dyed pieces of bright cloth. The Indians passed them around, talking but keeping their eyes on him. Cárdenas handed a small crucifix to the leader, who studied it without a word.

Cárdenas knew a few words in Nahuatl, the Aztecs' language so common on the trade routes. He hoped at least one of the Indians knew a little Nahuatl too. With some Nahuatl and signs, he told them as best as he could, "Go to your town and tell your people that the Christians are coming in peace and want to be your friends." He wasn't sure if they understood him. When they began walking away, he turned and rode back down the hill.

Aztec scouts ranging even farther in front of the expedition reported finding Indians in a stone village on a grassy plain ahead. That would be the expeditionaries' goal. At last, they had come to the Seven Cities of Cíbola whose wonders Friar Marcos had talked about. Everyone cheered when Coronado announced the discovery. The word was passed back to other expeditionaries who took up the cheer echoing off the sandstone cliffs around them.

Coronado stopped to establish camp and sent scouts forward again. They reported that the river they were following flowed through a narrow pass between high-walled mesas. The riverbanks there were thick with trees and boulders.

Upon hearing of the pass, Coronado turned to Field Master Cárdenas and the man he trusted most on military matters, Juan Troyano, one of the few men on the expedition with European battlefield experience. "What do you two think?"

Cárdenas shifted in his saddle. "Our expeditionary force is large but undisciplined and untested in battle. Many of our Indian allies speak different languages. As far as that goes, so do a lot of our expedition members. The pass sounds like it could be dangerous. Is there another way around?"

"We could climb out of this river's valley," Troyano said, looking up at the cliffs towering on each side. "But it could leave us vulnerable to attack struggling up those sides. It would be better to send a force to guard the pass until we can get there in the morning. With their horses, they can retreat if they meet an overwhelming force. Then if that happens, we would have time to decide what to do next."

Coronado looked around as if to take a better look at his advance force. He, his officers, and others who were wealthy enough, were the only ones wearing armor or chain mail and riding horses. Although every European had a sword, even most of the horsemen were equipped with leather or quilted cotton armor and Indian weapons. Of the Europeans on foot, just nineteen men in the whole expedition had crossbows and only twenty-one men carried the matchlock arquebus muskets. And not all of them were in the advance unit.

"Entering a possibly contested and restricted pass even with a professional army could be challenging," Coronado said. "With our inexperienced militia and headstrong Indian allies, it could be trouble. We must assume the Cíbolans are hostile. I think Juan is correct. We should send men to guard the pass."

Cárdenas nodded. "Yes, my lord. I will take twenty horsemen to guard the pass between the mesas tonight. We will see you in the morning when you arrive."

"Leave now while there is still daylight to get there."

"At your orders, my general."

—

That afternoon Hernando de Alvarado brought two Indians into camp that he said had met him peacefully. Because they brought corn meal and game meat to the famished expeditionaries, Coronado ordered that they be allowed to stay. All the men stayed close to their weapons. Expeditionary Pedro de Ledesma later would testify, "The Indians wandered about looking over the army like men who had come to see what people were in the camp and how they were organized."

Coronado gave them some large glass beads and small cloaks. Through Nahuatl and Pima interpreters, he tried to make them understand he was a friend coming to bring them a new ruler, a new religion, and a new way of life. Coronado thought that should be welcome news. Once they seemed to understand what he was saying, however, the Cíbolan Zunis reacted with frowns.

That night, they slipped away from the expedition, never to return.

# 6

Poquis emerged onto the rooftop at dawn. He looked down into the Middle-Heart Place, the open interior area surrounded by Ghufoor's walls. There he saw Ghufoor's bow chief, Xauían, pacing alone.

Xauían pulled the iridescent turkey-feather cloak, a badge of his rank, closer around him to ward off the morning coolness. Sun Father soon would rise above Turtle Mountain. Darkness already was giving way to dawn's soft glow. Poquis watched the feather tips of Xauían's cloak flutter in the morning breezes.

Poquis breathed in the scents of the river and Mother Earth. The eastern horizon glowed with shades of red, tinting the soft clouds above the mountain. Small finches chirped in the cottonwood trees, and seven geese flapped over the river, sending their raucous calls across the village. Poquis took one long, last look at the sky. Then he walked to the roof's edge.

He paused at the squawk of a large bird that ambled sideways across a waist-high wall toward him. The scarlet macaw seemed to glow in its adornment of red feathers on its head, breast and back, with yellow and blue feathers on its wings. The red feathers of its long tail shifted to blue on the tips. The bird lifted one clawed foot as if asking Poquis to untie the leather cord that restrained it. Grinning nearby were two small boys taking their turn at protecting the macaw from hawks while it was outside on summer days. Poquis held out his palm with the seeds that he carried each morning to the treasured bird. It squawked and tilted its white face for a one-eye stare at him. Then it snapped the seeds one at a time out of his hand with its large bill. The tribe had traded several turquoises and buffalo robes for the macaw. Traders had brought the bird from far to the south where macaws lived in thick forests among mighty rivers and eternal summer. Each Tiwa village cared for its own macaw, gathering the birds' molted feathers of bright colors for ceremonial decorations.

Poquis lowered his head and breathed in the musty scent of the bird's feathers. The feathers felt smooth to his fingers.

Smiling at the boys, Poquis descended the ladder into the open expanse of the Middle-Heart Place. Four women stoked a fire near its center. Smoke swirled in wisps around their stooped bodies as they worked at the edges of the fire on several pots made of orange clay. He smiled at Panpahlu, who'd joined other women sitting on the ground to paint designs onto pots. A group of boys gathered with a small dog in a corner, readying themselves for a rabbit hunt with throwing sticks and small bows and arrows. Two turkeys, trailed by a covey of chicks, strutted across the open area as if in a dance line. Chips of broken pottery littered the ground.

As Poquis walked toward the kiva's low walls and cavity, he passed nine men sitting cross-legged in the open space surrounded by Ghufoor's walls. They specialized in chipping obsidian and heat-treated flint for arrowheads, scrapers, and knives. He nodded a greeting. Three younger men nodded back, but the older ones ignored him. As he walked across the dusty open area, he could hear the faint talk and laughter of men already hoeing cornfields by the river at the bottom of the cliff.

Poquis realized he was limping from favoring his cut side and bruised back. He did his best to straighten himself and block out his wounds' pain.

Xauían was twice Poquis's age. Ghufoor's war leader and defender of the people. He stepped toward Poquis. "The elders are waiting," he said. "Again."

"I will speak to them."

Xauían curled his lips and repeated what Poquis said in a mocking tone. He added, "Men are preparing themselves for an honor dance. Yet you have not even given a report on your battle to the elders." Xauían scowled. "This is unacceptable, Poquis. You disrespect the elders."

"I mean no disrespect."

"Follow me."

Ahead of them a watchkeeper stood beside the ladder that descended into the kiva, his feet spread apart, his hands on his hips. Two uneven prongs of a ladder extended ten times the height of a man, piercing the sky to encourage rain to fall.

Once Poquis saw the watchkeeper, he knew that the aged sun priest would be in the meeting. This was more serious than he thought. It seemed clear now he should have met with the elders last night.

The pulsing of a drum began in the kiva below him, announcing his arrival. The muffled drumming vibrated like Mother Earth's heartbeat on the soles of his feet. The solemnity of the drum transformed the dark chamber of the subterranean kiva. A place where men wove at looms and boys were initiated into clans had become a holy space where men gathered to pray to the Creator and to katsina spirits.

The morning's strengthening light streamed ahead of Poquis as he descended the ladder, facing the rungs as he stepped down. Dust motes drifted in the light around him. A small fire behind him flickered light through the interior and radiated heat onto his bare back. His face remained impassive, never betraying the pain stabbing at his side with each step. As he stepped off the final rung onto the sandstone floor, he paused and acknowledged the sun priest with a tip of his head.

The old man's head was haloed by dry, white hair, and his face was cross-hatched by deep wrinkles. He was so thin that he seemed birdlike as he sat on the floor against the sides of the circular kiva. A blanket in the sacred colors of red, blue, yellow, and white draped over his shoulders. He gripped a cane, its high end shiny from being handled by generations of religious leaders. A cross, symbol of the ancestors' emergence from within Mother Earth, was carved on top of the cane, while a leather whip to symbolize his authority hung below. The priest watched Poquis with quiet dark eyes. On each side of him sat elderly men who led Ghufoor's two social groups and helped the sun priest rule the village in a council with other old men.

Walking to his left around the kiva's curving wall, Poquis greeted and paid respects to each of the sacred katsina figures painted half life-sized with their prayers for water. The supernaturals on the wall, some wearing high feather headdresses, stared into the kiva's interior with their rectangular white eyes and square black pupils. They'd been painted wearing katsina masks, deerskin shirts, white moccasins, and black kilts encircled with white belts of cotton fastened with tassels and shell rattles.

Poquis's eyes adjusted more to the dim interior. The image of the katsina Shulawitzi, the fire spirit, emerged from the shadows. The spirit's left hand grasped a spruce tree, on which three black-tipped, white eagle feathers were tied. A red gourd curved next to his right hand to represent his torch. A bald eagle flew toward the fire spirit, with raindrops showering from the bird's beak. A rattlesnake slithered along the wall above the eagle. Near the floor a black pot had been painted nestled on eagle feathers. Bolts of lightning fell into it. A shower of snow curved out of the top from the pot's one side, and rain poured out the other side.

Then, as Poquis kept turning to his left, there appeared Kochininako, the yellow corn maiden. By her side stood Meleyonako, the blue corn maiden. Each swung a small pot from which cascaded two streams of water. Lightning bolts zigzagged across the wall between the maidens above another water pot.

Another bald eagle seemed to glide across the wall, this one flying in the opposite direction from the first, its beak spewing seeds. A swallow flew, spraying droplets above another water pot filled with lightning bolts and cascades of water. A red line curved from the eagle's beak to a black fish leaping into the air, its mouth issuing a backward stream of water. Beyond the fish stood the katsina Kupishtaya, lightning man, holding a feathered planting stick in his left hand and a long cord lined with feathers. A white goose walked at the katsina's right foot, spewing water from its beak. Farther on the wall, a jackrabbit pierced by an arrow gave its life to feed the people.

Poquis paused before a katsina with a red and white hand painted on its chest—Oyoyeway, the elder Warrior Twin. He touched the painting lightly with his fingertips.

Between the sitting elders, katsina masks used in dances honoring the spirits leaned against the walls. Their silent faces recessed into the shadows.

As Poquis revolved to pay his respects to the katsina spirits, he also passed his gaze over the shapes of elders. They hunched in blankets as they watched him from where they were seated on the floor. All was quiet except the rhythm of the drummer, who sat beside the small fireplace's flickering fire. On each side of the drummer stood ponderosa tree trunks that ancestors had carried on their shoulders from the mountains. Together with two other pillars at the opposite side, the trunks supported the ceiling of wood beams and branches.

Xauían also had descended the ladder into the kiva. He motioned for Poquis to sit on the other side of the fireplace from the drummer. The drumbeats stopped when Poquis sat cross-legged on the floor.

The kiva chief stirred. His name was Shur-fa. He was a man with a voice that increased in speed and volume as he spoke. He chastised Poquis for not coming to the kiva to report his deeds to the elders as soon as he returned. The healer had been forced to leave the kiva and go to Poquis's home to treat him. Poquis's behavior was disrespectful to all.

Turshán stood, his cut and bruised head wrapped in a cloth bandage. He thanked Poquis for coming to his aid. He assured the elders that Poquis had showed great respect for the ancestors' spirits when they'd gazed through the cones of burned rock into the inner world.

Eye-Black Leader rose from his seated position. The other elders leaned forward to hear his words. He was the tallest man in the kiva, deep-voiced, and with his once-muscled skin now wrinkled with age. He had been a strong warrior as a young man and respected for his leadership in battle. He scowled. The mate of Poquis was barren, Eye-Black Leader said. He reminded the elders that a warrior like Poquis owed it to his tribe to take another mate so he could produce children for the future. Eye-Black Leader turned his head to look into Poquis's eyes staring back at him.

"Poquis defies the community will," Eye-Black Leader said. "No one else is allowed to do this. Why do we allow him to bring a black cloud with no rain among us, darkening the life of all of Ghufoor? Why do we allow him to not give us children?"

Other elders spoke their thoughts. Some gave long speeches. Others spoke in a few words.

Several were critical of Poquis, calling him stubborn and disobedient. Others excused him because he was from Puaray, and everyone knows the Tiwa people there have peculiar customs.

Xauían placed a hand on the ladder. After a long silence following the final speaker, Xauían asked for patience with the rebellious young man from Puaray.

"Grandfathers, Poquis does not always follow the ways of Ghufoor. Perhaps he should be lashed for punishment." Xauían paused. "But then, perhaps not. It is true he was not at our priest's side. But he was not far away. He did not pick up his bow and fire arrows from a safe distance. He jumped down to the side of Turshán to prevent a killing blow. Although outnumbered, he placed himself before the enemy. He fought until our other young men returning from a hunt could join the battle. To punish a man who made up for his mistake does not seem just. Poquis has odd ways. But he tends our crops, loves us, and defends us with his life. That is what I want to say."

An elder rose, lit a branch of cedar at the fire, and walked about the kiva, wafting the sweet purification smoke with a fan of eagle feathers in the six directions. East, south, west, north, the heavenward zenith, and the nadir of the inner world.

Stillness enveloped the room like dusk, soft and complete, as filaments of scented smoke drifted through the chamber. No one spoke for as long as it would take Sun Father to move the width of a hand across the sky.

Each elder contemplated silently, striving to understand the will of the Ghufoor community:

*What shall we say to this young man? He is not one of us. He comes from our brother Tiwas at Puaray. And yet he risks his life for us. He has saved us from our enemies even before this. He is already a leader in the Warrior Society. The priest Turshán, he of the Hummingbird Clan, still lives because of the courage of Poquis. And yet, Poquis dreamed while the enemy warriors approached, allowing the attack to occur. But then he saved the priest's life when he ran to his defense. Poquis brings honor to Ghufoor from his battle. He fails to respect many of our ways. Yet, who can criticize a warrior such as he? We need brave men such as Poquis, even if they walk their own path and not our path always. He won't take another mate to add to the life of our tribe. He puts his own judgment over the counsel of elders. We have never tolerated a man so rebellious, so given to outside ways. But we cannot exile him. Can we? The Zunis have warned us of strangers approaching their lands with hairy faces and riding man-eating beasts. If they come here, perhaps the Creator has sent Poquis the warrior to defend us.*

For a long time, no elders spoke their thoughts aloud.

After the long silence, the old sun priest conferred in a whisper with other priests sitting on each side of him. The others were his advisers, but the sun priest would have the final word. He gathered his blanket around him and spoke, his voice trembling from age but made certain by the people's confidence in him.

"We will honor the warrior Poquis with a dance and hold him close to us," said the old man. Approval murmured around the kiva. It was the will of the people.

Everyone rose and followed the religious leader's slow climb up the ladder. Poquis was the last to leave. He'd never said a word. Sun Father now neared the middle of the sky.

Poquis found Ishpanyan outside the wall with five other warriors. He descended the ladder to join them.

He looked at their bows and arrows. "Where are you going without me?"

Ishpanyan laughed. "We have been told to hunt deer in the mountains for your honor ceremony. Deer, and maybe bear and the curled-horn mountain climbers. I thought you would be in trouble for not seeing the elders last night, but now we hear you are a hero."

Poquis grabbed Ishpanyan's arm. "I will walk with you for a way. I have news to tell you. All of you. The elders have learned of a large group of invaders approaching our trading partners in the Zuni villages. They are the bearded light-skinned people we have heard about for so long, and many warriors from far to the south are with them."

Tiwas in the village could hear their excited chatter long after Poquis and the hunters descended the cliff toward the river.

# 7

The earth and rock walls of Hawikku rose three and four stories high atop a knoll that commanded a dry grass prairie in all directions. This holy time of the year had started many days earlier. That's when the setting sun struck the sacred point on the mesa on the horizon northwest of the Zuni town for five consecutive evenings. That marked the start of the summer solstice ceremonies that beseeched the katsinas to intervene with the Creator and send summer rains for the Zuni cornfields.

Outside the south wall, old Nayuchi squinted his eyes in the sunlight. He remained disappointed that his frailness had prevented him from making the pilgrimage of three long walks to Ko'thluwalawa, where katsinas lived under a rare desert lake. He held a feathered prayer stick as he chanted a prayer asking the rainmakers to water the earth. He looked to the southwest. Last night he had seen the fires lit by returning pilgrimage walkers in the distant heights, letting smoke plumes rise like breath clouds to the Creator.

They would be back tonight, expecting to see joyous faces and prayerful retreats for the ceremonies to come. As bow priest, it was up to Nayuchi to explain why the village was almost deserted instead, and why the ceremonies and dances could not be held.

He heard the rustle of Bartolomé's footsteps in the grass behind him. The young man sat in the grass beside Nayuchi. Just as Nayuchi could not go on the pilgrimage because of his age, Bartolomé had been denied the right because he was not a Zuni. He was a Guasave tribesman from Petatlán in Mexico. He had arrived the previous year with Esteban's entourage and remained with the Zunis.

"Grandfather," Bartolomé greeted Nayuchi. "What will you tell them?"

"I will say strangers are coming from far to the south like a bad wind. So I sent the women, children, and old people to our sanctuary." He jerked his chin toward the tall mesa in the distance—Dowa Yalanne—Sun Father's Shrine, also known as Corn Mountain. It dominated the central part of Zuni lands, its red rock radiant at the top and bottom with a belt of white sandstone around its middle. "I will remind them what you have told us about the bearded people who are approaching. When you came here last summer with the black man, Esteban, you told us he was a spy for these strangers. You said they are a cruel race that will make war against us. You said they are slave-hunters and merciless in war."

Bartolomé touched Nayuchi's arm. "The Zunis were right to kill Esteban after he found them. But the word went back anyway in the mouths of men with him. I remained with my new friends, the Zunis, but my companions ran away. Now men with light skin and hair across their faces know we are here. They are coming to punish the Zunis."

"Do you believe they will make slaves of us to dig into the mountains in the south, as they have so many others?"

"Even the long-distance traders, not just me, have told you for many years how these metal people called Castilians have killed so many people to the south. They lead their captives away, tied at the necks like a line of rabbits, and work them to death digging rocks in the mountains."

"This must be true. Our scouts say these invaders approaching our country have many slaves with them. They say those slaves have black skin like Esteban."

"I have seen the metal people keep spreading in all directions. Now they are coming to Shiwana."

Nayuchi gestured to the southwest. "More of our men are returning from the pilgrimage. Many warriors from our other villages as far away as Kyaki'ma, the House of Eagles, came here for the summer solstice ceremonies. They have remained. Soon we will have many men with shields, spears, clubs, bows, and arrows. The strangers will leave us alone when they see our force. Then I can call back our women and children and our ceremonies can continue."

"You do not listen to me, because I am not Zuni. You do not have the imagination to realize the power of these strangers. They come with metal clothes and metal weapons you have no imagination to understand. Their metal sticks erupt with fire and thunder and can bore holes through men from long distances. Our clubs are no match for their long metal knives. They ride on the backs of horses, which are like elk but with no antlers. You can no more stop them than you can stop an avalanche of boulders roaring down a mountainside."

"This metal you keep speaking of since we adopted you. Tell me more."

Bartolomé pulled his bow and an arrow from the quiver on his back. He strung the bow and shot at a rock. The arrow broke into pieces, its stone head shattered and shaft split.

"Their metal shirts and the coverings on their head are as hard as that," he said. "Please believe me. My people at Petatlán far south of here were once powerful like the Zunis. When the metal people came many years ago, they killed most of our warriors. They made slaves of women and children like me. They make us feed them and work for them. I came with Esteban and the man called Friar Marcos, who was like a Zuni sun priest, to escape from the misery."

Nayuchi tightened his lips and looked at the broken arrowhead. "You should have saved that tip of a lightning bolt. You might need it when the strangers arrive."

Both looked to the south and southwest. Miles of grass prairie swept from the base of Hawikku to a horizon lined with the gray profiles of high mesas.

Several minutes of silence passed before Nayuchi made his decision. "You know these metal people and what they are like. Our scouts say the metal people are following the river into our country. Take some men tonight to the place where the river cuts between two mesas. Perhaps you can scare them away or delay them long enough to give the rest of our elders and our women and children time to reach safety."

"They will not stop. But I will go and report back to you."

"I do not think they will stop either. That is why I have already sent other men to their camp with food to find out what they can."

—

The next morning, Nayuchi arranged for Bartolomé to meet with the pilgrimage walkers and priests. The pilgrimage walkers were still stunned by their return to a Hawikku filled only with men and the news of approaching invaders. Few could sleep that night. The kiva was not large enough to hold everyone who needed to know quickly, so they met in one of the open areas inside Hawikku's walls.

Nayuchi beckoned to Bartolomé to make a report on what he and the food delegation had learned.

"The strangers have come ready for war," Bartolomé said. He spoke loudly so he could be heard by the blanketed priests sitting on the ground before him and all the bare-chested men standing behind them. "We yelled at them in the dark last night from the tops of the mesas, ordering them to go away. But as soon as they heard us, they attacked. They mounted their horses and fired deafening thunderclaps at us. We escaped because we know the country and they do not. They will be here soon, perhaps today."

Nayuchi stood. It was impolite to interrupt a speaker, but he felt an urgency. "Tell them about the warriors from the land of the macaws," he said.

Bartolomé straightened his shoulders. "The strangers come with many warriors from the Land of Everlasting Summer to the south. Too many to count."

Eyes widened. They had heard how light-skinned strangers had arrived a generation ago in tall towers floating on the sea. The strangers had conquered their world's strongest tribe, the Aztecs, in their city of Mexico-Tenochtitlán. Indian traders had brought the astonishing news. Even in this desert, so far to the north, the cruel way Aztecs sacrificed their captives by cutting out their hearts was legendary. If the strangers and Aztecs were approaching together, the danger was greater than anything they had known before.

A war captain sprang to his feet. "Seize your weapons. At my command we will meet these invaders on the grassland. We must delay them as long as we can or they will go after our women and children still trying to reach Dowa Yalanne."

Another day passed before the strangers came within sight of Hawikku. Seventy-five of them rode horse-beasts. Others came in a crowd of hundreds around the horsemen. They stopped on the prairie. They had come close enough, however, that the Zunis could see sunlight flashing off armor, hear the flapping of banners in the wind, and listen to officers' shouted commands.

Out of the mass of strangers, two men rode horses forward. They wore metal shirts that sparkled like quartz rocks. Beside them walked two bald, pale men wearing gray robes billowing in the wind. There also was an Aztec war leader with his black hair wrapped in a topknot. The Aztec wore a shoulder harness to which a long pole topped by brilliant and exotic feathers was attached against his back. On his left arm, he held a round shield hung with long feathers. In his right hand he carried a spear edged with sharpened obsidian blades.

Nayuchi and two other elders, along with Bartolomé as a possible interpreter, stepped forward from the lines of two hundred armed Zuni defenders. As Nayuchi walked, he smelled the scent of dry prairie grasses crackling under his feet. He looked toward the gathered strangers in the distance beyond the small group approaching them. He noticed the armor of one man on horseback glowing yellow.

## 8

Among those on the hilltop that July 7, 1540, the standard-bearer boy Alonso Álvarez watched. The Spaniards had come excited by stories Friar Marcos had brought back the previous year of large Indian cities filled with gold and precious jewels. Surely, they thought, not far beyond would be China with its silk, spices, and dyes. They had been sustained on the grueling trip of four and a half months since leaving Compostela, Mexico, with dreams of riches like Spaniards had taken from the Aztecs at what now was Mexico City and from the Incas in Peru. Some even thought that northern Indian villages could be the wealthy Seven Cities of Spanish legend.

After all, upon hearing of Esteban's death, Friar Marcos said he had continued onward. He claimed to have stood on a hill overlooking Hawikku, which he called Cíbola.

Alonso remembered the Franciscan's words:

"I continued my journey till I came within sight of Cíbola. It is situated on a level stretch on the brow of a roundish hill. It appears to be a very beautiful city, the best that I have seen in these parts. The houses are of the type that the Indians described to me, all of stone with their stories and terraces, as it appeared to me from a hill whence I could see it. The town is bigger than the city of Mexico ... When I said to the chiefs who were with me how beautiful Cíbola appeared to me, they told me that it was the least of the seven cities."

Marcos had gone on to describe a valley in Mexico. Like many others, Alonso had assumed Marcos must still have been talking about Cíbola when Marcos wrote:

"I saw, from the mouth of the tract seven moderate-sized towns at some distance, and further a very fresh valley of very good land, whence rose much smoke. I was informed that there is much gold in it and that the natives of it deal in vessels and jewels for the ears and little plates with which they scrape themselves to relieve themselves of sweat."

Bigger than Mexico City. So much gold that the natives use it for everyday vessels and trinkets. Pleasant valleys and good land for farming. The Seven Cities confirmed!

Explosive as a volcano, Marcos's report excited Spaniards. But now the friar's words seemed hollow as the expeditionaries stared at the mud and rock Indian village before them.

The horseman Pedro de Castañeda would later recall Hawikku as "a small village crowded together and spilling down a cliff. In New Spain there are ranches that from a distance have a better appearance. It is a village with three and four upper stories and with up to two hundred fighting men. The houses are small and not very roomy."

Spaniards began muttering with anger and disappointment.

"When they saw the first village, which was Cíbola, such were the curses that some hurled at Friar Marcos that may God not allow them to reach him," Castañeda said.

Coronado, wearing his plumed helmet and armor gilded with gold, watched his advance party in the distance stop before the ranks of Indians. His horse stamped its feet. Coronado could hear the men around him checking their lances, swords, and shields in preparation for battle.

Rodrigo de Maldonado leaned toward Coronado and asked if the men he'd sent forward were in danger. They watched Cárdenas and Hernando Bermejo on horseback with the Aztec war chief and the two friars walking with them.

"I have asked them to tell the Indians that we were not going to do them any harm but will defend them in the name of the Holy Roman Emperor," Coronado replied. "These barbaric Indians killed Esteban last year. But if they lay down their weapons and accept the king and the Catholic faith, I will pardon them. Don García López de Cárdenas will read them the *requerimiento* so they will understand they are now subjects of His Majesty in Spain and of the pope."

"I doubt there is any gold in there," Maldonado said.

"Truth. But there is food." Coronado shifted in his saddle. "And we need that more than gold today."

As Cárdenas began to demand submission to Spanish arms on the plain ahead of them, Coronado turned and ordered his men to be ready. The men's fighting mood intensified the longer they beheld the disillusionment of the crude village ahead.

—

The Zunis would learn that the main horseman was the expedition's *maestre de campo*—the field master—García López de Cárdenas. In his late twenties, he was older than most expeditionaries.

Zuni eyes focused on the horses, which only their scouts had ever seen. They also stared at the Aztec with the high staff strapped to his back topped with macaw feathers.

After stopping in front of the Indians, one of the gray-robed men walking beside the horsemen handed a folded, thin sheet to Cárdenas. He unfolded it. Astride his horse, he began speaking in an unintelligible language, his eyes going back and forth from the sheet to the Zunis.

Bartolomé leaned toward Nayuchi in front of him. He whispered to Nayuchi in Zuni. "I speak some of their language, Castilian. They call this the requerimiento. I do not understand all that he says, but I do know he is ordering us to surrender and become Christians."

"Christians?" Nayuchi wrinkled his forehead in puzzlement.

"It is their religion. It is why each of those men in gray robes carries a cross."

After Cárdenas finished, the Aztec leader spoke, summarizing what Cárdenas had said.

"He speaks in the Nahuatl language, which I know," Bartolomé said, turning to Nayuchi. "He says we must put down our weapons. He says we must feed all the men with him, for they are very hungry."

"We will feed the strangers, but they cannot cross this line until our ceremonies are over." An elder beside Nayuchi handed him an orange bowl painted with black designs of birds, clouds, and rain. Nayuchi took the bowl. He bent and sprinkled a line of white corn meal from it across the ground.

When Nayuchi looked up, it surprised him to see the horsemen and gray-robes scowling and muttering angrily. Then Cárdenas and the other horseman stepped their horses across the line, shouting words Nayuchi could not understand.

Nayuchi and the elders backed away from the horses' advance. Nayuchi turned to the Zuni men behind him and nodded. As planned, the Zunis fired warning arrows above and between the strangers. The symbolic barrier of corn meal must be respected.

Cárdenas turned in his saddle and waved. The yellow-glowing man led scores of horsemen thundering down the hill, pulling up behind Cárdenas in a choking cloud of dust. Behind them ran more bearded men on foot and hundreds of Aztec warriors. Once everyone had arrived, the horsemen began advancing. They lowered their lances. The men on foot drew their long metal knives. Zunis fired more warning arrows near the shouting strangers. One arrow snagged in the oldest gray-robed man's loose frock. Another gray-robe shouted to the horsemen.

The man in yellow armor directed two of his men to seize Nayuchi. Then he shouted a command, *Santiago y a ellos!*—"For St. James and at them!" The Spaniards spurred their horses into a charge. The elders who had walked beside Nayuchi were the first Zunis lanced and trampled.

# PART II – SPANISH DOMINANCE
## July to September 1540

### 9

Alonso Álvarez's ship had landed in the New World in 1538. Since he was just fifteen, Coronado had made Alonso his standard-bearer. Now he resented being ordered onto the plain clearing away Cíbolan bodies.

Alonso looked across to the stone and mud walls of Cíbola. The village was built in tiered clusters up the sides of a hill, which rose above a rolling desert prairie of bunch grasses and cactuses. The landscape was vast. The sky blended into the desert in the distance except where high mesas interrupted the horizon.

An arquebus musketeer, he adjusted his bandoleer sash. It was weighted with containers of lead balls, powder, fuses, and wadding for his matchlock muzzle-loader. He also owned a chest-high forked pole on which to rest the gun's heavy muzzle when aiming. For the task before him, he'd left both his arquebus and its forked pole at the tents others were erecting. Not able to afford steel armor, Alonso wore a quilted jacket that reached to his thighs. Padded three fingers thick with dense cotton, it had already proved its worth by stopping an Indian arrow while he was making his way through the northern provinces of New Spain that spring. His green, floppy hat protected him from the sun. Striped, bloused trousers and leather shoes protected him from cactus spines.

Even as the expedition's youngest fighting man, he was strong. He had to be to carry a smoothbore musket as long as he was tall all the way from central Mexico. His father, Rodrigo Álvarez, carried one of the expedition's crossbows. Alonso felt he represented the future with an arquebus, while his father's crossbow represented the past.

Coronado had left Alonso in a rear guard when the general and most of his advance force proceeded toward certain battle at Cíbola. So Alonso had missed the short fight. Now he had to deal with the aftermath.

He hesitated at the carnage in front of him. Of course, the horsemen who had done most of the killing a few hours before weren't about to dirty their hands by cleaning up afterward. No, that was a job for the commoners in the rank-and-file. Alonso and the expedition's men on foot had been ordered out onto the plain in front of Cíbola. The general had pitched his headquarters tent nearby, so the infantrymen had to drag the bodies away.

The Indians wore loincloths with moccasins or sandals. Most carried round leather shields, which proved useless against swords and lances. The Indians' weapons were clubs, weak bows, and a few spears. It surprised Alonso to see that several of those lying on the plain were unarmed old men. At least forty Indian bodies lay sprawled in a line back to Cíbola's walls. Many had their heads and torsos mangled by the horsemen's lances. Others were lying in bloody smears among legs, arms, and heads severed by flailing swords.

"Oh, you should see the battlefields in France and Italy if you think this is bad," said a veteran named Juan Galiveer. His Spanish carried a thick English accent. He was clad in upper-body leather armor. He leaned over and picked up a decapitated head by its black hair. Alonso turned away so he wouldn't see the open eyes.

"You add cannon balls and grapeshot to the mix, and some of the bodies in Europe start looking like bloody meat stew," the man continued. With his free hand, he grabbed an arm of a corpse to which the head seemed to belong. He dragged the already stiffening body toward the deep ravine where the dead Zunis were being dumped. The ravine, a dry streambed that had cut through the desert, provided an open grave. They could shovel sand out of its sides to cover the bodies when they were through.

The stench of blood and bowels under July's hot sun sickened Alonso. But he had no choice except to help clear the bodies because the field master stood off to the side, hands on his hips, watching them. Alonso looked down at the body of a Cíbolan, a boy about his own age. Like other warriors, the boy had died facing the charging horses, a war club still tied to his wrist. A metal-tipped lance had pierced his shield and ripped apart his chest when it twisted out as the horse galloped past. Alonso began pulling the body by both arms.

Just before spilling the body over the ravine's edge, Alonso freed the war club from the dead boy's wrist and thrust it under his own belt. He pushed the body over the edge with his right foot as he would roll a log. Atop Cíbola's walls, expeditionaries were throwing bodies to the ground below. Alonso turned in that direction.

He felt lucky that Indians were all he might need to fight. The Englishman had been right. Fighting men like him were little more than cannon fodder, their lives spent cheaply, on the grisly European battlefields. These Indians were dangerous enough for him. Thank God they didn't have armor, horses, and steel weapons to back up their courage in battle.

The Franciscans were along to convert and protect the Indians. However, Alonso could see no evidence of the friars' safeguarding role on the battlefield.

Then there were the horsemen. Several were already rich from the forced labor and confiscated goods of Indians on encomiendas in Mexico. They hoped to acquire even more encomiendas for their expedition service.

Alonso now was a part of the conquest of the Indies, which had been the obsession of two generations. Alonso and others sought promising new land on which to settle. He had to admit he had not seen much to encourage him so far in the deserts and rugged mountains he'd crossed. He hoped to find something better.

—

An hour before the sun would set, several expeditionaries sat in Hawikku's dusty plaza. Multistory stone walls surrounded them. The famished men gorged on tortillas they had fashioned out of the corn meal and piles of corn and beans found inside the Indian village. They had moved into the village and been told to rest for a few days and regain their strength.

Alonso sat with Juan Pastor, his best friend, even if Juan was a cavalryman. The distinction of being among the expedition's youngest members drew them together in the odd combination of a footman-horseman friendship. Alonso suspected it helped his status that Coronado lent him a horse whenever Alonso performed his standard-bearer duties. Alonso poked Juan in the side and nodded his head toward an older footman approaching the group.

"He is the one I told you about," Alonso said in a low voice.

"The Englishman?"

Alonso chuckled. "He is English, so most Castilians have little to do with him. But I hear he is the scourge of God with his sword."

The Englishman accepted a tortilla from one of the group's older men and sat with a thud beside Alonso, greeting him with a slap on the back. The man had a round face, unlike the angular profile of so many of Alonso's countrymen. He had a red beard so thick that it covered his mouth and climbed toward his eyes.

"Juan Galiveer," Alonso said, "this is my friend Juan Pastor. With me, we are two of the youngest fighting men on the expedition."

"And men you are if you are with this expedition," Galiveer said, his Spanish so accented with English that both Alonso and Juan strained to understand the words. "Glad to meet you, Juan."

"I missed the battle," Alonso said. Galiveer already knew that, but Alonso felt an explanation was necessary. "Even though I am standard-bearer for the general, and served him as a servant in New Spain, he sometimes treats me like a boy because I am only fifteen."

"Well, you look bigger than fifteen. At least you got here in time to clean up the mess." Galiveer laughed.

"Truth. But Juan here was one of the lancers in the thick of it on his horse."

"Good for you, Juan. By the way, my name actually is Gulliver. No one seems to be able to pronounce it around here. No offense, Alonso."

"Gulliver," Juan repeated, struggling to pronounce the odd combination of vowels.

"That is right. But you can relax and call me Galiveer. Everyone else does."

"Take off your armor and let your skin breathe a little," Alonso said, tapping his knuckles on Galiveer's hard, elk leather tunic.

"I would like to, but orders of the general. Those savages could come back at any time with reinforcements. All of us need to stay on high alert."

With only about sixty footmen on the expedition, Alonso knew Galiveer. However, he didn't know much about him because of their difference in ages. "You are from England, yes?"

"That's right. Some years ago. I am the only English-speaking member of the expedition other than Tom Blake. Tomás Blaque, to you Castilians. But he is a Scot, so we do not get along well."

"I have been meaning to ask someone," Alonso said. "I am surprised there are so many foreigners on the expedition."

"Blake and I are not the only ones. There are a few Portuguese, you know, and others from Germany, France, Italy, Corsica, Sicily, Greece, and Crete. Some of us are professional fighters. We are welcome everywhere."

"If you are talking about foreigners, never forget that lying French monk," Juan added. "Friar Marcos. May he burn in hell for his lies."

A man with a cut on his face leaned forward toward the group and snorted. "I lost faith in him weeks ago," he declared. "If you ask me, he never knew where he was leading us. How many times did we almost starve or die of thirst?"

Galiveer nodded in agreement. "Friar Marcos guided us all the way here, and for what?" He gestured at the terraced walls of Cíbola around them. "Does this look like the wealthy Seven Cities of Antilia to you boys?"

Several men around them began cursing Marcos's name. "I heard the general is sending the friar back to Mexico City the first chance he gets," one declared, as others chimed in with more denouncements. They were staggered by the disappointment of finding a mud-and-stone Indian village instead of the Seven Cities that the Franciscan had talked about. They had no reason to expect other Indian villages in the area to be any better.

Alonso asked Galiveer about the battle. Alonso had heard just rumors about what happened.

"Well, I heard they tried to ambush some of our men at a narrow pass between high mesas the night before. What treachery. They say some of the lancers got so excited that they put their saddles on backwards. Oh, I wish I could have seen that." Galiveer reared back and roared with laughter.

"Anyway, we figured we would not be welcome after that. And when we got to this village, all the women and children were gone. There were only men of fighting age."

"So you knew there was going to be a battle," Alonso said.

"Yes, but we had to go on. We were starving. Capturing the pueblo looked like our one chance to get food. When we rode up to Cíbola, at least two hundred of them lined up in a formation in front of the village. The general sent Don García López de Cárdenas up ahead with two friars. We offered them peace if they would accept King Carlos and Pope Paul as their rulers and convert to the true faith. But these heathens drew a line on the ground with some white stuff. Friar Padilla told me it was corn meal. Here we were starving, and these savages were dumping food on the ground. Satanists telling Christians that we dare not go any farther. Imagine that. When we advanced, they shot some arrows. Well, sir, the general and the rest of us Christians and hundreds of our Aztec allies came running up. The barbaric Indians just shot more arrows and started advancing on us. One arrow even hit the robe of Friar Luis, which it pleased God did him no harm. I think I do remember seeing you on a horse, Juan."

Juan became animated. "Yes. One of the priests yelled at the general, 'Take your shields and go after them!' That's when the general called out the Santiago and we charged. Our horses terrified them and they turned and ran. They know better than to fight horsemen on an open plain now. Praise God, we lanced forty of them before the rest escaped into the village."

"I could hear arquebuses firing," Alonso said, "but I could not get here fast enough."

"That came later when we surrounded the pueblo and attacked the walls. We had to get the food that we knew was stored in there. The general was knocked senseless when they threw rocks down on him, but it took less than an hour for the rest of us to force our way in."

Galiveer paused to scowl. "But the pueblo's Indians escaped. The field master let them go."

Galiveer reached for some shattered boards painted blue with images of bears, deer, birds, and other animals on them in a variety of colors. "Friar Padilla was happy to let us break up these heathen altars of devil worship to use for firewood," he said with a loud laugh. He tossed two painted boards onto the campfire.

When the flames flared around the drumstick of a turkey he'd caught inside the village, Galiveer pulled a metal ramrod with its skewered meat out of the fire. He showed the turkey leg to them before biting off a chunk. He took a swig of water at the same time to cool the meat. He wiped his mouth with his sleeve as he chewed. "Truth. We found what we needed more than gold and silver. Corn and beans and fowls, better than those of New Spain. And salt, the best I have tasted in all my life."

Juan Pastor motioned and Galiveer handed the turkey leg to him. Juan bit off a mouthful of meat.

Galiveer turned to Alonso, "How is the general? Is he well?"

Alonso smiled, knowing the men considered him a good source of command-tent gossip because he was with Coronado so much as standard-bearer. "He remained unconscious for three hours. But he revived a while ago. He is covered with bruises and has an arrow wound in one foot."

"We are relieved to hear he is recovering," Galiveer said. He turned to Juan. "I killed one of the infidels with my sword. How about you?"

"I lanced two," said Juan, a grin spreading across his boyish face.

Alonso looked sideways at both of them. Such up-close killing bothered him whenever he thought about it. He preferred fighting from a distance with the arquebus.

The Englishman's face twisted in disgust. "I still cannot believe that our officers let the Indians escape. We should have killed them all."

# 10

Poquis and Xauían stood atop a second-story rooftop of the Tiwa town of Ghufoor. They watched the runner sprinting down the desert trade road, descending the miles-long slope from the high plains to the west. Xauían adjusted the cloak of turkey feathers protecting his back from the already hot morning sun rising above Turtle Mountain behind him. "Stay with me," Xauían told Poquis. "He probably has more news to add to what yesterday's runner told us. The strangers must have arrived at Hawikku by now."

Poquis saw the runner the size of an ant in the distance with the ridge of grasses and shrubs rising high behind him. The orange streaks of sunset were just beginning to rise like flaming arrows above the ridge's top. As the runner came on, the ant changed into an older boy with long running strides. "I think the news will be bad," Poquis said.

"If it is bad news, I need you to report it to the Warrior Society while I tell the sun priest and elders." Together, they descended by ladders.

Three other village elders joined Xauían and Poquis in front of Ghufoor's thick, adobe wall. They wore cotton blankets dyed in red, black, or yellow draped over their backs. All of them watched as the runner drew closer to the village. No one spoke.

A rooftop sentinel had spotted the runner in the distance and sent a boy to alert Xauían in the underground kiva. The sentinel had come down to stand by the wall with his bow and a quiver of arrows. A blue strap of cloth encircled his waist and secured a short loincloth made of dyed cotton. Like most young men, he went shirtless through the spring, summer, and fall. In his left hand he still held the turkey-bone flute he had been playing to entertain himself while on his watch.

The teenage boy running toward the village was a Tiwa, just like Xauían and the others in Ghufoor's two-storied adobe complex of apartments, storage rooms, and the interior open area of the Middle-Heart Place with its kiva. He was from Maigua, another town farther south on the other side of the river. The boy had departed with a trading group of Puebloans from the dozen

Tiwa villages along this stretch of Big River. That had been more than ten suns earlier.

Perched on Big River's western bank, Ghufoor was one of the main villages in the Tiguex Province, situated on an easy ford across the river for anyone traveling the east-west trade route. The trail reached from the eastern village of Pecos, near the edge of the buffalo prairie, past Ghufoor to the Zuni towns that included Hawikku to the west. From there, the Indian traders' footpath dipped southward to the tropical lands of macaw parrots with their feathers of sacred colors.

The young runner picked up his pace once he spotted the observers on Ghufoor's walls and rooftops. He wanted to impress the elders with his speed and endurance. The runner slowed to a trot and then to a walk as he approached the group awaiting him among the bunch grasses around the village. The runner greeted them with a hand signal.

He had come from the Zuni towns, running since before sunup. He'd stopped briefly at times to refresh himself from water pots and caches of corn meal buried at intervals along the trail. In the time of one sun, he had covered a journey that a trading party would need six or seven suns and sleeps to travel.

The runner had a barrel chest and muscled legs. He wore deerskin moccasins and a cotton loincloth, which his father had woven for him on the kiva's looms with the designs of the swift hare and the eagle. Xauían and the three elders waited for the runner to regain his breath, their arms folded across their chests. Poquis stood behind them. Other Tiwas looked on from Ghufoor's rooftops and walls, murmuring to each other.

Tiwas who had been tending the fields of corn, beans, squashes, and cotton down by the river climbed the fifty-foot bluff at the east edge of the village. They gathered behind the elders. Some men were bare-chested and in loincloths, while others wore shirts with either moccasins or sandals. The women wore embroidered cotton blankets of white or dyed in colors. Some blankets were draped over one shoulder and fastened at the waist with a cotton sash. Others wore their blankets wrapped around their bodies under the arms. Some of the older women also wore a shawl over their shoulders. Several children and unmarried young women were nude.

What the runner told them startled the crowd.

One sun ago, he reported, alien men wearing rock-hard clothes and riding fearsome beasts had attacked their Zuni trading partners at Hawikku. The invaders had arrived during summer solstice ceremonies. The runner told how Zuni priests had spread the traditional line of corn meal before the strangers to mark where they could not pass. But the strangers continued to press forward with their beasts. Their faces were hidden under beards and they wore shirts of thick leather or shining metal.

He said warriors had fired a volley of warning arrows, missing the strangers by close margins. The strangers charged forward on the backs of huge beasts they called horses, killing many Zunis, including some of Hawikku's priest leaders. They stabbed the Zunis with lances whose points had the same hard smoothness of the clothes, which they called metal. They used weapons that flashed lightning and thunder and bored holes through warriors. They also used long metal knives that slashed off heads, arms, and legs with a single stroke. A horde of fierce Aztecs from the land of macaws fought alongside them. Other Zuni warriors fought from the village walls. There were so many invaders, however, that resistance was hopeless. When the Zunis fled, the invaders plundered the village of its food and sprawled a camp of striped tents around it.

The boy had run to warn the Tiguex villages of these bearded metal people. The trade routes from Hawikku included this northern branch that led straight to Ghufoor. It was certain the strangers would come to Ghufoor soon.

As the other elders continued questioning the runner, Xauían stepped backward to stand beside Poquis. "When I was your age," Xauían told Poquis, "I had listened in disbelief to stories from long-distance traders that strangers such as these had defeated the mighty Aztec nation. Now strangers and Aztecs are allies and have come together into our country."

Poquis stared at the coloring western horizon before he responded. "All my life I also have heard such stories as if they were dreams. I have heard how they were men with light skin, their faces covered with hair like animals, who wore metal clothes and had powerful weapons. We had hoped that the metal people riding war beasts would not look for us in this vast desert. But now they are at Zuni, and the Warrior Society must be alerted that soon they will be here."

Xauían nodded. "For two cycles of seasons I have come to rely on you more and more as my most able warrior. You have always shown the most courage and the best mind in battle. For this crisis, I will need your leadership and advice."

"I am honored by your praise. The Warrior Society should send out a series of runners to Zuni to keep us informed about the strangers and what they are doing. We must stock our mesa-top fortresses with provisions and make sure we have many arrows in case we are forced to defend ourselves. And we need to contact the warrior societies of the closest Tiwa towns to see if they will help us if needed."

"After what happened to the Zunis, I agree we would be foolish not to prepare for the possibility of war. We will try to be brothers in peace with such powerful enemies, but such efforts could fail. If peace does not succeed, we must be ready. I will talk to the sun priest and the elders. Once they agree, we will start preparations as soon as possible.

Xauían clasped both of Poquis's shoulders. "Your last suggestion to seek a confederacy with the other villages will take more effort. Ghufoor has about fifty warriors. Kuaua has a few more. Of the ten other closest towns, most have fewer. We are used to fighting off bands of the wandering tribes of the desert and mountains and even those who have come into our country from the great grassland to the east. Now we might need to face an enemy where we will be greatly outnumbered, who have powerful weapons, and who wear metal that our arrows shatter against."

"There is much to do in little time."

"After I give the Warrior Society their instructions, the older warriors will assist me in making sure the tasks are completed. I have introduced you to leaders at the other villages so they know you have my confidence. It is you who must go to each village and convince them to be ready to join us in arms if necessary."

Xauían turned to climb a ladder against the wall into Ghufoor. He would first report news of the metal people's attack at Zuni to the aged sun priest. Then he would take the news to the elders and Katsina religion priests for permission to put his plan into action. It might take more than one sun to reach agreement, he thought, but he felt an urgency to begin.

## 11

Nayuchi was horrified at the sight of his people so quickly killed on the field. He struggled against the two bearded men who'd seized him. But he was an old man, and they were young and strong. The two Spaniards dragged Nayuchi away and afterward never left his side.

His guards took him into a tent three days later to meet the young man he would learn was named Francisco Vázquez de Coronado. Nayuchi held his head high and stared hard-eyed at the man responsible for the deaths of so many of his people.

Coronado sat behind a table. A boy stood on the right side holding a staff of colored cloths. Nayuchi would later learn the boy's name was Alonso. On the left was a bare-chested native from the southern lands of everlasting summer and treasured macaw birds. Coronado said something unintelligible to the Aztec, who then spoke to Nayuchi. At first the words were meaningless sounds. The Aztec tried again in what sounded like another language. On the third time, words Nayuchi recognized as the Aztec language of Nahuatl, he thought he could understand. The Aztec was asking, "Do you understand me?"

Never taking his eyes off Coronado, Nayuchi said he could understand a little.

The Aztec told that to Coronado, who told the interpreter what he wanted to know next.

It took several attempts back and forth with the interpreter, each trying to find words the other might know in languages other than Zuni.

"Are you the cacique?"

"I do not know that word."

"Are you the leader of the Cíbolans?"

Nayuchi finally realized that Coronado was using the word Cíbolans for all Zunis. He said he was just one of the leaders. The principal leader was safe elsewhere.

"Who is the young man I saw talking to you who seemed to understand Nahuatl?" Coronado asked through the Aztec. "He escaped the battle. I need him as an interpreter."

Nayuchi pretended not to understand the question.

Coronado leaned across his desk. The Aztec interpreted each sentence, one at a time. "We let you talk to that very old man who came as a messenger from your people last night. Now you need to talk to me. The Aztec chief who met you on the field tells me that he is sure the young man next to you was a Guasave Indian from Petatlán in Mexico. Did he come here with the black man who arrived last year? You know what I am saying to you."

Nayuchi's expression never changed. "Your people killed that young man," he said. The Aztec interpreted his answer back to Coronado.

"Did you capture him last summer when the black man came?"

"Yes. But you killed him. He is dead."

Coronado leaned back into his chair. "I do not believe you. I promise your messenger will not be harmed. When he returns tonight, tell him to bring us the young Indian from the south. I also want to meet your leader."

—

It had surprised Coronado that he could not find any house in the pueblo in which a leader lived who would have superiority over others. All buildings and rooms seemed equal. How can people be ruled without a king, he wondered? He was astonished to meet the old and frail man who entered Coronado's tent two days later. The old man said he was the village's leader. He wore a blanket made of many pieces and many colors. He knew more words in Nahuatl than Nayuchi, making the Aztec interpreter's job easier.

The elder confirmed they had killed Esteban the previous year. He showed Coronado some of Esteban's possessions.

Coronado asked why they killed Esteban. "Because we asked him if he had any brothers," the old man said. "He told us he had an uncountable number of fair-skinned, bearded brothers. He said they had powerful weapons and were not far from here. We could not allow him to tell his brothers where we live."

For the rest of the time, Coronado and the elder argued. The elder kept insisting that Coronado leave his country. Coronado kept telling him he was there to stay.

After Coronado declared he would be angry if they did not turn over their captive who had come with Esteban, the elder left. The next day, he brought Bartolomé to Coronado. Dressed like a Zuni, but with the tattoos of a man from the Guasave tribe in Mexico, Bartolomé stood before Coronado and his retinue of Castilians. He spoke the language of Petatlán and also much of the Nahuatl of the Aztecs. He even could speak a little Spanish. Coronado watched as Bartolomé conversed in Zuni with Nayuchi.

Coronado turned to his head groom, Juan de Contreras, who bowed when Coronado addressed him. "We are fortunate to have found an interpreter," Coronado said. "He understands much in many languages. See to it that he is well taken care of and does not wander off."

Pleased at gaining an interpreter, and wanting to reassure the Cíbolans, Coronado allowed the elders to wander freely in their previous home. Expeditionaries were told to treat them with courtesy or face severe punishment. Every day Coronado called them for meetings and tried to convince them they should bring their people down from the high mesa they'd fled to. He told them they should come back to their villages.

In their last meeting, Nayuchi decided to try a new strategy to convince Coronado to leave. After he'd learned the strangers were looking for a place with seven cities, he had tried to interest them in the Hopis to the west. As a result, Coronado had sent two exploring groups to Hopi. Now Nayuchi steered the interpreter into talking about the weather at Hawikku.

"Winter is terrible," Nayuchi said. "Men freeze to death if they walk to the river of ice, a cold wind blasts against our walls every day, and the snow piles up to our rooftops. You must have seen the many fireplaces in our rooms to warm us during the winter."

It pleased Nayuchi that Coronado seemed worried when his words were translated. He began again, saying, "There is a large river toward where Sun Father rises each morning. It is not too far. Sun Father makes the winters there mild. Spring comes early. The people have much food for your men and much grass for your horses."

The next night, Nayuchi and the elder with the many-pieces blanket, along with others who accompanied them, disappeared. The only Zunis left in the pueblo were some boys who offered to run messages back and forth.

—

The domed pavilion tent with its sides of striped colors fluttered in the hot summer breezes of August 3, 1540, beside another abandoned Zuni pueblo. Francisco Vázquez de Coronado sat at his desk inside enjoying the pleasant summer day. It had been about a month since the first pueblo had been overcome. He decided he could no longer delay his report to Viceroy Mendoza. He picked up his quill pen and began writing with the elaborate flourishes of sixteenth-century penmanship.

Never did the young conquistador doubt he would loom large in history. He came from a prominent Castilian family in Spain. Skilled in the politics and confidence of the privileged, he also became experienced in battle against the New World's natives. They had courage but their weapons were weak. Coronado was governor of the frontier province of New Galacia northwest of Mexico City. And the friendship he had curried with Viceroy Antonio de Mendoza had reaped still another great reward.

He remembered his audience with Mendoza when Coronado had delivered the exciting news brought back by the Franciscan friar Marcos de Niza about rich Indian cities to the north. He'd bowed to the man who controlled all of New Spain from Mexico City. Friends already had told Coronado of the favor that Mendoza intended to bestow. The Coronado and Mendoza families had been associated for a quarter of a century, going back to the fathers.

Who would go north to explore and conquer the northern land? Friar Marcos promised it was filled with new souls for God and in native cities wealthy and populous enough to pay tribute to anyone brave enough to conquer them. There were reports of many riches.

Contenders included the greatest conquistador of all, Hernán Cortés, conqueror of Mexico. Then there was the conqueror of Panama and Nicaragua who also had assisted Francisco Pizarro in Peru, Hernando de Soto. There also was the famous conquistador Pedro de Alvarado. Another who wanted to go north, Nuño Beltrán de Guzmán, remembered in Mexico as "Bloody Guzmán," was eliminated from contention when he was arrested in 1537. Guzmán had been charged with war crimes against the Indians and sent to Spain in shackles.

But Coronado knew that Mendoza saw Cortés, Soto, and Alvarado as dangerous rivals. That left an opening. Coronado exploited it by demonstrating his loyalty to the viceroy. He insinuated himself more into Mendoza's favor, becoming Mendoza's favorite provincial governor.

Mendoza had conferred the rank of captain-general on the young Coronado at that audience, entrusting him to find and conquer the lands that Friar Marcos had described so glowingly.

Coronado shook his head, discouraged. They had come all this way, and for what? Friar Marcos had called the first village Cíbola. Coronado renamed it as Granada, reserving Cíbola as the name for the entire province of towns. Coronado frowned. How should he break the news to the viceroy? Instead of large and prosperous cities in Cíbola Province, his force had found Indian apartment buildings occupied by religious farmers.

In the weeks they'd spent crossing the desert country, the only natives they'd seen were nomads who lived around temporary camps. The expedition had passed numerous ruins of buildings, but no villages. His expeditionaries began then to suspect that conditions would not improve. These Indians in Cíbola, however, lived in multistory towns, wore cotton clothes in addition to tanned leather and robes, cultivated cornfields, and lived as well or better than rural and small-town Castilians in Spain. But there was no gold or silver to be found.

He sighed and dipped his quill into the ink jar before continuing.

Referring to Friar Marcos, Coronado wrote to the viceroy, "In brief, I can assure you that in reality he has not told the truth in a single thing that he said, but everything is the reverse of what he said, except the name of the city and the large stone houses."

Coronado described how his expeditionaries were disappointed by what they found along the trail even before reaching Cíbola because so much of what Friar Marcos had reported had turned out to be wrong. Many expeditionaries had gone into debt to invest in the expedition and now were worrying about financial ruin.

"I tried to lift their spirits the best I could by telling them ... that we should focus our anticipation on those Seven Cities [of Cíbola] and the other provinces about which we had information—which were the goal of our undertaking."

He put the letter aside. He needed to make sure he wrote everything in the most positive way. Viceroy Mendoza had begun to have second thoughts about sending Coronado out when he'd heard another scouting party's negative reports. Despite the discouraging appearance of Cíbola, Coronado needed to make sure he left enough hope for encomiendas and even the friar's rumors of riches so Mendoza wouldn't recall him.

# 12

Coronado relied on the veterans with him, especially two men with long military experience: Juan Troyano, and the tough field master, García López de Cárdenas. But after the July 7th battle, there were few Indians in sight. Coronado couldn't even send friars to preach to them. All the Cíbolans had fled to a stronghold on top of a high and steep mesa about twelve miles away. Once he'd learned where they had gone, Coronado had reconnoitered the mesa from its base on July 19th and decided it was impregnable.

He took up his quill to finish his letter to the viceroy, describing the battle for the pueblo.

"I did not find a single woman or any young men less than fifteen years or men older than sixty, except two or three elders who remained to command all the other youths and fighting men," he wrote. It was now obvious the Indians had evacuated their population and most of their provisions before the expedition arrived. He had fought a diversionary force.

Coronado sighed. He dreaded having to write such news to Mendoza.

His advance force had traveled more than four months through Mexico and the mountainous desert beyond, banners waving in the wind, mounted on Spanish barb warhorses with armor, swords, and lance points reflecting the sunlight, representatives of the world's most powerful sixteenth-century nation.

Weeks behind him was the bulk of the largest expedition that Spaniards had ever launched north of Mexico.

There were herds of fifteen hundred horses and mules and about six thousand sheep and cattle. Food on the hoof. Coronado himself brought at least twenty-two horses and several mules.

In all, Coronado commanded three hundred and fifty men at arms who hailed from all over Europe, with most from the Spanish province of Castile. Coronado's European fighting men included few professional soldiers. The rest could be termed militia. There were mercenaries and adventurers from several other European countries mixed in with the Spaniards.

The greatest part of the force consisted of up to two thousand Aztecs from Mexico City, Tarascans from Michoacán, and other warrior cultures in central and western Mexico. The warriors outnumbered Coronado's men-at-arms by as much as five-to-one. And because many of the Europeans also wore Indian clothing and carried Indian weapons, the expedition resembled a massive Mexican Indian force more than a European army.

There also were hundreds of family members, paid servants, and African slaves. Coronado had brought seven of his African slaves: four men and three women.

Coronado lowered his head into his hands. All of that effort and expense for this. The other cities of Cíbola Province were no better than Hawikku/Granada and just as empty of inhabitants. Even if they could be talked down from the mesa, there weren't many of them to pay tribute with goods or provide forced labor. There probably weren't enough for a decent encomienda for even one of his officers.

Coronado knew he needed to justify fighting the Indians for the first village. He'd already convinced himself that it was the Indians who started the fight. He set the stage by telling the viceroy that, instead of just yelling at Cárdenas and his horsemen at the pass, the Indians had launched an assault, firing arrows at the Spaniards and their horses.

Then he went on to describe the encounter at Hawikku. "In order to comply with Your Lordship's advice," he wrote, "I did not want them to be attacked ... And I said that what our enemies were doing was nothing and that it was not right to do battle with so few people."

Cortés or Pizarro would have killed as many enemy warriors as possible, of course. Coronado wanted to make sure the viceroy knew his expedition was showing more restraint, as the viceroy had ordered.

"When the Indians saw that we did not move, they took greater courage, and grew so bold that they came up almost to the heels of our horses to shoot their arrows. On this account I saw that it was no longer time to hesitate, and as the priests approved the action, I charged them."

Coronado leaned back in his chair. That was good, he thought, noting that he had the Franciscans' permission to attack. Mendoza couldn't argue with that. Coronado could still hear the friars' voices pierce the din of shouting men and snorting horses, urging the men to attack the Indians.

His horsemen had surged forward, running the natives through with lances, cutting them down with swords, and trampling them beneath the horses' hooves. Coronado smiled, remembering the looks of consternation his battle-eager horsemen had given him when he called off the charge.

Coronado went on to describe how his men then attacked the village.

"As that was where the food was, of which we stood in such great need, I assembled my whole force and divided them as seemed to be best for the attack on the city, and surrounded it. The hunger which we suffered would not permit of any delay."

Coronado ordered his men to shoot Indians off the walls with their arquebus muskets and crossbows. Then, eager to impress his men with his leadership, and being one of the few expeditionaries protected by metal armor, Coronado had climbed a ladder he found leaning against the wall. But the ladder had been placed there as a trap. Coronado was battered twice to the ground by slabs of rock tossed down on him. He'd been knocked unconscious despite wearing a helmet.

"I think that if Don García López de Cárdenas had not come to my help, like a good cavalier, the second time that they knocked me to the ground, by placing his own body above mine, I should have been in much greater danger than I was."

After carrying the unconscious Coronado to safety, Cárdenas sent hundreds of Mexican Indian allies into the attack. The outnumbered Zunis gave up the fight in less than an hour. Again the expedition had shown uncommon mercy. Cárdenas also knew the viceroy's orders of leniency toward Indians. He realized Coronado would not want him to do more than necessary to capture the village and gain the food stored there. Against all his previous experience as a conquistador, Cárdenas let the survivors escape.

Coronado went back to his letter, noting, "But it pleased God that the Indians surrendered. And Our Lord saw fit that this city was captured." He never mentioned the overwhelming force of Aztecs and other Mexican Indian allies.

Coronado, his head aching from his injury, also had a painful arrow wound to his right ankle.

"I am now well, God be praised, although still somewhat battered by the stones," Coronado wrote. He told Mendoza of four Castilians wounded by arrows in the assault on the village. "Also in the battle we had in the countryside, two or three other companions-in-arms were wounded. And three horses were killed ... There were seven or eight other horses wounded, but now these men, and the horses as well, have recovered." Coronado gave no accounting of casualties among the Mexican Indian allies. He knew Mendoza would not be interested.

He told Mendoza that the Cíbolans were a strange race and hard to understand. They didn't seem to realize there would be peace if they would simply become Christians and serve as vassals to the holy Roman emperor and king of Spain.

"When three days had passed after this city was captured, some Indians came from those settlements to offer me peace. They brought some turquoises and poor, little blankets. I welcomed them in His Majesty's name with the best speeches I could, making them understand that my purpose in coming to this land, in His Majesty's name and by Your Lordship's command, is so that they all the others in this province may be Christians and know the true God as their lord and His Majesty as their king and earthly lord." Coronado shook his head in exasperation as he continued: "[The elders] returned to their houses. But suddenly, on the next day, they packed up their belongings and food and fled to the hills ... leaving their towns almost deserted."

Coronado told Viceroy Mendoza that he was sending groups out to explore the countryside in hopes of finding a better place to establish his headquarters. "The land is extremely cold," Coronado added, thinking back to his conversation with the Cíbolan elder. "The snow and the cold are usually very severe. I report this because the natives of the land say this, and it seems likely that it is so ... Because of the nature of the country, the type of rooms they have, and the hides and other things these people have to protect themselves from the cold."

Coronado pondered what else to report. He had to be careful with bad news, such as Cíbola being a poor province with no riches or even much possibility of Indians making tribute payments or providing forced labor.

Perhaps, he thought, he should tell the viceroy that the failure was not for lack of trying. He put his quill to the paper again.

"God knows I would have wished to have better news to write Your Lordship, but I have to tell the truth ... You may be certain that if all the wealth and treasure of the world were here, I would not have been able to do more in His Majesty's service and that of Your Lordship than I have done in coming to where he has directed me. My companions and I carried our food supply on our backs and on our horses for three hundred leagues, traveling on foot many days. We made routes across cliffs and through rugged mountains, along with other hardships I will omit telling. Nor do I intend to leave here short of death, if it be of service to His Majesty and Your Lordship that it be so."

He knew the shame of failure would follow him forever if he turned back now. And the money he and his wife had invested would be lost. He needed a way to salvage the expedition. He needed to look farther for gold and potential encomiendas that everyone believed must be in the north. The valuable spices and other rich trade goods of India and China also had to be in one direction or the other. The riches Mendoza had sent him to find must be near.

The best idea was to finish on a positive note. Coronado started the conclusion to his letter:

"From what I am able to conclude, there does not appear to me to be any prospect of obtaining gold and silver, but I trust in God that if it exists here we will obtain it. And it will not remain for lack of seeking it."

# 13

Poquis remained at Xauían's side as the bow chief met with the Warrior Society. Xauían told them that the strangers who attacked the Zunis would come to Ghufoor soon. The elders would try to meet the bearded metal people in peace. However, seeing the warlike nature of the invaders, the elders also needed the warriors to be prepared in case they were attacked as their trading partners to the west had been.

Xauían set the warriors to work supervising and protecting the women carrying more food and water to the fortress villages on the mesa. He made sure there were plentiful supplies of bows, arrows, shields, and clubs, and he began sending runners back and forth to Zuni to monitor the strangers.

"Again your judgment and advice are strong," Xauían told Poquis. "Now while we complete preparations here, I am sending you to the other villages to ask if they will help us if we are forced to fight."

He told Poquis to take a group of runners as well as warriors with relatives or friends in the other Tiwa villages. First Poquis was to go a short walk north to Kuaua, then cross the river and visit Watche. They both thought the closest villages would be the easiest to convince to aid Ghufoor if called. Then Poquis was to proceed south visiting nine other villages on both sides of the river and all within short walks from each other until he reached the southernmost village in the concentration, which was the largest village of all. For reasons he kept to himself, Xauían did not ask Poquis to go on the longer walk to the last Tiwa village, Tsugwaga.

Carrying Xauían's turkey feather cloak over his arm as a sign he spoke for Ghufoor's bow chief, Poquis visited each of the other Tiwa villages.

His visit to Tuf Sheur Teui, on the east side of the river a short walk to the south, was typical of each village.

Poquis was well known at Tuf Sheur Teui because his exploits as a Ghufoor warrior had become celebrated throughout the Tiguex country. He also was a native of the Tiwa village of Puaray a little farther south. He gained permission to speak to the Warrior Society there.

They met in a grove of cottonwood trees outside the village walls, far enough away that the women would not know of the business discussed—even though their mates might tell them afterward. About a hundred warriors and the elders who advised them sat on the ground on both sides and before him. Poquis could see the life-giving waters of Big River sparkling beyond the trees in front of him. Behind him rose the village's brown, solid walls. They rose at the base of sand hills that rolled up a long plateau to the mountain. The trees along the river cooled the late summer day.

Poquis thanked the Tuf Sheur Teui men for meeting him. Then he brought forward a Zuni man who spoke Tiwa. The man had fought in the battle against the metal people and Aztecs. He told how the horsemen with their lances slaughtered forty Zunis on the field and how hundreds of invaders attacked Hawikku's walls. The invading force was overwhelming, he said, and now it was known that many more strangers would arrive in a moon or two.

The warriors and elders sat silent through the Zuni foreigner's presentation.

Poquis stood and thanked the men again, this time for their attention. "We can expect the strangers will come here eventually, perhaps sooner than we can imagine. Our runners tell us that the strangers are sending out exploring parties all around the Zuni country. We hear that they also have attacked the Hopis. They will come to Big River next."

A murmur went through the crowd. Then an elder stood. "This is disturbing news, but why do you come to tell us this? The Zuni country is far away. Perhaps the strangers will not come this far."

"Not come? It is more likely our great river will dry up and fill with sand. The trade route runs from the Zuni villages to Ghufoor and our other Tiwa villages. The strangers will come with the falling leaves and the first snows."

There was another murmur, for it was unexpected that a young warrior such as Poquis would contradict an elder. Poquis realized the disturbance, and he held up Xauían's turkey-feather cloak. "I do not speak for myself," he said. "The words I speak were placed on my tongue by Xauían, the bow chief of Ghufoor. He sends me to ask the brave men of Tuf Sheur Teui and other Tiwa villages to prepare for the arrival of these bearded strangers. They come with horses, metal weapons, and many warriors from the Land of Everlasting Summer."

Angered by Poquis's challenge of his authority, the elder swept a similar cloak off his back and waved it at Poquis. "I am the bow chief of Tuf Sheur Teui. These men are my warriors. I talk to the katsinas with my prayers. I listen to them, not to Xauían. Do you think my warriors will follow Xauían instead of me and fight these metal people? He can lead Ghufoor warriors, but he cannot tell the men of our village what to do."

Poquis sat, deferring to the elder, who remained standing. "Do you wish me to tell you the wishes of Xauían?"

"I will listen."

"Xauían tells me to say that all the Tiwa villages should pledge to one leader. He does not seek to be that leader. The sun priests can decide. He tells me to say that it is important we meet these strangers together, united in strength, if they turn violent."

The elder walked to Poquis to stand over him. "So Xauían thinks there will be a war."

"Xauían does not know. The metal people are very strong in numbers. They have weapons we have never seen before. He wants to greet them in peace when they come. He also wants the Tiwa people to be prepared in case these strangers attack us."

The elder gathered his turkey cloak around his shoulders. "I will tell the sun priest what the warrior Poquis has said. I also will tell him that appearing warlike might cause them to attack us as they did the Zunis and the Hopis."

"Xauían says preparation must be as invisible as the air. The strangers must not see it."

The elder stared into Poquis's eyes for a long moment. Then he walked away. All the Tuf Sheur Teui warriors rose and followed him back to their village. They flowed around the seated form of Poquis as if they were a stream parted by a rock.

—

Many suns later Poquis sat alone in the dim light of Ghufoor's second kiva whose walls did not have painted katsinas. He waited for Xauían to join him. He had sent runners before every setting of Father Sun to keep Xauían informed. The only message Xauían ever sent back was to keep trying. Poquis had visited every village at least twice, and sometimes more often. All valued their autonomy too much to agree to follow one leader.

Poquis was beset with doubts. What must Xauían think, knowing that he had failed to persuade the Tiwa villages to join in an alliance? Many in Ghufoor's Warrior Society looked to Poquis for leadership, but he felt he had failed them. There in the kiva's silence Poquis felt a weary loneliness. The Warrior Twins were not here. They had given him the strength he needed in his many battles. But now, as he sat surrounded by the bare earth walls, he felt all the katsina spirits had abandoned him.

He looked up at the sound and then sight of Xauían descending the ladder into the kiva. They greeted each other, and Xauían sat cross-legged on the other side of the small, flickering fire at the adobe altar. They sat for a long time, each whispering a quiet prayer to the spirits and the Creator. Poquis tried, but his prayers seemed unworthy.

Xauían looked over to Poquis. "You have done well," he said. "It is better than I expected."

Surprised, Poquis frowned. "They will not join behind one leader. Not you or anyone else. They say they do not fear the strangers. Many say they do not think the strangers will even come here. They argue, why should they come here? We have none of this yellow rock and things called silk and spices that the strangers keep asking the Zunis about."

Xauían smiled. "The metal people will come. When they do, I hope they will soon leave to look farther for whatever it is they want. No one promised to join together if there is war. But each village promised you that they would send food and gifts so we can greet these strangers in peace. For that, you deserve honor. It could not have been easy. These invaders are much stronger than we Tiwas, so we must try for peace."

Poquis felt a draft against his bare chest from the vent opening into the kiva. "What if they attack us? There are too many of them."

"That is why we must not make the mistake the Zunis made. We must not show force. We must meet them in peace. Then perhaps they will leave us."

"I think there will be a fight sometime." Poquis leaned back a little. "The Zunis say the metal people and the Aztecs have come ready for war, not peace."

"What did your Zuni companion who speaks our language tell you?"

"He left to return to his people on top of Dowa Yalanne. Before he left he told me what the elders had told him."

Xauían waited, saying nothing.

Poquis leaned forward. "The elders told him that one of the strangers came down into a kiva at Hawikku where they were meeting. The stranger wore a shirt and hat of metal, and he had the long metal knife that they call a sword. His pants were puffed out and striped with many colors. He spoke to them in words they could not understand. They said he sat on his haunches like a dog, staring into the kiva fire. They gave him rabbit meat to eat. Then an elder started singing a chant that allows witches to change into animals. As the stranger ate the rabbit, his beard began growing longer until it covered his body. Then the elders saw that the stranger had vanished. In his place was a wolf."

Poquis sat upright again. "That is what the Zuni said he was told."

# 14

The trail had been pounded into a wide, sandy line by generations of feet. It coursed across a desert of bunch-grasses and short bushes for more than two hundred miles from Pecos to Zuni, linking with a network of other trails spreading out for much farther.

From a hilltop, the Pecos leader could look behind him and see a column of twenty of his companions walking along the trail in a late summer, rainy-season journey. They were drenched with rain many afternoons and baked under the sun the rest of the time.

No one knew the trails better than that tall man at the front of the column. He was a trader. He was followed by hunched-over companions, a padded leather strap across their foreheads to help carry the weight of leather packs on their backs. The packs bulged with turquoise jewelry, cotton blankets, buffalo hides, and painted pottery of many designs. Often he exchanged goods with other long-distance traders like himself whom he met on the trails. But sometimes, out of curiosity, he walked the trails to the outer limits. He had been east to the grassland plains to trade with nomadic tribes and seen the immense buffalo herds. He had walked all the way to the western sea, where undrinkable water rolled on past the horizon. He had made his way to the mountainous jungles of the scarlet macaw parrots far to the south, trading for live birds to bring back. It was there he had first heard tales of pale people with beards who rode horse-beasts and conquered everyone wherever they went.

In addition to the Towa language of Pecos, he spoke Nahuatl, the language of so many of the people far to the south and common on the trade routes. He also knew some Pima and Zuni, the main languages to the west. He could converse with the plains tribes in sign language. And he knew Tiwa and a bit of other languages spoken among the flat-roofed towns along Big River.

As he strode forward, he thought with pleasure at how the Pecos elders had praised his skill with languages. His ability with so many, they said, made him the best man to meet the strangers who'd arrived in the Zuni country. For the last twenty cycles of winter, spring, summer, and fall, he'd been preparing himself for this rendezvous by traveling the trails and trading with different tribes. All tribes gave him safe passage so he could continue bringing the trade goods they desired. And they let him return with macaw birds and copper bells from the south, sea shells from the west, and buffalo hides from the east.

"Find this tribe of strangers," the old sun priest had told him at the kiva council. "Find out how strong they are, where they are going, and what they want. Perhaps they will become trading partners who will give us new and wonderful things in exchange for what we can give them. Ask if they will help us against our enemies."

Behind him walked a Pecos elder, who was a Katsina religion priest. But as the one in front, the tall man was the real leader. He knew it. Without him, none of this would be possible. And he knew what the elders thought even though it had gone unsaid. Because he had that rarity of Indian facial hair, the bearded strangers might be more receptive to him. Though his cheeks and chin were as smooth-faced as his companions, he sported a long and wispy mustache. He took pride in its distinctive look.

From Pecos, the group had traveled down from the mountains and into the desert. They crossed Big River at Ghufoor, walked past the village of Zia, and on toward the west, in a journey taking fifteen suns. When they had come close to Zuni country, the elder had sent a runner ahead to the Zuni sanctuary atop Dowa Yalanne. The Pecos group had rested until Zunis could come to explain what had happened about two moons before. Then the elder had sent another runner to the bearded strangers with a Zuni the invaders knew.

The next day, the mustachioed man led the group on the move again.

In the afternoon, he stopped the column with an upraised hand. In the distance he could see their Pecos runner coming down the trail with another man.

The Pecos bearers took off their bulging trade packs and rested on both sides of the trail. The young man with their runner was dressed like a Zuni, but he did not look like one. He identified himself by the alien-sounding name of Bartolomé. He stared at the tall Pecos man with the mustache and spoke to him in a mix of Nahuatl, some Zuni words, and sign language he had picked up.

The Pecos man understood the combination. Bartolomé was telling him that the strangers wanted to meet and trade with his Pecos people.

"As soon as they heard you described," Bartolomé said, "they began calling you Bigotes. That is a word in their language for growing hair on the lip. Their leader is named Coronado. He wants to meet you."

The elder interrupted in the Pecos language, which Bigotes translated into Nahuatl for Bartolomé: "Are they dangerous? Will they greet us in peace?"

Bartolomé's face turned serious. "They are very powerful in war. I ran away when they attacked the Zunis. When this Coronado heard I was from Mexico, he took me from the Zunis to be an interpreter. You can come in peace."

—

Alonso Álvarez planted one end of the staff that flew the expedition's colors into the sandy ground under the late August sun. He'd gathered with other expeditionaries when word came of the impending arrival of Indians on the trade road toward the Spanish encampment. In preparation for their visit, Alonso and others had erected a multicolored canopy that flapped and shook in the wind. Coronado waited in a chair carved with Christian and royal symbols. Several expeditionaries stood in a semicircle behind their general. Lancers sat on their horses a short distance away. Alonso stood beside the chair holding the pole flying Coronado's banner and pennons as the Indians were escorted forward.

Wearing his gilded armor and plumed helmet, Coronado had surrounded himself with swordsmen who had been able to afford shining steel breastplates and metal helmets shaped like a ship's prow. Many of the hand-picked horsemen also wore metal armor or chain mail vests.

Alonso stared at the Indian leader's long mustache. As the Pecos man stepped forward to stand before Coronado, Alonso felt vulnerable in his quilted tunic. He was the only Spaniard not wearing metal armor near Coronado. Alonso heard the Indian utter unpronounceable sounds that he decided must be the man's name. Like everyone else, however, Alonso remembered just the name that Coronado called the Indian: Bigotes.

Bigotes acted so friendly that Alonso and the others relaxed their guard. Bigotes opened his hands and held them out toward Coronado.

Coronado motioned to Bartolomé to step forward and interpret. Bartolomé spoke to Bigotes in his combination of Zuni, Nahuatl, and even some Pima. Even Alonso recognized some words used from the Aztecs' Nahuatl language. It helped that both Bartolomé and Bigotes spoke slowly and repeated words, because neither was fluent in all the languages. They filled gaps with the limited sign language that Bartolomé had been able to learn and many alien words. In turn, Bartolomé explained things in Nahuatl to an Aztec interpreter, who then translated to Coronado in rapid-fire Castilian Spanish.

"Tell them," Coronado said in Spanish, "that I will give them water and food and gifts. But first they must swear obedience to the holy Roman emperor and king of Spain, in whose name I come. They must become Christians by pledging their allegiance to the pope and know the true God."

Alonso listened as the Aztec translated Coronado's message into Nahuatl to Bartolomé. The man from Petatlán then turned and spoke in a mix of languages to Bigotes, who alternately frowned and smiled in confusion. Then Bigotes replied. The Aztec translated back into Spanish. He said Bigotes had agreed and wanted to be friends with the Spaniards.

Coronado beckoned several Spaniards. They moved forward with baskets filled with Spanish trade items. "Tell them I am pleased to have their obedience. Tell them I welcome them to the province of Cíbola with these gifts."

Coronado motioned for the other Indians in Bigotes' group to come forward. Alonso stiffened in tenseness and other Spaniards gripped the hilts of their swords. Coronado leaned forward in his chair and presented the Indians with glass beads of many colors, polished metal hand mirrors, and small copper bells. The Indians delighted in showing the gifts to each other. In turn, Bigotes told several bearers to present Coronado with tanned hides of a large, curly-haired beast.

Coronado pointed to Bigotes and asked in Spanish, "From where do you come?"

Through an awkward combination of sign language and Nahuatl words that followed, even Alonso started to sense the gist of the reply. In the final Spanish translation, it was said Bigotes had come from a village called Pecos because they had heard of the expedition. The mustachioed Indian picked up a stick and drew a map in the sand. His map situated Pecos amid forested mountains. Bigotes scratched a line from there to a box drawing of a building, which he indicated was Hawikku. Then he drew a curvy line intersecting the route, representing a large river about a third of the way from Pecos to Hawikku.

Coronado unrolled one of the great woolly hides. "Ask him what kind of animals these are and where they live," he instructed the translators.

—

These metal people are bizarre, the Pecos man thought, as he struggled to understand what Bartolomé said to him. Why did they keep calling him Bigotes even after he told them his name? And why had they started calling the elder with him by the word cacique? Once he realized that Coronado wished these words to be their names, he shrugged. Perhaps these alien people did not use names but gave people new ones, he thought. How odd.

Bartolomé began speaking about how the Pecos people must obey the man wearing yellow metal, agree to be ruled by people with titles unfathomable to Bigotes, answer to a mysterious God, and honor beings that were called saints.

Bigotes tried to puzzle it out. The king and the pope that Coronado mentioned sounded to him like the Warrior Twins, but with different names. A true God? This Coronado must be talking about the god who spreads mist in the mountains, he decided. And he thought that perhaps the saints that Coronado referred to were katsinas. These strangers used such different words that Bigotes became unsure how to respond.

He used a mixture of some Nahuatl words, some sign language and even some Zuni and Pima words he had picked up, splicing them together to come up with a statement. Bigotes ventured to talk in this communication mixture to Bartolomé, looking toward the seated Coronado. "Say to him that we come in peace. We wish to be allies with the metal people against our enemies. Say to him we have come so we can know the metal people better and to trade with them. Tell him we have gifts to seal our alliance."

Bartolomé turned to the Aztec interpreter. Bigotes could not follow the combination of languages. Back and forth Bigotes and the interpreter went with questions, trying to decipher what each was saying to the other. Then the Aztec interpreter rephrased everything to Coronado. He spoke in the other language so rapidly that Bigotes could tell even Bartolomé was deaf to it. The smile on the man in yellow armor, however, reassured Bigotes that his visit would be a success.

Gifts were exchanged. It was then that Coronado had unrolled the buffalo skin with another question: "What is this animal, and where is it found?"

Bigotes spoke the Pecos word for a buffalo. When the strangers seemed perplexed, he walked in among his bearers. Finding a man with an image of a buffalo tattooed on his arm, Bigotes led him before Coronado. He showed the arm with the tattoo. He indicated the height of the animal with a hand. He spread his arms out, walked to the farthest point, and spread them out to indicate a buffalo's length.

He said the animals lived on great grasslands east of Pecos in numbers so large they were impossible to count. To get to Pecos and the buffalo herds beyond, he retraced the route backward on his map, drawing more boxes for buildings like Hawikku's to show the flat-roofed towns that lay along Big River. That was the country known as Tiguex, he said. The people grew cotton and food in the desert with water they channeled from the river. Pecos was at least four more suns of travel past Big River, he said. And two or more suns of travel after that were the buffalo herds. He picked up a buffalo hide. He used a stick to punch numerous holes in the sand, representing a large herd of the beasts beyond Pecos.

Coronado asked Bigotes through the interpreters about the numbers of people who live along the river to the east and in his own village.

"Many people live in the flat-roofed towns up and down the river," Bigotes replied, once he understood the question. He stood taller in pride. "But Pecos is the largest and most powerful."

—

When Bigotes and his companions left to set up a camp close to the abandoned Hawikku, Coronado turned to Alonso, still holding the pole of banners.

"Leave the colors here and go find Hernando de Alvarado. Bring him to me."

Within minutes, Alonso returned with the young officer, twenty-three and already a captain. Alvarado entered Coronado's headquarters tent and bowed as Alonso stepped aside and retrieved his standards pole. Sunlight diffused through the tent's fabric, reflecting the interior of the tent on the officer's steel breastplate. Alonso took his position behind the general as Coronado recounted to Alvarado what the Pecos Indian called Bigotes had said.

"Make preparations to go to the east," Coronado told him. "Bigotes leads me to think that in this, at least, the old Cíbolan man told the truth about better prospects in that direction. Take twenty men on a commission for eighty days. I will have Bigotes guide you. I want you to leave Sunday and go as far as you need to find the cows he describes."

The general handed Alvarado a copy of his orders. "Report back what you have found. I want to know about this Tiguex Province along a large river. Bigotes said there are several farming villages. See if it's suitable for the expedition to spend the winter there."

Coronado looked through his tent flap at the still-abandoned Cíbolan/Zuni pueblo outside and at the desert, already turning cold in the nights. "We don't want to spend it here," he said, more to himself than to anyone else.

—

For his journey east, Hernando de Alvarado wanted the toughest men. He hand-picked twenty horsemen, making sure to include Juan Troyano, a thirty-year career military man and the veteran of many European campaigns. Troyano's beard was dark brown with white streaks, which he favored as a mark of his experience. Coronado also sent the teenaged Alonso Álvarez as a standard-bearer. Alvarado was pleased that the leader of the four Franciscans and the most militant of them, Friar Juan de Padilla, volunteered.

On foot with Friar Padilla and Bigotes' group were about a hundred Indian allies from central Mexico. Three wore their fearsome warrior regalia of jaguar skins, with the warriors' faces visible through the open jaws and teeth of the heads. One had donned a carved wooden eagle's head, and his body was decorated in eagle feathers. The Indian allies carried round shields painted with curved or geometric line designs, long feathers dangling from the bottom edges. Their weapons of choice were wooden paddles embedded along the edges with sharp edges of chipped obsidian, like broken glass. Called a maquahuitl, a Nahuatl word, the weapon was as long as an arm and deadly when used to slash. Some warriors carried wooden poles sharpened to a fire-hardened point.

Alvarado remained disappointed that Coronado would spare only four arquebuses and no crossbows. Coronado said he needed most of the long-range weapons because it would be many days before the expedition's main force led by Tristán de Luna y Arellano arrived. Coronado was left with about thirty infantry and thirty-five horsemen to hold Cíbola Province after sending Alvarado east and other exploring parties west. Coronado also kept several hundred Mexican Indian allies at Hawikku even after sending so many of them with Alvarado.

Bigotes led Alvarado and his men along the trade road, pausing at times to investigate ruined buildings of ancient Indian dwellings. When they came to a fork in the road, Bigotes explained through Bartolomé and the Aztec interpreter that the left trail went to a Keres pueblo called Zia. The right trail led to the mesa-top fortress of Ácoma, also a Keres pueblo. They had been traveling for five days. Alvarado turned the group to the right. Bigotes seemed to be known in all the villages. Alvarado told Bigotes to move ahead to explain to the Ácoma people that he would be arriving soon.

Ácoma was in a spacious valley of tall, tottering sandstone formations a hundred or more feet perpendicular. The mesa with the village on its top rose like a solid-walled platform more than three hundred feet high. It was accessible by a small path that ascended through a split between cliffs and gigantic boulders where notches had been cut for the steep ascent. After they arrived at the valley, Alvarado could see buildings on top of the mesa. He realized Ácoma must be ancient.

# 15

Caoma stood at the edge of Ácoma's northern precipice. The Pecos trader, who was guaranteed safe passage by all tribes for the warm buffalo hides he brought, had been welcomed to the top of Ácoma the previous day. But the trader brought no buffalo robes this time. Instead, he said the strangers who'd attacked the Zunis were coming to visit Caoma's people of the white rock.

Ácoma and Zuni runners had been traveling back and forth for weeks with information about the bearded strangers and their native allies from far to the south. The Ácomas had feared that the strangers would come east to visit them soon. Caoma had heard how the man Coronado had sent exploring parties westward from Zuni to the Hopi villages and the great canyon beyond. Elders had met that night and given Caoma his instructions.

As bow chief, it would be Caoma who would take his warriors to meet the strangers for the first time.

He looked down from his mesa-top home and watched the long line of strangers and foreign warriors descend the trail threading between the boulders and hills to the west and into the valley. Nothing surprised him. In anticipation of this day, Caoma had once walked to Zuni and seen for himself the horses, the metal weapons, the wind-whipped colorful banners, and the great numbers of foreign warriors. The awe he felt at the sight helped him to understand why the Pecos trader now preferred to be called by the name of Bigotes that the strangers had given him.

It was hard for him, however, to understand how such an overwhelming force had appeared at Zuni so suddenly.

Ácoma warriors had long ruled here, secure from attack in their impregnable mesa-top fortress. At the slightest hint of disrespect, Caoma had led Ácoma warriors to attack and discipline the flat-roofed towns along Big River to the northeast. Other tribes throughout the area feared his warriors. However, these strangers, who were sure to be his enemies, were a new power that the proud Ácoma people now needed to consider.

He turned and walked through swarming activity among the villagers preparing for the arrival. Warriors awaited him at the top of the long rock stairway that descended to the mesa base. Older men with women and children made piles of food, pottery, and other supplies to take down if necessary.

Caoma crouched beside a great rock reservoir of water. He hooked his fingers through the handle of a drinking cup and scooped some water. Generations before, the Creator had flown a cottonwood seed-fluff to the top of the mesa and set it beside the pool. Now that lone tree's trunk and leaves blessed the people with shade. Caoma said a prayer, drank, and prayed again.

*The strangers are a terrible threat,* the elders had told him. *Take great caution.*

He rose. For reassurance, he patted the stone club in the blue cotton sash around his waist. He would leave most warriors at the top. He would lead a hundred warriors down the stairway.

—

Despite Bigotes' introduction, Ácoma warriors armed with bows and arrows, clubs, and spears confronted Alvarado's group at their mesa's base. The Ácomas drew a line on the ground with corn meal as the Zunis had done, forbidding the expeditionaries to cross.

Alvarado spread his Mexican Indians around to the sides. His horsemen lowered their lances and prepared to charge as they had at Cíbola, the horses pawing the ground and stomping with their iron-clad hooves.

Bigotes dashed forward and began talking in sign language and rapid words. The Ácoma leader was taller than most of the warriors but still not as large as the average Castilian.

Alvarado leaned down from his saddle to the Aztec interpreter and Bartolomé who stood beside his horse. "What is Bigotes saying?"

Bartolomé watched. Then he looked up at Alvarado, replying through the Aztec interpreter, "He is telling them not to resist. He says you Castilians will attack as you did against the people of Cíbola and kill them all. They have already heard about the battle there. This is a bluff, and their leader is having second thoughts. Bigotes is telling them we need food. He promises that then we will leave and go to the river in the east."

—

Caoma raised his hand, as if to ask everyone to stop where they were. He looked at the hundred or more Aztec warriors, who stared back, holding their shields and obsidian-edged clubs. They alone seemed a match for the warriors he'd brought down from the mesa. There were also the twenty bearded strangers with horses, lances, swords, and sticks of thunder and lightning that he'd studied in his trips to Zuni.

He looked back at Bigotes. "Is it true they will leave if we give them food?"

Bigotes told him the metal people were in a hurry to see the villages along Big River and then go find the buffalos. He said they needed more supplies.

*We want them to leave,* came the words of the elders. *Do not fight them unless we must.*

Caoma sent a warrior dashing up the rock stairway. Soon several men descended carrying bread, piñon nuts, and corn meal. They presented the food to the man Bigotes said was named Alvarado. As gifts were handed out, the Ácoma warriors walked among the horses. They rubbed the horses' sweat on themselves. They made the shapes of crosses with their fingers as their sign of peace.

Caoma stood back to watch the expeditionaries pack the food in bags on their beasts. He saw the young, bearded man on the closest horse talk to Bigotes. Then Bigotes walked toward him.

"He wants to go to the top and see your village," Bigotes said.

*They will want to climb to the top. Allow only a few.*

Caoma gave his assent. He said Alvarado and five others could climb up.

—

Alvarado chose Juan Troyano and four men with armor or chain mail to make the climb with him. They found the way treacherous, handing their arquebuses and lances from one to the other as they pulled themselves up through the series of hand- and toe-holds. Their Ácoma guides scampered up the path without using their hands.

Alvarado would later write to Coronado that Ácoma "is one of the strongest places that we have seen, because the city is on a very high rock, with such a rough ascent that we repented having gone up to the place. The houses have three or four stories. The people are the same sort as those of the province of Cíbola. They have plenty of food, of corn and beans and fowls like those of New Spain."

The climb and the weight of their armor soon had Alvarado and Troyano gasping for breath.

"Look up there," said Troyano, pointing to the top of a curving face of solid rock towering above them. "It would take a very good arquebus to fire a ball that high."

"Let alone hit anything," Alvarado added, wiping the sweat running down his face from under his metal helmet.

As they neared the top, Troyano pointed to a rock face overhanging the climbing trail. "See that," he said. "There's a wall of large loose rocks that can be dropped onto the trail. I think that's why they let us come up. They wanted us to see that."

Alvarado paused in his climbing to look. The wall was positioned so defenders could drop boulders onto any invader trying to climb the steps. He resumed climbing. He said to Troyano behind him, "Entry is by invitation only, I see."

Once on top of the mesa, the Ácoma leader led them to the open area between walls of houses. Alvarado called the area a plaza, and he could see a rock depression to store rain and snow for water. The message was clear. The Ácoma Indians had lived on top of the mesa for hundreds of years because no one could dislodge them.

Descending was as treacherous as the climb. One Castilian lost his footing and fell onto another, but they suffered just bruises plus jokes about their clumsiness.

In preparing to leave Ácoma, Alvarado presented colored glass beads to the leader of the Ácomas, who raised his eyebrows in half-circles in admiration of the gift. He asked in sign language where Alvarado and his party were going next.

"To Tiguex and Pecos, and then to the great grasslands beyond," Alvarado told Bartolomé to reply.

Shortly after Alvarado's group left Ácoma behind, Friar Padilla ran to a nearby spring. He kneeled beside a cross two palms high and as thick as a finger that had been stuck in the ground.

"Look," Padilla exclaimed to Alonso, who rode one of Coronado's horses over to the Franciscan. Padilla pointed to the first cross and numerous smaller crosses with feathers tied to them amid withered bouquets of cut flowers. The friar's eyes lit with excitement. "In some way they must have received some light from the cross of Our Redeemer, Christ." He rubbed his chin, looking at the crosses and feathered sticks. "Perhaps it came by way of India, from which they proceeded."

Fifteen miles northeast of Ácoma, Alvarado's force encountered ponds surrounded by cottonwood trees. The water was a welcome sight in the weeks of travel across deserts since Mexico. Then, after three more days of desert traveling, they topped a miles-long ridge and halted in surprise at the sight ahead. The rest of the way was a long, gradual slope descending to an expansive valley. On the opposite side rose the rocky, blue mountains they'd been traveling toward for several days. Down the middle of the valley, a broad river of sun-spangled water undulated through a desert of brown grass, gliding through narrow groves of cottonwood trees with leaves turning golden. The Europeans held their breath.

"We must call this the River of Our Lady," Friar Padilla said, standing by Alvarado's horse and looking up at him. "We have seen it on September seventh, the eve of her feast day. Praise Jesus and His holy mother."

"It's a big river for the desert," Alvarado declared. *"Un río grande."*

From the ridge the expeditionaries could see on each side of the river half a dozen apartment-block complexes, each one a separate Indian village, and each one near vast areas of irrigated corn fields. In the distance to the south, more green patches and columns of smoke held the promise of more pueblos. Alvarado rose from his saddle and counted the pueblos he could see on each side of the river. He would later find there were twelve, all of the Tiwa nation, in a cluster thirteen miles long from north to the south.

Bigotes stood on the ridge's crest. He put his hands together and then spread them apart to take in the whole scene before them.

"Tiguex," he announced.

# 16

Poquis reported to Xauían. Alerted by a runner from Ácoma, Xauían had dispatched pairs of warriors in several directions. Their orders were to report back to him as soon as the metal people riding horses were seen.

"They are coming on the trade road," Poquis said, nodding his head toward the miles-long slope to the west.

From the Ácoma runner's report, Xauían already knew twenty strangers were coming on horses with at least a hundred foreign warriors. He turned to two young runners. "You go down this side of the river, and you go down the other side," he said to each in turn. "Tell our people in the other villages that the time to seek peace has come. All are to send delegations at sunrise, as the elders have agreed."

As the messengers sprinted away, Xauían turned back to Poquis and touched the healed knife wound on the warrior's side. Marked now with a scar, it still was sore. "Let us hope we can meet these invaders in peace so you don't end up with something even worse," Xauían said.

Later in the afternoon, Xauían stood in front of Ghufoor's walls with Poquis, Ishpanyan, and other warriors to greet the trader from Pecos with a mustache. All the river tribes knew the man who now called himself Bigotes was a leader of the Pecos people, against whom everyone fought occasionally.

As Bigotes approached, Xauían turned to Poquis with a grin. "And we thought you act strange sometimes," he said, using his finger to trace a mustache on Poquis' bare upper lip. Poquis stared ahead as other Tiwas chuckled. Xauían turned back to greet the Pecos man and others with him.

Three Aztec warriors were dressed in the skins of jaguars, the elusive big cats that the Tiwas revered as Spirit Hunters. They brought forward a tall wooden cross and set it upright. Bigotes greeted Xauían in the Tiwa language. Bigotes said he came to speak for Hernando de Alvarado of the metal people, who wanted to bring the Tiwas to obedience to a new ruler and to teach the Tiwas about the true God.

Bigotes handed a small cross to Xauían. "They send this as a symbol of their religion," he said. "The Zunis call these strangers

'Bundle of Body Hair People,' but they call themselves Christians."
Xauían took the cross. He studied it, frowning. Bigotes continued,
"I don't know what it means. They said it is a sign that they come
in peace."

Xauían scoffed. "We have heard how they killed our trading
partners, the Zuni, and later killed some Hopi. We have heard
how they threatened the Ácoma warriors. How can you say they
come in peace?"

Bigotes motioned with his eyes sideways toward Bartolomé.
"Be wise and careful," he said in a low voice in Tiwa, "for that man
there named Bartolomé is from far to the south. He lived with the
Zunis for a year. He will see your anger and will report it to this
Alvarado, who even now waits to follow me."

Xauían acted as if he were looking over all of the Indians
accompanying the mustachioed Pecos trader. He noticed as he did
that Bartolomé was dressed like a Zuni. Switching to the Zuni
language, so Bartolomé would understand what he was saying,
Xauían said the people of Ghufoor would be pleased to meet the
strangers.

Bigotes stayed while Bartolomé and the Aztecs ran back to tell
Alvarado that he would be welcome.

Xauían motioned to Bigotes to follow him to one side. They
walked along Ghufoor's high walls. They paused along its south
side by a steep slope, the river coursing below them. Xauían
asked, "What do these strangers want?"

"They will attack you if you resist them. Beware of the ones
who ride the horses. In a fight on open ground, the riders will
destroy everyone with their lances and long knives. If you must
fight, then fight from your walls. But I warn you. There are so
many of them that even walls did not save the Zunis. Better that
you make peace with them. Then they will move on. I am taking
them to Pecos, so they will not be here long."

"All towns of Tiguex will send their people here tomorrow with
gifts. We will treat them as friends until they prove otherwise."

"I hope your people bring food," Bigotes said. "These
Christians are always starving and demand that we feed them.
Pecos will welcome them as well. I already have talked these
strangers into going out on the buffalo prairie. Maybe they will
keep going or, even better, wander lost forever."

# 17

Bigotes and Xauían waited beside Ghufoor's walls for the strange visitors. Poquis, Ishpanyan and all of Ghufoor's fifty-some members of the Warrior Society stood in a rank behind the two leaders. They were bare-chested with war clubs under their belts and quivers on their backs. Their round shields hung from neck slings, accessible in an instant to the warriors' hands. A hundred Aztecs stood silent to one side, holding their shields and obsidian-edged maquahuitls. The Aztec shields were painted with stripes and circles and long feathers draped from the bottom edges. The smaller Tiwa shields were made of thick buffalo hide and were about an arm's length in diameter. Most were decorated with designs symbolizing mountains, clouds, rain, and lightning. Poquis's shield was divided in half horizontally by a broad band of cloud designs that were topped by a painting of two black buffalo horns. Aztecs and Tiwas stared at each other as the bearded metal people walked forward.

Bigotes tried to explain what he knew about the strangers as they approached.

"They are very warlike and superstitious," Bigotes told Xauían. "They carry crosses everywhere they go and build even larger ones when they camp. Their priest, that grim man wearing the gray robe, is always with them. They want us to worship their three gods, which they call Father, Son, and Holy Ghost. And they have many katsinas, which they call saints and angels. They sometimes call themselves Castilians, from the world they came from. That land is beyond the water that meets the sky. Sometimes they call themselves Christians, from the name of one of their gods. Behind these are many more who are bringing animals that they eat. Animals you have never seen before. These light-skinned strangers call themselves children of the sun. With them are black people, who are their slaves. When they get here, you will see they are an arrogant and aggressive people. These Aztecs with them are fierce in war."

Alvarado and six of his men approached on foot with stern faces. They left their horses beside the tall wooden cross they had erected upon their arrival. Other men remained mounted on horseback, aiming their long lances with shiny points to the sky.

The sun reflected off the steel breastplates and helmets worn by Alvarado and his officers. Other strangers wore links of metal or thick, quilted cotton jackets, as well as helmets or leather hats. A sturdy-looking boy carried a staff from which fluttered colored cloths. All the strangers wore long metal knives hanging from wide leather belts.

Alvarado's Zuni interpreter, Bartolomé, did not understand Tiwa words, but Bigotes knew many of the Aztecs' Nahuatl words from his travels on the trade route. He was almost as fluent in Tiwa as he was in his native language at Pecos. However, the conversations were laborious and often confusing. When Xauían spoke, Bigotes translated into Nahuatl, which a tall Aztec named Quauhtli then translated into Spanish for Alvarado. Translations went the other way when Alvarado spoke.

Alvarado told Xauían that he represented many more Christians. The Aztec warriors were his allies, he explained. He came in peace, Alvarado assured Xauían. Then he added that his men wielded powerful weapons that would destroy anyone who made the mistake of becoming their enemy. They needed food to continue their travels up the river, across to Pecos, and on to the buffalo prairie. Alvarado finished by saying he wanted to see more of Ghufoor.

Xauían ignored the militaristic threats, as Bigotes had advised him. He assured Alvarado that his people were always happy to feed travelers. He said all Tiguex villages would send people with food to greet them in the morning. He said he would show them Ghufoor.

Xauían nodded in turn to Bigotes, Poquis, and Ishpanyan, asking them to follow him. Alvarado motioned to Juan Troyano, Quauhtli, and the boy Alonso with the staff carrying colored cloths to also accompany him.

Xauían led everyone down the steep slope on the pueblo's east side to the floodlands next to the river. A large field stretched toward cottonwood trees along the river's edge. Several stalks of corn grew from each of hundreds of mounds. Around and between the hills of corn, leafy stems of squash twisted, their yellow and purple fruits plump in ripeness. Bean vines spread over the ground and twined up the cornstalks. The squash and bean plants were bright green, but the cornstalks already were lightening as they matured toward harvest. White puffs of cotton adorned bare stems that stood knee-high along the water's edge.

Several Indian women stared down from rooftops at the visitors' beards, light skins, and shiny metal clothes. Some backed away, fearful of the strangers' alien appearance. A group of Tiwa men continued digging an irrigation ditch and weeding. The river swept against the edge of the red clay cliff upon which the pueblo perched.

Alvarado and his men looked at the crops and chattered among themselves, excited expressions on their faces.

Xauían returned the group to Ghufoor's walls. They climbed a ladder to the top of the first wall. The group walked across the first roof and descended another ladder into the enclosed open area. At Ácoma, most people had stayed inside their houses. Here, however, young and old Tiwas crowded the open area inside Ghufoor's walls and regarded the strangers with curiosity.

"That must be your hot room in the plaza," Alvarado said, pointing to a low, box-like construction in a corner of the Middle-Heart Place. A ladder descended through an opening into a subterranean chamber.

Xauían looked puzzled when the Spaniard's comment was translated to him.

"What does he mean?" Xauían asked Bigotes in Tiwa.

Bigotes replied in Tiwa so the interpreters could not understand him. "They think we use our kivas for hot rooms. They think the kivas are just a place where single men live and tell stories. They will insist on going down. Just let them think this is nothing more than a place to stay warm in winter and cool in summer. They know nothing of our religion and would not understand the paintings of katsinas in your other kiva. Take them into that unpainted kiva but not the painted one."

This time Xauían laughed. "Tell the hairy strangers in metal that there's an old man down there right now keeping warm. I will send Poquis to alert him."

Poquis moved ahead of the group while Bigotes translated to Bartolomé. Poquis descended into the kiva and alerted the religious leader about the strangers coming to see him.

Xauían led the rest down the ladder.

Xauían introduced the sun priest as the pueblo's leading elder. The old man began speaking in Tiwa.

—

Alvarado scowled, unable to understand the old man's words. He glanced at Bigotes and Bartolomé, waiting for a translation.

Translations went back and forth between Bigotes and Quauhtli, trying to match the words as they conversed in Nahuatl and sign language. Finally, Quauhtli spoke in Spanish to Alvarado: "He says he is the oldest man in the pueblo. He says he watched us walk here from Ácoma."

Alvarado turned to Troyano, his eyes wide with alarm. "This cacique is a sorcerer who can fly," Alvarado exclaimed. "We should have brought Friar Padilla in here with us to protect us from the devil who speaks through this man."

Troyano made the sign of the cross by touching his forehead, chest, and both shoulders. "Let us go," he said.

—

After Bigotes translated the strangers' alarm to him, Poquis thought about the confusion. Poquis was the last to leave, following the others up the ladder. How could the Christians think the sun priest's description of runners keeping him informed on their progress across the desert be twisted into the idea that the old man could fly? The misunderstanding didn't make sense to Poquis.

When they emerged from the pueblo, Poquis looked toward several Castilians and Aztecs on their knees in front of the cross silhouetted against the blue sky west of the pueblo. Poquis could hear the gray-robed man called Friar Padilla singing words as he stood before them. The Castilians and Aztecs chanted back in unison. Why were they on their knees and singing? It seemed very odd to Poquis. Beside the cross, the strangers had also erected a white tent like the ones the prairie tribes used. However, Indian tents were conical and made of buffalo hides. This tent was long and high and made of a heavy cloth. Breezes tugged at the tent's fabric.

Poquis watched Xauían climb a ladder back into Ghufoor as Alvarado and most of the other strangers returned to the camp where the Castilians and Aztecs were kneeling.

Poquis looked over at the boy with the banners standing alone. He watched as the boy carried his standard over to Bigotes, Bartolomé, and Ishpanyan by a wall.

Poquis studied the banners along the pole. Communicating through Bigotes and then Bartolomé, he learned the boy's name was Alonso Álvarez. Poquis asked Alonso for the meaning of the colored cloths with unfamiliar symbols.

"They are like the designs painted on your shields," Alonso replied. "These cloths hold important meaning for the Castilians. I am sure the designs on your shields are important to you in the same way."

Poquis nodded as Alonso's words were translated to him.

Alonso pointed to the fresh scar running along Poquis' side. "Please do me the favor and tell me how you injured."

"The wild desert raiders," Poquis replied through the interpreters. "I fought four of them with my club." He patted the club in his waistband. "One of them cut me with a knife."

"That is remarkable," Alonso said. Poquis looked at Alonso when the response was translated back and said nothing.

"We crossed only an empty desert since Cíbola," Alonso said. "Except for Ácoma and now here, we have not seen any Indians. Who are these wild desert men?"

The answer went back through Bigotes and Bartolomé: "They are all around. You will not see them unless they want you to see them." There was a pause. "Or unless they want to kill you." Poquis and Ishpanyan laughed

Alonso held up his hand to get their attention. Then he reached down and pulled up the trouser on his right leg, showing an indented scar on his calf. He stood and touched an arrow in the quiver crafted from mountain lion skin on Ishpanyan's back. "Flecha," Alonso said in Spanish, pulling the arrow part way out of the quiver and dropping it back in again. He leaned back down and tapped the concave area on his leg. "Flecha," he said again, grinning and driving a forefinger against his leg.

Poquis pulled an arrow out of his own quiver. He held the arrow out in front of him. "Flecha," he said, looking at Alonso's face.

Alonso nodded. "Sí. Una flecha."

Poquis stepped back and held the arrow in both hands. "Sí," he repeated. "Una flecha."

Bartolomé nodded and laughed, saying something to Bigotes.

Poquis grinned, not sure of what Bartolomé said. Bigotes translated it to, "You are speaking his language, called Spanish."

Alonso pointed to his chest, saying, "Alonso."

Poquis patted his chest. "Poquis."

Alonso touched his hand. "La mano," he said.

Poquis touched his hand, then Ishpanyan's. "La mano," he repeated.

Alonso and Poquis laughed, but Ishpanyan glared at them. He snatched his hand away from Poquis. He gave a dismissive wave as he walked away, just as Alvarado called from the tent for Bartolomé. Bigotes left with Bartolomé. Alonso turned to leave as well, but he stopped when Poquis held him back by the arm. Poquis touched his own nose.

"La nariz," Alonso told him. Poquis repeated the words.

For the next two hours, they sat in the shadow of Ghufoor's wall with Alonso teaching Spanish words to Poquis.

# 18

Hernando de Alvarado and Juan Troyano both agreed that Tiguex was the best place they had seen since Mexico. Zuni and Hopi pueblos seemed to have been built in the most inaccessible and inhospitable places. Food and water had to be carried from a distance for survival along small rivers. But the Tiwas had built their community houses on a large river beside cottonwood trees and clearings of irrigated cropland. The forested mountain range on the other side of the valley promised even more resources.

That night Alvarado and Troyano sat inside their tent around a candle-lit camp table. The pueblo's walls were a short walk away. Light from campfires outside glowed against the tent's fabric.

"Their leader looks very much like Juan Henche the German back in New Spain," Alvarado said, referring to Xauían, and using the Spanish word of *Alemán* for German.

"Juan Alemán. That's what we should call him," Troyano said. "It's a lot easier to remember than his heathen name. These Indians make me nervous. I feel they only tell us what they want us to know. They are not honest with us. They are ignorant and godless and possessed by the devil."

"Friar Padilla says they are heretics and great idolaters. He was outraged when I told him of the masks I saw in the underground hot-room here. He wants me to burn them. He says they are masks of the devil, just like ones he destroyed belonging to the Zunis. But I begged him to be patient. There will be time for that later. For now, we are under orders to explore beyond Pecos. We do not have time to get into a fight here."

The two officers stepped out of the tent to gaze at the pueblo, a massive apartment complex. Unlike the Zuni towns built of stacked rocks, the walls of the Tiwa pueblo were smoothed by a mud plaster, hard and brown. This pueblo was two stories high all around with towers rising in places. There were no doors because ladders through ceiling holes gave access to the rooms. The outside of the rooms were joined in a solid wall. They discussed the military situation. There was a small entrance in the south wall where a person could squeeze through on hands and knees— an access easily blocked. They agreed that ladders were the only way to reach the roofs. They couldn't see well in the darkness now, but during the day Troyano and Alvarado had noticed small openings along the walls through which arrows could be shot. The pueblo was not as benign as it might first appear.

Stars sparkled, and the Milky Way spread overhead like a river of silver. The air was warm with the spicy smoke of campfires. Splashes of light came from the fires around which the Spaniards and the Aztecs clustered separately in conversation and laughter. Alvarado looked at Ghufoor's town walls, rising like a lighter shadow lit by the moon. What did the savages call their town? "Coofor" was the closest he could come to the pronunciation.

He looked forward to the morning. The Tiwa leader he now called Juan Alemán had said all the Tiguex pueblos along the river would be sending people to Coofor to welcome the expedition. He would tell them to pledge their obedience to King and Holy Roman Emperor Carlos. He would leave it to Friar Padilla to have them swear fealty to the pope. Later the friars could give them knowledge of Jesus Christ.

Alvarado re-entered his tent and sat at his camp table. He wrote another installment in the report he would have a horseman deliver to Coronado at Cíbola. He wrote of how his group had left Cíbola on August 29th—"the day of the beheading of Saint John the Baptist"—and visited Ácoma before arriving in the Tiguex Province on the river.

Alvarado wrote that the Tiguex people "have a good appearance, more like laborers than a warlike race." He could see that they were farmers, traders, and artisans whose glazed clay pottery was widespread and admired by even his own men. The idea of them being laborers rather than warriors like the Aztecs was worth noting. Alvarado knew that Castilians in search of encomiendas would be encouraged by the peaceful appearance of the Tiguex people they could use for forced labor.

Alvarado wrote, "It is the old men who have most authority among them. We consider them sorcerers because they say they can mount up to heaven and other things of this nature." He remembered Friar Padilla's description of the Indians as superstitious idolaters. "They venerate the sun and rain," Alvarado wrote, shaking his head in disgust.

—

When morning came, Hernando de Alvarado was pleased at the homage the Tiwas offered to Spanish power. He walked to the door of his tent at sunrise. A crowd of Indians milled around the outside walls of the Indian village, bringing gifts of food and supplies to the expeditionaries.

Alvarado already sported a full beard at age twenty-three. His eyes were as hard as his steel helmet and breastplate.

Upon Alvarado's appearance, scores of Indians began playing music on turkey bone flutes, notched rasps of bone and wood, gourd rattles, and drums. They honored the twenty Europeans and the expedition's Aztec allies in a festive atmosphere.

Both men and women from all twelve pueblos in the Tiguex Province had come together.

Alvarado watched as the Tiwa leader he called Juan Alemán, rather than by the man's real name of Xauían, organized the Indians into groups from each pueblo. Each pueblo's religious leader took his place at the front. The Indians began walking in lines toward the Spanish encampment next to the pueblo Alvarado had renamed as Coofor. The village's religious leader, an old man wearing a turkey-feather robe, spoke to the Indians while Alvarado listened to his interpreters' translation. They told him the cacique described how the Tiwas were pleased to welcome the metal people to the land of Tiguex.

The Tiwas walked around the tent, several young men playing the same tune in unison on their flutes. They filled the air with notes like warbling birds. Smiling Tiwas carried gifts in their arms or clapped their hands in time with the flute music.

Each woman wore a blanket tied around her body with another over her shoulders and back. Many blankets were dyed in different colors. Their hair was tied with cloths into a coil on each side, decorated with turquoises. The older men wore blankets or buffalo robes with the fur turned inside and the hide outside painted with designs. Young men were bare-chested, wearing cotton loincloths and leather moccasins or plant fiber sandals.

Alvarado greeted each of the twelve pueblo groups as they entered the tent. The people told him the names of their pueblos. Expeditionaries would come up with Spanish names easier to remember.

The Puebloans presented corn flour, dried game, turkeys, squashes, bread, piñon nuts, and beans, along with blankets, deerskins, buffalo hides, and painted clay pots.

There were so many Tiwas that Alvarado had to dig deep into his supply of trade goods. He handed out colorful glass beads, mirrors, and other trinkets new to the Puebloans.

A few hours later, the Tiwas returned to their homes with their laughter, songs, and conversations echoing through the wide river valley.

That night, looking at the piles of pottery, robes, and food inside his tent, Alvarado added to his note to Coronado. He knew

Tristán de Luna y Arellano would be arriving at Cíbola soon with the bulk of the expedition, including several hundred Tarascan and other Mexican Indian allies. Arellano also was bringing thousands of sheep and cattle. Everyone was worried that Cíbola's grass would never suffice for the expedition's livestock.

Alvarado urged Coronado to move the entire expedition to Tiguex Province for the winter. He cited the friendly people, the abundance of corn, the large river, and the shelter they could find in the Indian buildings. They would also be closer to everything else they sought to the east: the buffalo plains, the lure of the silk and spices of the Indies, and the many Indian souls for Franciscans to save. Alvarado already had heard of many other flat-roofed house towns up and down the large river that ran beside Coofor. If larger than this, the area's population held the promise of future encomiendas enriched by forced labor and tribute payments extracted from the Indians.

Hernando de Alvarado smiled, knowing the general would be relieved to hear that the country was much better in this large river valley.

# PART III – PRELUDE TO WAR
## October 1540
## 19

At about the same time Coronado was in Cíbola, Dominican Friar Bartolomé de las Casas was in Spain awaiting his appointment with the king.

He had completed one of his several perilous journeys across the Atlantic Ocean to report to the king about his horror over the Indian genocide in the Americas. He had spent the past forty years of his life raging against Spanish destruction of the native inhabitants. He struggled in a no-man's land. The Spanish crown and Vatican were on one side, passing laws and making proclamations that the natives of the Americas should be treated humanely. On the other side were the conquistadors and colonists from Spain who wanted to get rich even if they had to ignore the king and pope by killing and enslaving the Indians to do it.

Las Casas took pride in being called "Defender of the Indians." He welcomed the hatred that fellow Spaniards in the Americas heaped upon him.

Conquistadors and colonists alike considered the Indians to be subhumans. Both felt they had just one way to a wealth they never could achieve in feudal Spain. That way was by terrorizing and killing enough original owners of the land. Then they could use the rest for forced labor and tribute payments and make themselves rich.

Las Casas sat at a crude table in his small and bare room in the Dominican monastery. By candlelight Las Casas wrote with a quill what he wanted to say once he was granted his audience with the king. In Spain, he could present his remarks with the power of his persuasive personality. In New Spain, he often had to smuggle his letters to the king, protesting the inhumanity of the conquest all around him.

Las Casas wanted the existing law enforced throughout the Americas to protect the Indians. "And till now," he wrote, "the king has not succeeded because all, small and great, go there to pilfer, some more, some less, some publicly and openly, others secretly and under disguise. And with the pretext that they are serving the king, they dishonor God and rob and destroy the king."

The king, pope, and citizens of Spain remained unaware of the conquistadors' atrocities against the Indians, Las Casas added, explaining, "They [conquistadors and colonists] always have exercised diligent care to hide the truth from our Lord the King about injuries and losses to God, to human souls, and to his state."

He paused and thought back to his meeting the previous fall with Viceroy Mendoza. He prayed that his visit would make the expedition already underway to the north more humane than other Spanish expeditions.

In his bare cell in Spain, it amused Las Casas to think of the sumptuous office and governmental home that Mendoza lived in at Mexico City. The velvet drapes, the European paintings, the stained glass windows, sculptures, and Indian servants.

Months had passed since their meeting, but the details were still clear in Las Casas's mind. The viceroy had been dressed like a king in splendid blue and white linens and silks. Indeed, he almost was a king in the Americas, answering to His Majesty many weeks away across the Atlantic. Even so, Mendoza had bowed to the priest. Everyone in New Spain knew Las Casas was known to whisper in the king's ears. Mendoza poured a small measure of French cabernet into the priest's crystal wine glass. Then he sat across from the priest at the shining mahogany table made by a fine Italian craftsman. Unlike the austere Las Casas, who had the shaved head of a monk with a ringlet of hair around the middle, Mendoza's hair flowed, luxurious and dark, to his shoulders.

After the exchange of courtesies, Las Casas had gotten to the point that most concerned him.

"I have heard, your excellency," he'd told the viceroy, "that you have appointed Francisco Vázquez de Coronado, your governor in New Galacia, to investigate the Franciscans' claims of great and rich cities to the north."

Las Casas did not touch his wine glass, which Mendoza would have considered an affront if his guest had not been a priest of Las Casas's stature. Instead, Mendoza sniffed at his wine's bouquet and enjoyed a sip.

Mendoza smiled. "I wish, Father, that you would not grimace every time you mention your fellow brothers in Christ in the Franciscan order. You seem to think them villains."

"I do not consider them villains, Don Antonio. I consider them grievously misguided."

Mendoza smiled at the priest's candor.

"It is not a secret that those of us in the Dominican order are very upset with many Franciscans," Las Casas said, still with diplomatic pleasantness. "We have our differences, as you well know. They look the other way while Indians are used for forced labor on the evil Spanish encomiendas, which also demand tribute payments so large that the Indians are kept in poverty. That is exceeded in gravity by their willingness to accede to merciless and greedy conquests of Indians, which the Franciscans rationalize by converting the few survivors."

"You judge the Franciscans harshly, Father." Mendoza sipped his wine.

"Yes, I judge them, but my opinion is nothing." Las Casas sat up straighter in his chair and adjusted his long Dominican robe. "Pope Paul has declared infallibly that the Indians are humans. I will tell you his exact words. He said, 'The Indians are truly men. Indians and all other people who may later be discovered by Christians are by no means to be deprived of their liberty or the possession of their property, even though they may be outside the faith of Jesus Christ. Nor should they be in any way enslaved.' Las Casas sighed and bowed his head for a brief prayer before continuing: "But our conquistadors and colonists wage pitiless war against them and treat them like chattels without souls. The Franciscans must answer some day to a much higher authority than me, the king, or the pope."

"I have no choice with the Franciscans, Father. Yes, Francisco Vázquez will be leading the expedition toward the Indian cities to the north that Friar Marcos tells so many wonderful things about. I will leave soon to meet him at Compostela, from where he will leave in late February. Friar Marcos will be his guide. Other Franciscans will go with him as well to convert the Indians and save their souls."

"What Franciscans will go?"

"I plan to send at least five, and I have three volunteers already. Friar Marcos de Niza will lead the Franciscans. He will be accompanied by Friar Juan de Padilla and a very devout lay brother, Luis de Úbeda, a man of constant prayer who lives a good and holy life."

"I have concern about Friar Padilla. He is an impatient ecclesiastic and his mind is obsessed with finding the Seven Cities of Antilia here in the Indies. I hear that he is already calling the Indian towns discovered by Friar Marcos as the Seven Cities of Cíbola."

"He will be fine. That is one reason for the expedition, of course. It is to learn whether this Cíbola is the Seven Cities."

"The Seven Cities are a myth. Are we to believe that seven Catholic Portuguese bishops fled over the sea to escape the attacking Moors many centuries ago? And can it be that they built seven magnificent and rich cities in an unknown land? The story is beyond preposterous."

"You are in the minority to think so." Again, Mendoza sipped his wine and never took his eyes off Las Casas's eyes.

"Never mind that," said Las Casas, still not touching his wine glass. "I beseech you, Don Antonio, that this new expedition treat the Indians they encounter humanely, as our holy father in Rome has requested. Let us not continue this pattern of ruthless conquest. Humane treatment of the Indians will produce better results than violence. I beg you to promise me, Don Antonio."

"I do think you are right, Father. You know of my efforts to educate the Indians in the university and teach them music, writing, and our Catholic religion. All for the greater glory of God. I will include in Francisco Vázquez de Coronado's orders that he is to treat the Indians with humanity and dignity. I promise and give my word in the name of and on behalf of His Majesty and by the royal power which I hold that your wishes will be followed."

"Your word is sacred to me, Don Antonio. I will speak of your enlightened approach to King Carlos when I see him on my upcoming trip to Spain. God bless you."

———

Las Casas sighed. He believed the viceroy had been true to his word and given Coronado instructions to treat Indians he met humanely. He just was not sure Coronado and his men would be any different than other conquistadors once they were out of the viceroy's reach. He adjusted the crucifix hanging from a cord around his neck, set aside his statement to the king seeking abolition of the encomienda system, and moved another stack of papers toward him. For the rest of the night, with heavy heart, he picked up his quill to resume writing the book he hoped would inform the public and end atrocities in the New World. His Spanish title translated to *A Short Account of the Destruction of the Indies*.

# 20

Xauían lowered himself to sit next to Poquis on the kiva's ledge. "I now agree with you that we will be forced to fight these metal people and their warrior allies from the south." Darkness had arrived quickly after sunset. A nearby fire popped sparks at them in the night. Crickets chirped around them.

"If only to protect our food," Poquis agreed. "They have already eaten everything we gave them two suns ago. They say they will ask us for more tomorrow and again when they leave in a few more suns."

Xauían swiveled his head to look at Poquis. "How do you know they will leave soon?"

"I have been learning their language. The boy who carries the colored cloths on a stick is teaching me. Sometimes others do as well. I think it will be useful to know their language. It is too awkward and perhaps dangerous to trust a translator to tell us what they are saying, or to tell them what we are saying. We could say one thing and they might think we said something else."

"I heard you were learning their words."

"Sí," Poquis replied in Spanish, and he grinned at the puzzled expression on Xauían's face.

"How much do you know?"

"Not much yet. I want to go with them when they leave. Stay with them. Learn more of their language."

"No, Poquis. If the rest of these strangers come here and become enemies, I will need every warrior. There are other metal people still at Hawikku, and many more will arrive soon from far to the south. And even more foreign warriors as well. I fear for our people."

Poquis looked up at the night sky. "I will return when Moon Mother is shaped once again as she is now. No later."

"The strangers will not let you leave."

"They will not know I have left until I am gone."

"This is a bad idea, Poquis. These metal people are more warlike than even the wandering tribes of the desert and mountains. They brought none of the women from their Hawikku camp because they expect to fight. They carry their weapons everywhere and guard their horses. They condemn our elders as evil. But look at their priest, the Gray Robe they call Padilla. He looks at us with nothing but contempt."

"To know them better is our one chance," Poquis said. "They are strange and they talk too loud. They treat their allies from the land of macaws like inferiors, even though those warriors fight for them. We need to keep in mind that when the rest of the strangers come, even all the Tiguex villages together will be outnumbered. I ask your permission to go with them and try to learn more of their language. It might be important."

"You never learned more than a few words of our desert and mountain enemies."

"This is different. The wandering tribesmen are few, although there are more every season. And they sometimes trade with us. But these metal people demand our food. They pay for it with beads we cannot eat. They might destroy us with their horses and weapons, or enslave us, or drive us out of our country."

Xauían became silent. Then he stood and walked toward the kiva ladder. "I will speak to the elders. They will decide."

—

The warrior Ishpanyan stepped out from the darkness beside Ghufoor's high wall. He surprised Poquis with his sudden appearance. The moon cast a pattern of light and shadows across Ishpanyan's scowling face. "You spend all your time with these strangers," Ishpanyan said. "You should be helping us make more arrows in case they attack us. Now you say you want to go with them. You act like you think more of these strangers than you do of your own people."

"You know that is not true. I will defend our people to the death. But I—"

"Do not speak to me. I am too angry at you right now." Ishpanyan turned to walk away. He stopped and faced Poquis again. "Be careful, Poquis. Some do not like you learning to talk like the metal people. They say you might be turning into a witch."

—

In the morning, Poquis's mate, Panpahlu, returned from the community corn grinding with a clay pot filled with corn meal. She added water, making a thick batter. She poured that onto a thin stone griddle propped over the small cooking fire. After they had eaten breakfast, Panpahlu and Poquis sat side-by-side, cross-legged on the floor of their room, talking as they did each morning. The fire brightened the middle of the room, its smoke going up through the roof opening for the ladder. The flickering light from the flames danced shadows around the dim walls. Smoke and earthy scents mixed through the room.

Poquis caressed Panpahlu's face. "Listen to me and understand. So I can learn more of their language, I have asked the elders to let me go with the strangers when they leave in a few suns."

Panpahlu pulled her blanket tighter around her and nodded. "I know," she said. "The women told me at the grinding stones."

Poquis drew back. "How can the women know this? The elders met just last night in the kiva. Even I have not been told their decision."

Panpahlu laughed. "Men's secrets buzz out of the kiva like hummingbirds. We women do not need to attend your secret meetings."

Poquis shook his head. He asked in mock seriousness, "And what have the elders decided?"

Panpahlu leaned against him as he wrapped an arm around her. "They will let you go. I will miss you. But we need to know much more about these strangers and their language and customs. The elders are afraid. They don't know what to do."

"In thirty suns, perhaps sooner, that's when I will return to you. I will miss you, too."

Looking up at his face, Panpahlu asked him, "When will you leave with them?"

"I do not think they will leave for a while."

"Good. The people will feel more confident about you accompanying the strangers if you can join in tomorrow's corn dance."

## 21

As she waited at one end of the Middle-Heart Place's open space with the others, Panpahlu thrilled to the drum's deep-toned thoom, thoom, thoom at three beats per second. The drum vibrated the warming afternoon air. She and scores of Tiwas had gathered at one end of the walled open area, dressed in their finest clothes, turquoise jewelry, and feathers. They filed out to the drum's cadenced beat. Hundreds of seashells and turkey bones tied to arms and legs clattered. There also came a tinkling of a few small copper bells obtained in trade from the south. Gourd rattles chattered like cicadas buzzing in trees. The drumbeats echoed off Ghufoor's adobe walls surrounding the open space of bare earth, thoom, thoom, thoom. The dancers and singers kept time with their feet, their arms, and their bodies.

The ancient dance, its knowledge passed on from parent to child, transformed the great open space into a dusty haze. A god-bright sun blessed the dance, as it did in every month of Autumn Moon.

Twenty men stood around the drummer. In rhythmic pitches, they sang an ancient Tiwa prayer asking for the Creator's blessing on the cornfields so there would be a good harvest.

Two pueblo men with white handprints on their faces and wearing buckskin shirts with white kilts led the dancers. A fox pelt dangled from the back of every male dancer's kilt to remind the people of their dependence on animals. The men took small steps to the sound of each drum beat, pacing forward side by side, holding an ear of corn in the left hand and shivering a gourd rattle in the right as they advanced to the drumbeats. Thoom, thoom, thoom.

Behind them came a long line of other men dressed the same way, spaced between the women. The women wore blankets blackened with plant dye and tied with red sashes around their waists, their feet stepping to the drum beats. Each woman wore a large scallop seashell hung from a cloth strap or a heishe necklace of small beads crafted from white sea shells. Some had necklaces of the blue stone of turquoise. Most women wore a headpiece shaped like a small tablet and as blue as the sky. Each headpiece was pierced with a four-pointed star and topped with three pyramid points stepped up and down like clouds. Every woman also held an ear of corn in the right hand and a juniper bough representing eternity in the left. They dipped one hand and raised the other in time to the drumbeats.

The women wore their hair down to symbolize falling rain. Prized feathers from eagles, turkeys, and macaws hung in the hair of men and women alike and fluttered from their clothing. The men wore deerskin moccasins. The women advanced with bare feet so they could better send women's life-giving energy into the ground for the corn.

Panpahlu danced almost in a trance. The dancers stepped in lines. Tagging at the end of each line were children, costumed in miniature like the adults. Another generation coming along to the beat of the drum, thoom, thoom, thoom, the clicking shells and bird bones, the buzzing rattles, and the stamp of the dancers' feet.

Circling and walking among the dancers were four men with their bare torsos and limbs painted black. They helped fix costumes and shouted out directions and encouragement. Instead of free flowing hair decorated with red and blue macaw feathers like the dancers, these men piled their hair into a knot atop their heads. They tied their hair with rags and dry cornhusks.

Keeping time to the drum and voices of the singers, the men danced by stomping their feet. The women padded barefoot with light steps. The drumbeats kept pounding.

The dancers formed a pair of parallel files, turning their bodies to face one way and then another, their feet keeping time to the drum. Then the two files faced each other two arms' length apart.

Panpahlu stepped in place with the other dancers. Her heart stirred with expectation.

Then, exiting by ladder out of an underground kiva in the northwest corner, came men dressed as rain dancer katsinas. They were bare-chested with dangling leather pouches. They wore bands of fur around their arms, kilts fastened with woven hip-sashes of many colors and designs, and dyed leather moccasins with leggings. Long-haired, painted wooden masks with eye slits covered their faces. Macaw feathers, pieces of corn stalks, and beads decorated the masks. By donning the masks representing katsinas, each man temporarily became the katsina himself. Each katsina carried a miniature bow hung with dangling eagle feathers in his left hand. He shook a gourd rattle with his right.

Panpahlu faced straight ahead, but she cast her eyes sideways to watch the approach of the katsinas as they came walking between the two lines of dancers. At last Poquis had attained the acceptance to be masked as one of the katsinas. Now he was a costumed representation of the ancestors who had become holy spirits to care for the people and carry their prayers to the Creator. She wondered if she would be able to tell which katsina was her loved one.

Flutes sounded like bird melodies upon arrival of the katsinas, the drum pounded, and the Tiwa singers continued chanting.

A reverent murmur rose from the dancers as the katsinas filed between them. The dancers sprinkled white corn meal on the katsinas' shoulders. Panpahlu watched each one until at last she saw the katsina with an enemy's knife scar on his side. She sprinkled an extra portion of corn meal on the white mounds atop Poquis's shoulders. She could not see his eyes behind the mask's slits, but she knew he looked at her. She knew it. Drumbeats, flute notes, and singers' voices drifted in the air.

—

When Alvarado had heard the drum beats inside the pueblo, he summoned Juan Alemán and learned a corn dance was taking place. The Indian leader invited Alvarado to enter the pueblo and watch from atop the walls. Alvarado sent five armed Spaniards. They dangled their legs over the roof edge as they watched the dance in the plaza below.

The Spaniards relaxed after becoming satisfied the dance was not a pretext for attacking them. Alvarado had sent enough men to ensure defense if the invitation was a trap, but not so many as to alarm the Tiwas.

Sitting among the Spaniards on the first terrace beside the lay brother, Friar Luis, Father Padilla recoiled in disgust when he saw the masked Indians emerge from one of the plaza's underground chambers.

"This is an abomination," Padilla said through gritted teeth, rising to his feet. "Look at these pagans. Dressed like demons straight from hell. Where is Alvarado? He must stop these devil worshipers. While he lets this iniquity go on, all the saints grieve at the sight of such sacrilege. These Indians are worse infidels than the Turks and Moors."

Luis sighed. "I agree this is offensive to all devout Christians. But even Spain's Laws of Burgos declare we must let the Indians perform their dances."

"The laws do not apply to us here, Brother Luis. We Franciscans are here to do God's work, not the king's. Dominican trouble-makers like Bartolomé de las Casas would serve the Lord far better if they would preach to the Indians instead of to the court in Seville. Let Las Casas and the other Dominicans wring their hands and spout legalities. Remember, it is we Franciscans who suffer so we can bring God's word and save the souls of these devil worshipers. These idolaters. These pagans." He ran out of names to call them.

Luis shook his head. "But at what cost? I wonder. All those Indians killed at Cíbola. The rest fled to the top of a mesa where we cannot go and preach the sacred word to them."

"They will come down eventually, and then we will convert them. The deaths of those at Cíbola will open the door for them to know the true faith."

"But I ask again, at what cost, Father Padilla? We have killed an unimaginable number of Indians in Mexico, and now in Peru and the great lands in between, with our arms and diseases. At what cost will we convert them?"

Padilla scoffed at the frail old man sitting at his feet. "You are of little faith," he said, his voice rising in anger. "As St. Augustine told us, the loss of a single soul without baptism exceeds in gravity the death of countless pagans, even were they innocent."

Luis watched the masked Tiwas. They passed below him in a line to the beat of the drum in the plaza below him. "May God convert them," he prayed softly.

"You always say that, Brother Luis, but perhaps it is up to us to convert them." Padilla stood, stalked across the roof, and descended a ladder. Luis turned to watch the priest stride back to the camp.

In a few minutes, Padilla returned with a cross six feet high that he had dragged from the camp and wrestled to the top of the roof. He placed it on end and stood beside it, towering over the plaza. He shouted, "Blessed be Jesus." The Tiwas below him raised inquiring, then frowning, faces.

Luis rose to stand beside Padilla. Luis was a skinny scarecrow in a voluminous robe next to the stout priest. "I must protest, Father," he said. "What you are doing embitters them against us."

Padilla glared at the lay brother. He continued to stand beside the cross, but he stopped shouting at the crowd. "When I return from the buffalo plains," he vowed, "I will put a stop to this devil worship. When conversion of the Indies is complete, we will see the glory of the Second Coming of Jesus Christ, whose thousand-year reign will be a Kingdom of God on Earth before the final judgment."

Brother Luis said no more. Unlike the priest, he was not a believer in the Millennial Kingdom of many Franciscans. They thought discovery of the Americas was a sign that the Second Coming was imminent once its natives were converted to

Catholicism. Luis prayed for peace between the expeditionaries and Indians.

When the dance ended and the drumbeats stopped, the dancers uttered a cry of approval. They walked out of the plaza and scattered back to their rooms in the pueblo.

# 22

Three days later Bigotes led Alvarado's expeditionaries and Aztec warriors out of the Tiguex Province. They followed the river by traveling north. Poquis walked with Bigotes and the other Pecos men, keeping his distance from the surly Aztecs. The Christians had made a new tall cross from cottonwood branches along the river. Two of the expedition's African slaves took turns carrying it before Friar Padilla. The Franciscan walked with his gray robes fluttering in the wind, always carrying a small cross in his hand. Brother Luis plodded farther back, a man-sized cross laid across his back as he dragged the end along the ground, mumbling his prayers.

Poquis made one last backward glance at Ghufoor as he left, hoping for a glimpse of Panpahlu. All he could see were Ghufoor's tan walls and the wooden cross erected beside the town.

Friar Padilla had spent all three days urging the Tiwas to bring offerings to that large cross. When Xauian and the sun priest realized the importance the strangers gave to the cross, they'd told the Tiwas to honor it. Several Tiwas complied because they respected a cross anyway as a symbol of the emergence and peace. Poquis recalled the pleased look on Friar Padilla's face as he watched Tiwas climbing onto the shoulders of others or up ladders so they could place flowers and bits of turquoise on the cross. Some even draped blankets over the arms of the cross. Expeditionaries took away the blankets each night for their own use.

Pottery of all shapes and sizes, painted with abstract designs representing rain, clouds, birds, and other important elements of Tiwa culture, also were placed at the base of the cross. Most of the pottery was made of red clay with black designs. There also was white pottery painted with black lines that had been acquired by trade from other villages. There were cooking pots, bowls, large jars, cups with handles, seed storage vessels, and pitchers. All displayed an artistic touch the expeditionaries marveled at. Expeditionaries removed the pottery at night. They found more the next day.

Poquis and Panpahlu had taken painted prayer sticks carved from cottonwood to the length of a man's hand and decorated with feathers. But they placed their offerings onto the cross for a different reason than the others.

Poquis recalled how Ishpanyan had challenged him after he'd climbed down the ladder from the cross.

"These others are fools," Ishpanyan had said, grabbing Poquis's arm as he jerked his chin toward some Tiwa women approaching with pottery. "But you, Poquis, why do you bring gifts to honor this cross the strangers put up?"

"I have left prayer sticks, not gifts." Poquis motioned with his head toward feathers fluttering from carved sticks he'd tied to other Tiwas' offerings. Ishpanyan looked up. Poquis watched as Ishpanyan's face softened with realization. "My prayer sticks are to send prayers to the Creator and our katsinas, not to the gods of the strangers," Poquis said. "I am asking the Warrior Twins to give us strength and to cancel the offerings of people too weak to understand."

Poquis looked back at the tall cross as he accompanied the strangers. The twenty metal people rode horses. Foreign warriors enveloped them. It disturbed him that the cross was becoming popular among the people of Tiguex. He wondered why it was so important to the Christians.

# 23

Alvarado's group walked along a trail on the west side of the river, arriving soon at the adobe-walled apartment building complex of Kuaua. Larger than Coofor, Kuaua perched like a fortress on the west bank overlooking the river. It faced the mountain range on the other side of the valley. Behind its walls lay a large rectangular plaza almost bisected by an extension of housing compartments three stories high, with two smaller plazas leading off the main one.

Although his mules and extra horses already carried a burden of supplies collected at Coofor, Alvarado decided to pick up more at Kuaua. He wanted to train the Indians to always give gifts to the Spaniards. The inhabitants came out to greet the convoy. Alvarado sat on his horse and sent Bartolomé and Bigotes forward with bags to demand more corn and corn meal. After he dismounted, Tiwas escorted him on a quick walk around the interior plazas. He studied the fires for hardening pottery. Several compartments at ground level had ladders poking skyward to mark the rooftop entrances to subterranean rooms. The Spaniards now called each plaza's below-ground rooms *estufas*. Hot rooms.

When on the march again, Alvarado's force reached a point where steep mesas blocked progress and a smaller river intersected the large river. They crossed over to the east side amid mounded sand hills. Later they passed by several towns on both sides of the river belonging to the Keres and Tewa nations. All were walled, flat-roofed towns like Coofor and Kuaua. The residents of each pueblo, alerted in advance by Bigotes and stories they had heard from runners, came out to regard the visitors with cautious curiosity.

Alvarado stopped long enough to claim each tribe's pueblo and the surrounding land for the king of Spain, taking the Indian lands by decree. Friar Padilla paused at each pueblo for another reason. Upon arrival he always opened a clay vessel of water he had blessed. With a wet finger, he traced the sign of the cross on the foreheads of puzzled, shy children. He told everyone he'd saved their souls should they die before reaching the age of reason.

Bigotes was able to arrange for peaceful passage past the many pueblos in every case except two. At those pueblos, warriors emerged to fight. In both cases, however, the mounted expeditionaries killed many Indians in cavalry charges with lances.

After seven days, Alvarado and his horsemen reined to a stop before the northern-most pueblo. It lay at the base of snow-covered mountains. To the west, a river gorge cut more than six hundred feet deep, as if a knife had sliced open the flat plain. At the bottom of the gorge, the river tumbled in churned chaos around boulders between narrow rock walls on its way to Tiguex Province and the sea beyond. Alvarado's men had arrived at Taos. It was the most unusual pueblo they had seen.

A horseman sat in his saddle and contemplated the scene before him. Unlike the other pueblos, a low stone wall encircled Taos instead of having the sides of the Indian housing complex serve that purpose. The other pueblos they'd visited had enclosed plazas, but not here. Taos was composed of two large block-like buildings. One to the north and another to the south faced each other. A small stream ran through the plaza between them. Later the horseman would write:

"The houses abut each other and are of five and six stories, three made of mud walls and two or three made of thin wooden walls. The buildings get narrower as they rise. On the exterior, on the levels made of mud walls, covered passages made of wood extend out all the way around on each level, one above the other. Because they are in the mountains, the people in this pueblo do not harvest cotton or raise turkeys. They dress only in buffalo and deer hides. It is the pueblo with the most people in all that land."

# 24

Poquis spent the four suns walking beside Bigotes or moving up among the horses and visiting with Alonso.

The teenaged Alonso carried the standard on horseback the entire way, the large banner flapping above him with the Virgin Mary and coat of arms. With Bigotes, Poquis tried to increase his knowledge of the Aztec language of Nahuatl. With Alonso, Poquis practiced his growing knowledge of Spanish, memorizing words and phrases from the boy, who seemed to enjoy being a teacher.

Visiting Taos for the first time in years put Poquis in high spirits. The Taos people also were Tiwas, although they spoke a northern dialect of the language. Poquis had to concentrate to understand their words.

Taos was built at the edge of the high desert plain extending southward to Ghufoor and beyond. Towering over Taos were pine-cloaked mountains and steep ridges already capped with snow.

One of the kiva chiefs, a man named Shirpoyo, invited Poquis and Bigotes to his home for dinner when he heard where they were from. That evening they climbed three ladders to reach the flat roof where they could descend into the single-room apartment.

They sat on buffalo hides around the cooking fire. Whitewashed walls reflected the firelight. Shirpoyo was a man who laughed easily. His mate had looped several strands of turquoise around her neck and even her wrists for the occasion. She wore a colorful blanket over a soft deerskin dress. They had three young daughters with happy chatter and a son of about fourteen. The boy volunteered to run along Big River to Ghufoor the next day to tell Panpahlu that Poquis had arrived in Taos safely.

"Neither of us has eaten so much in a long time," Poquis told the woman, pointing with his chin to Bigotes. She handed each of them another piece of venison, hot from the fire.

Shirpoyo smiled at her. "She is very afraid of these metal people and the foreign warriors," he said. "What can you tell us about them? What do they want?"

The discussion went late into the night. Bigotes and Poquis told everything they could about the metal people and their odd ways. The metal people are a warlike race, they said. But if people did not resist, they would just put up a large cross and not attack. However, they would demand so much food and clothing that the only thing to do was encourage them to move on. Not even Bigotes, who had known them the longest, was sure where they came from. He knew they wanted yellow rock and other things he'd never heard of. The metal people's horses, weapons, and Aztec allies meant that every town's warriors were outmatched. The Zunis, the Hopis, and two other pueblos along the river on this trip had learned that hard lesson in defeat. Even Ácoma's feared warriors decided that the wise strategy was to provide supplies and not fight.

Toward the end of the evening, Shirpoyo draped a buffalo robe around his back and leaned against one wall. "You are welcome to stay with us while you are here," he said. "We might not eat this well every night. Even so, we will do our best to strengthen you for the rest of your journey."

He grinned and fingered a necklace of twenty bear claws draped around his neck and dangling over his deerskin shirt. "I visited both your villages on the great adventure of my youth."

Poquis looked up. "Where did you go?"

"Yes, tell us," Bigotes said.

He told them how he and a friend named Tután decided as young men about twenty years earlier to follow Big River all the way to the south sea. When they reached the Tiguex country where their Southern Tiwa brethren lived, they stayed three nights each in Kuaua and Ghufoor. Tután complained they would never reach the end of the river if they kept delaying. They paused for two more nights at Tsugwaga, hesitating before leaving that southernmost Tiwa town. From there on, it was a world unknown to them.

Poquis smiled. Alonso had told Poquis that the metal people referred to Tsugwaga as Isleta, a word in their language meaning Little Island. The village was on high ground that Big River flowed around on each side during floods. But he did not want to interrupt Shirpoyo's story or steer discussion to the strangers.

"We were gone for six moons," Shirpoyo said, laughing. "Everyone at Taos thought we were lost or dead." He looked at Bigotes. "We came back by way of Pecos and stayed a few nights there, too. Both of you were just children then."

"I would like to meet Tután," Poquis said.

Shirpoyo shook his head. "A bear killed him in the mountains the winter after we returned. That is why you should have your adventures when you are young. Some say I should not do this, but I keep his memory alive by talking about him with you. I believe my memory of him strengthens him in his spirit journey to the west to meet the ancestors."

—

They journeyed east for five suns after leaving Taos, resting for more than a day at Kua' p'o-oge before entering the mountain passes. Kua' p'o-oge was an Indian ruin beside a snowmelt mountain stream. Poquis heard the Franciscan name the stream as *Río de Santa Fe*. It took two days from there to reach Pecos, the largest and easternmost village in all of Pueblo country.

Situated on the back of a pine-scented but treeless ridge, Pecos was built from slabs of rock. The village dominated a bowl-like valley with forested mountains and towering ridges on all sides. Snow already smothered the tops and whitened long streaks down the slopes. Pecos was the first pueblo since the Zuni villages and Ácoma built of stone. Poquis overheard Castilians saying Pecos reminded them of a fortress in their own land.

Poquis remained wary of the scores of plains Indians camped in the meadow at the ridge's base. Ponderosa pines and junipers brought a rich cover of greenery up to the edges of the meadow's tall grass. Because it was just one long walk to the buffalo prairie, plains tribes came to Pecos to barter tanned buffalo hides for Puebloan pottery and corn.

"I have never seen so many in front of one of our villages," Poquis said. He followed Bigotes on the trail up the ridge, looking downward at the plains tipis.

Bigotes kept walking up the hillside. "They must stay in their camp. We do not dare let them inside because they cannot be trusted. We call these people Teyas, or brave men. They are strong warriors and have destroyed other villages between here and Ghufoor." Bigotes told Poquis to notice the sentinels keeping watch over the encampment from the Pecos flat roofs. The sentinels carried conch shell horns from the western sea that they could blow into and sound an alarm if the Teyas turned threatening.

—

Alvarado left the horses at the base of the hill. When he saw the Teya camp of tipis, he posted all his Aztecs to guard the horses. Then he and several Spaniards followed Bigotes and Poquis single-file up the narrow trail that crossed the length of the ridge, angling ever higher. From the height, they could see miles in every direction.

A Castilian with Alvarado praised Pecos in his description, saying:

"There is one of the other kind of villages larger than all the rest, and very strong, which is called Pecos. It has four or five stories, has eight large courtyards, each one with its balcony, and there are fine houses in it."

Another wrote: "Pecos is in a little valley between mountain chains and mountains covered with large pine forests. There is a little stream which contains very good trout and otters, and there are very large bears and good falcons hereabouts."

Juan Jaramillo was impressed with the quantities of food and supplies stored at every pueblo the Spaniards visited, making special mention of Taos and Pecos. "They have corn and beans and melons, skins, and some long robes of feathers which they braid ... and they also make them of a sort of plain weaving with which they make the cloaks to protect themselves. They all have hot rooms underground."

Bigotes had arranged for his home village to give the warmest welcome of all the pueblos. As Bigotes led Alvarado's group along the trail up the hill, the residents poured out in a celebratory mood.

"The people of the pueblo came out to welcome Hernando de Alvarado and their captain [Bigotes] with demonstrations of happiness," the horseman Pedro de Castañeda reported years later. "They took Alvarado into the pueblo with drums and flutes, of which there are many there similar to fifes. And they offered him a large gift of clothing and turquoises, of which there are many in that land. Alvarado's company rested there for several days."

—

"I am leaving tonight," Poquis announced.

Bigotes looked up from watching the flames warming them in his family home inside Pecos. The mustachioed Pecos man coughed on the smoke. "They might try to catch you," he said. "But there is one good way where they cannot follow you on their horses. I will give you a guide to show you. Tonight is a good night to get away. The metal people want to go and find the buffalo herds tomorrow. I am sending a guide with them who is a war prisoner from those who live on the plains. He is from the far side. He will find the buffalo herds they are so eager to see."

"Is he the one who wraps so much cloth around his head?"

"Yes." Bigotes turned to his son sitting in a corner and talked to him in the Pecos language. The boy jumped up. He scampered up the ladder and through the roof hatch.

Bigotes grinned. "I told him to go to the Sun Kiva, find Chosa, and tell him I need him. Chosa can track anyone. So of course he knows best how to stop anyone from tracking him. Or you. He will take you out safely."

"A favor by you today and one by me some other day," Poquis said. He turned his attention back to a prayer stick he'd been working on since leaving Taos. He would hide the prayer stick in the mountain rocks to bless his journey back home. He kept tying blue and red feathers to the stick because birds were messengers to the spirits and could fly his prayer to them.

"Perhaps no one will even care if you leave. They are thinking about the plains and the buffaloes now."

"Perhaps," said Poquis, picking out small feathers. He concentrated on finishing the prayer stick in time for his journey.

# 25

Soon after Poquis returned to Panpahlu, runners arrived in Ghufoor saying that a large number of metal people and their Aztec allies were marching toward them from the Zuni towns. Mother Corn had been harvested, nights were cold, the days were turning cooler, and the cottonwood tree leaves had turned brown and were falling.

The Tiwas learned the stranger leading them was Field Master García López de Cárdenas. He glittered with reflected sunlight on his armor as he led his armed force to Ghufoor a few days later. The expeditionaries erected a large cross at Alvarado's old campsite west of the village. They spread themselves over the area in tents and brush huts for shelter against the onset of winter. They built numerous campfires for warmth and cooking. A fog of smoke wrapped around the tents from juniper wood that the expeditionaries had cut along the way.

As Xauían walked to the Spanish camp, he motioned to Poquis to come to his side. They walked across the desert plain toward the encampment west of the village.

"Now we will see how much of their language you know," Xauían said. "Stay with me. But do not let them see that you understand anything. Afterward, you and I will talk."

Cárdenas waited inside his tent for Xauían and Poquis to enter. Five Castilians stood silently behind Cárdenas with lances and swords. Cárdenas stepped toward the Indian delegation with an impassive face darkened by unsmiling eyes and a full black beard. Taller than the Indians, he tilted his chin upward. That gave the impression he was looking down at them from even more height.

"Juan Alemán," he demanded in his bass voice. Xauían stepped forward, responding to the name the strangers always called him.

Poquis looked around. The tent entrance flapped in the wind, battering the sounds of clinking metal and men talking in Spanish throughout the camp. The sour smell of unwashed metal people crept around the tent. A middle-aged Zuni man stood beside Cárdenas. He knew enough Tiwa to get by, and he addressed

Xauían. The Zuni said he'd learned Spanish over the last several months. He would interpret for everyone.

Cárdenas spoke in Spanish to the interpreter in a stern way. Then he faced Xauían. Through the interpreter, Cárdenas said he needed the Tiwas to provide clothing because the month he called November kept bringing ever colder nights.

They talked through the interpreter with Cárdenas for a short time. Upon returning to Ghufoor, Poquis followed Xauían into the kiva to consult with the elders.

The elders sat in silence, their forms dim in the shadows, making them indistinct in their blankets and buffalo robes. Light came from the fireplace. A shaft of dusty light also pierced the room through the opening in the ceiling from the outside world. With a motion of his frail hand, the elderly sun priest invited Xauían to speak.

"This new leader of the metal people is a man named Cárdenas," Xauían told the elders. "He is older than the one called Hernando de Alvarado."

Poquis noticed how Xauían struggled with the pronunciations of the alien names. Xauían continued, his gaze intent on the sun priest. "Where Alvarado smiled, this man glares. Where Alvarado asked questions, this man makes demands. We have fifty warriors at Ghufoor, and he already has many more Aztec warriors than that with him. He also has many Christians and horses. Even more are coming behind him."

A murmur spread like a ripple of water through the room.

"They have an interpreter who knows some of our language and some of their language. He told us the metal people come in peace. He said they will camp outside our walls. He also said we must give them corn meal and warm clothing until the rest arrive under their leader, whose name is Francisco Vázquez de Coronado. Their leader's metal armor is yellow."

Another murmur circulated around the room. Xauían waited until there was silence again. "It is as I have told you. Poquis from the Warrior Society has learned many words in their language. He tells me there is more to this than the interpreter is allowed to tell us."

The elders turned in the shadows toward Poquis. He felt as if even the katsina spirits painted on the walls were watching him with their black eyes. The darkness seemed to close around him, as if a blanket had muffled his senses. He felt a catch in his throat. The sun priest nodded toward him. Poquis drew in his breath and exhaled. He'd never been permitted to speak to elders in the kiva before.

"Grandfathers." Poquis spoke in a soft voice with deliberation. "I am doing my best to learn the language of the metal people. The Zuni interpreter with them does not know their language very well. So they speak slowly and use simple words when they talk to him. Because of this, I was able to understand what this Cárdenas told the Zuni interpreter just before talking with Xauían."

Poquis paused, waiting for a signal from the sun priest to continue. Everyone was as quiet and as still as the katsina spirits painted around the walls. When the old man nodded at him, Poquis took a step forward.

"This Cárdenas told the Zuni he would be hanged if he revealed that soon, because of the cold, the metal people will take our village from us."

# PART IV – POWER AND GOLD
## December 1540
## 26

About thirty Tiwa warriors stood on a first-story roof section of their village, bows and arrows in their hands. They watched dozens of Europeans, a score or more of them mounted on horses, plus hundreds of foreign warriors, spread across the desert prairie in front of Ghufoor's long western wall. The invaders also formed against the northern and southern walls.

Clouds of frosted breath burst from the horses' nostrils in the cold air of Night Moon. The beasts scraped at the recent snow on the ground, sounding like clubs rubbing against stones.

Ghufoor had been the Tiwas' home for almost two centuries. When the weather turned icy in a storm, Cárdenas had summoned Xauían. He demanded that the Tiwas abandon Ghufoor so Cárdenas and his men could be sheltered inside. The Tiwas refused. They told him they could not leave their homes, their fields, and the graves of their loved ones. They had known from Poquis's warning that it would come to this. They had spent the week since Xauían's first meeting with Cárdenas making more arrows. They would fight for their home.

Tiwa warriors manned the three sides facing the strangers. They lightly guarded the eastern wall, which perched on the bank down to the waters of Big River. It was late afternoon, and the Spaniards waited until the setting sun was at their back and in the Tiwas' eyes. García López de Cárdenas was in charge because Coronado was still camped at the Zuni towns. The Tiwas watched Cárdenas ride his horse forward, flanked by two other Christians on horseback. They were armored like him and carrying lances with colored pennants flying at the points. Friar Juan de Padilla walked beside the horsemen, along with a score of Aztec warriors carrying their shields and wooden paddles edged with slices of sharp obsidian—the maquahuitl weapons the Tiwas had come to envy.

—

Cárdenas unfolded a sheet of paper. In a loud and clear voice, as he had earlier at Cíbola, he read the conquistadors' requerimiento to the Indians. The document ordered them to become vassals of the king of Spain and the Catholic pope, to obey Cárdenas's orders, and to allow the Franciscans to convert them to Christianity.

"But, if you do not do this," he concluded in his reading in Spanish, "or maliciously make delay in it, I certify to you that, with the help of God, we shall powerfully enter into your country, and shall make war against you in all ways and manners that we can, and shall subject you to the yoke and obedience of the Church and of their Highnesses. We shall take you and your wives and your children, and shall make slaves of them, and as such shall sell and dispose of them as their Highnesses may command. And we shall take away your goods, and shall do you all the mischief and damage that we can, as to vassals who do not obey, and refuse to receive their lord, and resist and contradict him. And we protest that the deaths and losses which shall accrue from this are your fault, and not that of their Highnesses, or ours, nor of these gentlemen who come with us."

Cárdenas raised his head and looked toward the walls, frowning. A cold wind ruffled his horse's mane.

—

Poquis strained to understand the requerimiento's Spanish. He recognized several words, but Cárdenas read it so fast that the only clear meaning was a sense of the threatening tone. Tiwa warriors began shouting at the strangers, shaking fists, and calling them insulting names from Ghufoor's rooftops as Cárdenas and his group returned to their lines.

"We will stop them," Poquis shouted to Xauían, who was standing farther down the length of Ghufoor's roof. "Our warriors are ready."

Then the Aztecs began advancing toward the walls. A storm of arrows brought up their shields.

The Tiwas on the roof had seen the arquebus muskets pointed toward them. However, they had no knowledge of how death could be propelled from such a distance without drawing on a bowstring. A cloud of smoke billowed from the strangers' line. Thunder roared as the Tiwas had heard before only in lightning storms. A warrior fell backward gasping, a bloody hole the size of a man's thumb in his chest. Chunks of adobe flew from other impacts by lead balls. With a battle cry of *Santiago y a ellos!* the expeditionaries and Aztecs charged toward Ghufoor's three exposed sides.

Poquis notched an arrow and sent it flying at an Aztec warrior leading the charge.

The Aztec wore a spotted jaguar's skin. The claws were like bracelets around his wrists and ankles. His face was visible through the animal's teeth. He looked like a jaguar running on its hind legs. Poquis's arrow plunged through the warrior's throat, and the Aztec stumbled and fell. Warriors behind him jumped over his body and kept running toward the walls.

"Be strong," Poquis yelled to warriors around him. "They are only men and will die like us."

Arrows streamed from loopholes that looked out from several outside rooms around the village wall. Armored conquistadors on horseback galloped along the walls, dropping ladders. As the Aztecs and expeditionaries reached Ghufoor, they grabbed the ladders and leaned them against the walls. Tiwas on the flat roofs cleared the ladders of climbers by dropping large rocks stored around the village's heights.

Poquis jumped in front of a metal-clad Castilian as the man reached a ladder's top rungs brandishing his sword. Dropping his bow, Poquis lifted a granite slab off the terrace's roof. Raising it above his head, Poquis heaved the rock at the Castilian's steel breastplate. There was a metallic clang. The blow forced the Castilian backward and off the ladder, knocking others off below him as he fell. As Poquis lunged for the ladder and pulled it up, another thunderous volley from arquebus muskets struck down archers on each side of Xauían a short distance away. The war captain continued shooting arrows into the crowded prairie below. He fought alone until Poquis and half a dozen other bowmen leaped to his side. Shouts of pain and anger erupted into a throaty roar in the village and on the field outside.

A warrior to the right of Xauían drilled an arrow into a Spanish horse. The animal screamed like a man as it reared. The horse spilled its rider onto the ground before galloping back to the expedition's camp. Poquis looked to the bowman to praise him for his shot when he saw a crossbow shaft appear in the bowman's chest. The warrior staggered backward and dropped to his knees. Without a sound, he toppled backward, falling into the open Middle-Heart Place below.

The chaos of blood and rage ceased at the sound of a trumpet on the field. The attackers withdrew to their camp out of arrow range to the west, carrying their wounded and dragging their dead.

Poquis picked up a ladder on the roof along Ghufoor's west wall. He dropped it over the side and scampered down. From the battlefield, he snatched up three maquahuitls. Several Aztecs turned from their retreat and began running toward him until arrows from Ghufoor turned them back. From a distance, Spanish arquebusiers fired. The shots splintered the wall with mini-explosions of broken adobe around Poquis as he hurried up the ladder. A warrior hauled the ladder up while Poquis handed the maquahuitls to Xauían. The war chief used a thumb to test the sharp obsidian edges and nodded his approval.

—

While Tiwa warriors kept watch at the loopholes and walls, Xauían joined the women in carrying the dead to Ghufoor's inside open area. In honor to the bowman who wounded the horse, Xauían laid him on the ground floor of his own apartment in the west wall. The crossbow shaft had broken in the fall from the roof but still protruded from the warrior's chest.

After the Night People scattered like campfire sparks above him, Xauían descended into the painted kiva to meet with the elders.

"Grandfathers. I told them we could not leave our home and the bones of our ancestors," he told them. "But they mean to drive us out. They are many. Even more are coming soon from the land of the Zuni. We are few. Poquis led the fight, but some of our bravest warriors died today."

The fire crackled and sputtered in the hearth. Tension spread in the kiva's dim recesses as everyone thought about what Xauían said. A thought had so much power that it did not need to be spoken. They would reach an understanding in meditation, moving as one people, as one mind. An elder arose and stood in the circle of men. He lit a handful of cedar from the fire. Turning with slow movements, he drifted smoke over the men with a fan of eagle feathers. Men murmured prayers to the katsina spirits on the walls around them as the smoke scented the room.

Much later, Xauían moved next to the painted image of the Elder War Twin. The katsina seemed to stand beside him. "Our warriors fought well. We honor them. But the result is as sure as tomorrow's return of Sun Father. We cannot hold them out the next time. They are very brave as well, and there are many more of them. I can see them building more ladders in their camp for another attack."

There was a long silence until the sun priest spoke. Light from the fire illuminated his white hair, but the rest of him was shadowed in folds of his blanket. The consensus of everyone focused in him. He spoke their will.

"Our town has been stolen from us. You will go to Cárdenas at dawn. Tell him we will leave and live with our friends in other villages. The Creator knows and will give us strength."

They had never been defeated before behind their village walls. But all the men nodded as one. Xauían climbed the kiva ladder into the night. Poquis stood waiting for him. He saw the look of despair on Xauían's face and knew the elders' decision. The two of them stood silently, looking up at the shining Night People. Wind Old Woman caressed them. Grandfather Coyote cried out a sacred four times from the cottonwoods along the river.

# 27

In early December, Francisco Vázquez de Coronado set out from the Zuni villages for the Tiguex Province with another contingent of expeditionaries and Native allies. He arrived near the province's southern end at Tsugwaga, the pueblo the expeditionaries knew as Isleta. The residents greeted him with food, music, and gifts. They told him that by following the river north he would find others like himself. It took all day for Coronado and his men to travel on foot and on horseback up the river in a fierce, cold wind. They passed by other pueblos on or near the banks, making their way beside a narrow forest of winter-bare cottonwood trees. Cárdenas rode south to meet his general and escort him to their new winter headquarters. It was in the pueblo with a name Alvarado had said sounded like Coofor. Cold and tired, Coronado and his men were relieved to see the pueblo's shelter.

Upon his arrival, Coronado saw the battle casualties from a few days earlier. He and Cárdenas agreed they would report to the viceroy that the Tiwas had volunteered to vacate the pueblo so the Spaniards could move in and be sheltered from the winter weather.

In a way, they rationalized, the Tiwas had left voluntarily. They'd abandoned the village before Cárdenas could launch another attack. The viceroy might think his orders for leniency toward Indians weren't being followed if he knew every detail. Coronado and his officers felt the viceroy didn't understand what they were going through trying to deal with the natives in this desert wilderness. Telling the viceroy too much might lead to trouble when they returned.

———

Coronado felt a charge of excitement behind his table inside the commandeered pueblo. An Indian from the buffalo plains stood before him, brought by Cárdenas and Hernando de Alvarado. The news about this Indian had filled Coofor and its entire outside camp with gold-fever excitement all day before Coronado's arrival. At last, thought Coronado, there was confirmation that Indian lands rich in gold were indeed to be found in this desolate country. The greatest part of Coronado's wealth, which was gained through his wife's estate, was invested in the expedition. All in the hope that someone like this Indian might be found.

Coronado could see why Alvarado called this Indian "the Turk." The tattooed man wrapped his black hair in a cloth like the turbans that Turks wore. Coronado sat enthralled as Turk, a Pecos captive from the far end of the buffalo plains, regaled him with stories of a rich Indian civilization to the east known as Quivira.

Pedro de Castañeda later would recall: "The Turk said that in his land there was a river in the plain which was two leagues wide. There were fish as large as horses there. And a great many exceedingly large canoes with more than twenty rowers on each side, which also carried sails. The lords traveled ... seated beneath awnings. On the prow there was a large eagle of gold. He said further that the lord of that land slept during siesta under a great tree on which a number of small golden bells hung. In the breeze, they gave him pleasure. Further, he said that generally everybody's common serving dishes were worked silver. And the pitchers, plates, and small bowls were of gold."

Turk also said he once owned gold arm bands. He said Bigotes had taken them away.

That statement commanded Coronado's full attention. Bigotes has gold?

"Yes, my general," Alvarado replied, "but Bigotes denies everything. He says there are no gold arm bands. That is why I brought Bigotes, the cacique, Turk, and another Indian of the plains, Ysopete, back from Pecos in iron collars and chains. We must make Bigotes give up the gold arm bands."

Coronado's eyes widened. At last, after the disappointing appearance of the Indian pueblos, after it appeared there were not enough Indians for a rich encomienda, now there was hope for finding gold. Just to the east. A little farther.

Because of the gold excitement, most approved of Alvarado's forced removal of the Pecos captives. The horseman Castañeda, however, harbored qualms about the way his companions treated the Indians. Castañeda wrote about the incident years later, recalling how the Pecos Indians had greeted Alvarado at first as a friend. They'd tried to convince him that the Pawnee whom the expeditionaries called Turk was lying. There were no gold arm bands. Not believing them, Alvarado put Bigotes and a Pecos elder in chains and took them back to Coofor. They would remain prisoners for the next six months.

"This was the beginning of bringing discredit on the Spaniards' word when they offered peace from then on," Castañeda decided.

Now Pecos, the most powerful Indian village in the area with an estimated five hundred warriors, had changed from friends to implacable enemies over the imprisonment of Bigotes and the aged cacique.

Coronado knew that Dominican Friar Bartolomé de las Casas had met with Viceroy Mendoza in Mexico City just before the expedition started. Mendoza then had ordered Coronado to treat the Indians humanely. Coronado dispelled his concerns about what the viceroy might think about taking Indians as prisoners even though they'd caused no harm. News of gold would be more than enough to make the viceroy look the other way.

Coronado was further protected because Friar Juan de Padilla had approved kidnapping the Pecos leaders. The Franciscan even helped Alvarado question them about the gold arm bands. Padilla had told Coronado how important it was to His Majesty's service to learn as much as possible about Quivira. He insisted this could be learned from Bigotes.

Coronado would smile whenever he recalled how easy it was to excuse himself from the questioning and turn it over to Alvarado and the eager Franciscan priest. Coronado would find many reasons to reassure himself that Turk was telling the truth, that Bigotes was lying, and that vast riches of gold lay temporarily beyond his reach. Ysopete, another Indian from the buffalo grasslands that Alvarado had kidnapped, was from a different tribe than the Turk. He was a Wichita. He disputed Turk's stories of a wealthy country to the east, but Coronado and the other Spaniards ignored him.

—

A weakened Father Sun cast no warmth that morning early in the month of Night Moon. Its pale light shone through snow falling like feathers on the five Spaniards on horseback waiting outside Kuaua's walls. Many of Ghufoor's refugees had moved into that nearest village after losing their home. In answer to the Spaniards' shouts of his nickname of Juan Alemán, Xauían appeared on the terrace of the eastern wall and looked down at the strangers. The man he had come to know as García López de Cárdenas led the horsemen. Xauían had practiced saying and memorizing the name since he'd realized the man was second only to Coronado in commanding the invaders. Cárdenas wore a buffalo robe Bigotes had given him at Zuni. The other horsemen had wrapped themselves in two Tiwa blankets apiece against the cold that made the trees pop and turned the nearby river to ice.

All held long, metal-pointed lances and had sheathed swords hanging from their wide belts. Everyone's breath puffed like white smoke.

Bartolomé, the Mexican Indian who had been adopted by the Zunis, stepped forward and called to Xauían through the still air. "Coronado asks you to visit him," Bartolomé said in an accented combination of Zuni and Nahuatl words.

Xauían sent a man for warmer clothing and motioned for Poquis to come to his side.

"Find Ishpanyan," Xauían said. "You will go with me. Bring your clubs in your sashes. I am having buffalo robes brought for all of us."

When they were ready, Poquis lowered a ladder and the three of them climbed down. Other Tiwas pulled the ladder back up after they reached the ground. Swathed in their buffalo robes, the three of them crunched through the snow toward the Spaniards. Once everyone was together, the Spaniards turned their horses south toward Ghufoor.

Poquis had heard that the strangers renamed the village, some calling it Coofor and others calling it Alcanfor. The snow was knee-deep, so the three Tiwas walked in the track that the horses had broken both coming and going. Poquis pulled the buffalo hide tighter around him. Its fur was turned inside, and the outside was painted with symbols important to his people. There was no wind, but the icy air still numbed his face.

He could hear ducks and geese calling from the river to their left. In the snowy distance to his right he spotted seven pronghorn antelope.

Ghufoor felt like a foreign city after just a few days, crowded with the bearded strangers and the Aztec warriors. The three Puebloans walked through an entrance that had been cut into the wall. Horses, men, and piles of equipment filled the once open space of the Middle-Heart Place. Snow had been trampled into an iced surface over frozen mud. Cárdenas took them to the second floor room that Coronado had turned into his chambers along the west wall. They paused. They'd never seen a doorway closed with wooden planks. As they entered, they could smell freshly cut wood. The strangers had taken out four walls, making the room much larger than usual. The missing walls had been replaced with squared beams against the ceiling. New pillars of cottonwood trunks supported the beams. Smoke holes had been filled in with new ceiling construction.

In the wall opposite the doorway a fireplace had been built. Its flames filled the room with light, as did new window openings cut into the walls with their hide coverings parted. Poquis recognized stone slabs that once had been a kiva's floor and now were used to line the fireplace walls and chimney shaft.

Coronado sat on an elaborate, carved chair behind a desk. A swordsman stood on each side behind him. Poquis let his eyes connect with Alonso's eyes. Alonso held the staff with Coronado's banners, but he and Poquis never acknowledged each other.

Poquis listened for the Spanish he knew. But Coronado spoke too rapidly to Cárdenas for Poquis to understand him. Cárdenas stepped back to stand beside the door.

An old Aztec, his face wrinkled with age and his topknot of hair brightened with macaw feathers, walked from the fireplace and stood beside Coronado. The Aztec elder wore a yellow cotton shirt and yellow pants that reached his sandals. He had hung a folded Tiwa blanket over his left arm, not needing it in the warm room. Xauían took off his buffalo hide as well and held it in a bunch before him. His deerskin shirt and pants and his tall legging moccasins were all he needed as the fireplace poured heat into the room. Poquis and Ishpanyan kept their robes on.

—

Xauían looked toward the Aztec as the old man took a step toward him. The Aztec spoke Coronado's Spanish words in Nahuatl simultaneously with Coronado's voice. "I am glad you came, Juan Alemán," the Aztec said as if it were he who was talking. "I have an important request."

Xauían thought of his warrior with a crossbow shaft in his chest buried in a first-floor room of the west wall. Xauían stood as straight as he could. "You have our home," Xauían said in Tiwa. "I do not know what else we can give you."

The old Aztec reached out a hand to touch Xauían's shoulder. "I know you understand much in my language if I speak slowly," he said in Nahuatl. "Speak to me in my language. Then I will speak for you to this evil Christian who hates us both. But leave the anger in your heart." The Aztec smiled.

Xauían glanced at Coronado, who stared at him, not understanding his words or the Aztec's. He repeated what he'd said, this time speaking in Nahuatl, stumbling a little as he searched for the right words. The old man spoke in Spanish to Coronado.

"It is only for a short time," Coronado replied through the Aztec interpreter. "Some day I will build our own town."

Xauían frowned. "I thought you had come like the geese who fly here for the winter. I did not know you plan to stay here."

Coronado leaned back in his chair. "You think I will leave. But you are mistaken. You are now subjects of his majesty and the holy pope. You must give your obedience."

"Who is this majesty? Who is this pope?"

"The friars can tell you. But they tell me you will not speak to them. You must let them teach you about the true God."

Xauían watched the Aztec as the old man finished Coronado's words. Then Xauían turned back to face Coronado. "The Creator gave us this country. Your God gave you your country. Who knows? Perhaps we have the same Creator who wanted us to stay apart."

Coronado sighed. "I did not summon you here to argue about religion." He pointed to Poquis and Ishpanyan, who stood on each side of Xauían. "I sent orders for you to come. Why did you bring these warriors? Are you afraid of me?"

Xauían did not reply at first. Instead he turned his head to look at the swordsman to the left of Coronado. Then he turned his head to look at the swordsman on Coronado's right. He looked at Alonso and the interpreter, then he turned to look at Cárdenas standing beside the door and at a Spaniard with a lance standing in the doorway.

He turned back to Coronado. "I am not afraid," he said in Nahuatl to the Aztec, who translated his words for Coronado. "But you have many warriors here. I brought two of mine so I would not feel alone."

Coronado shook his head and scowled at Poquis and Ishpanyan. They looked back with no expression on their faces.

Coronado looked sideways to catch the eye of each swordsman. "Very well, Juan Alemán. I brought you here to make this request. My people are freezing. Soon many more will be here. I need you to tell your people to give us much corn and three hundred blankets."

Xauían's lips tightened. "My ears have heard that you are bringing animals with heavy hair. My ears have heard that Christians make clothes and blankets from that hair. You should make your own blankets."

Coronado's face flushed with anger. He glared at Xauían before replying. "I did not bring people who know how to make clothes out of sheep wool. And special tools are needed. That is why you must provide three hundred blankets."

The Aztec translated Coronado's words. Then he explained what Coronado meant by sheep and wool.

"Many of your men already wear blankets we gave you," Xauían replied. "They eat the corn we gave you. Even your horses eat our corn. Now you say many more of your people and animals are coming. Your hunger makes our corn melt away like snow in the spring. Will you also make us naked in the winter winds? We have little enough for ourselves. We cannot also feed and clothe all of you."

Coronado stood. His face stiffened and his voice turned hard. "You will get me three hundred blankets. That is less than thirty from each of your pueblos."

"I am a leader only of my own village," Xauían said. He didn't mention the sun priest because he didn't want Coronado to know about him. "I am not the leader of other villages. I cannot tell them to give you three hundred of their blankets."

"I have seen how everyone from the other pueblos respect you. They would give the blankets if you went to them."

"It is up to the leader of each village," Xauían insisted. "You must ask at each village for the corn and blankets."

The Aztec translated Xauían's response. He smiled at Xauían.

—

Supply concerns motivated Coronado to call a meeting the next day of his council, the circle of officers he trusted most.

The council included Coronado's second-in-command, the field master. García López de Cárdenas had saved Coronado's life at Cíbola. Cárdenas also had discovered the great canyon in the west, and convinced the Indians to leave Coofor so Coronado could move his men in for the winter. Coronado would never call a meeting without Cárdenas.

Alvarado's discovery of Turk's alluring stories of gold to the east guaranteed that young captain's place in the inner circle. Plus, he was the captain of artillery, in charge of Coronado's arsenal of six small bronze cannons.

And there was Juan Troyano, one of the expedition's few professional military men. He had served as a seaman and then as an artilleryman in Italy and other campaigns. He had accompanied Coronado's advance force in the assault against the Zunis and gone with Alvarado to the buffalo plains. Coronado and his captains never decided much without asking Troyano's opinion because of his military experience.

Pablo de Melgosa, a captain of infantry, was twenty-four. His men respected Melgosa for his fierceness in battle with the sword. Coronado's captains of cavalry included Rodrigo de Maldonado and Diego López.

There were also the royal financial officers, along to verify an accurate accounting of any discovered riches to ensure the king's twenty-percent share. They attended every council, as did at least one or two Franciscan friars.

Coronado turned to Cárdenas. "How is the collection of food and blankets from the Indians going?"

"Juan Alemán still insists he cannot order other pueblos to give us the three hundred blankets. So I am sending men to each pueblo tomorrow. Some of our Indian allies from Mexico and Africans already have died in this cold. We will collect blankets and buffalo robes as fast as we can and distribute them, starting with those still camping outside."

"Good. We have plenty of trade goods to pay for them."

"My general, that already has become a problem. These stubborn and disobedient savages say they need the food and blankets for themselves. It is more difficult every day to requisition what we need."

Alvarado spoke up. "I think they are hiding supplies at night in the mountains. That is why they don't have much to give us."

Coronado nodded at Alvarado, then turned back to Cárdenas. "We have no choice but to rely on the Indians for food and clothing. We now know we cannot expect any help from the ships the viceroy sent with our winter supplies. Melchior Díaz found a note at the base of a tree from the ship's captain, Hernando de Alarcón, saying they had given up and returned to New Spain. None of us realized how far away the sea is to the west. We need food and clothing now, not only for those of us here but for the rest that Captain Arellano is bringing. Soon there will be three thousand of us here, and the weather is getting colder."

"Yes, your Excellency. Praise God for the memory of his servant, Melchior Díaz. His accidental death was a great loss."

"If I may make a suggestion, General." Alvarado spoke from the line of officers. "If we cut off Juan Alemán's nose and then his hands one at a time, I am sure he will become more willing to help us get the supplies we need." Several officers voiced their agreement.

Coronado shook his head. "We are under the viceroy and king's orders to treat the Indians with benevolence. This is not Mexico City or Peru. Times have changed."

Pablo de Melgosa hitched up his sword belt and took a step forward. "Permission to speak frankly, my lord."

When Coronado nodded, Melgosa continued. "This most certainly is not Mexico City or Peru. Instead of grand cities, we find mud towns. Instead of gold and silver, we find turquoise stones. Instead of silk, we find animal hides. Instead of potential encomiendas, we find a scattering of pueblos with a few hundred people here or there. The one thing we have found of any value is the promise of incredible quantities of buffalo hides if we go and hunt them. The friars don't even see many souls for conversion. Most of us will be bankrupted by this expedition. We must find this Quivira of which Turk speaks, where the Indians are said to have much gold."

Coronado motioned that he agreed. "In the spring, we will go east across the buffalo plains and find Quivira. But first, we must force Bigotes to admit his lies and give up the gold arm bands. That will be proof that Turk is telling the truth about Quivira."

"Bigotes refuses to tell us anything," Alvarado said. "He won't give up the gold easily. That godless old sorcerer the cacique is no better."

Coronado's mouth twisted with anger. He half rose out of his seat behind the camp table. His voice became louder as he pointed at Alvarado. "Throw Bigotes to Pedro de Tovar's dogs. But do not let the dogs kill him. Not this time. The dogs will persuade Bigotes to give up the gold arm bands."

# 28

Shocked by what he'd seen at Ghufoor, Ishpanyan ran toward Big River. He broke through the ice in a spot thinned by fast current. With difficulty, he pulled himself out of the freezing water and reached the other side.

He stopped to shout to some villagers at Watche about what he'd seen. He raced south, pausing again to make a report at the village of Tuf Sheur Teui before continuing his run to Puaray beyond.

He encountered Poquis starting from Puaray on the trail northward.

"Ishpanyan, did you fall in the river?" Poquis pulled the buffalo robe from around his own shoulders and threw it across Ishpanyan's back.

"The Castilians," Ishpanyan said after regaining some of his breath, every word a puff of white air in the cold. "They let one of their large dogs attack Bigotes. I ran here as soon as I saw it happen."

"Who? Which one of them did it?"

Ishpanyan sneered. "Your friend, the one called Alvarado. He yelled at Bigotes, who was bound in their chains, and then he set the dog on him. Maybe your friend used the dog to attack the Pecos elder as well."

"No metal person is my friend. What are you—"

"You traveled to Pecos with him. You say you returned without his permission, but he did not punish you when he saw you here. You listen to them and understand their strange words. Are you a witch, Poquis?"

"I am learning their language so we will know what they say. You must realize—"

"I do not know what to think. But I know we must fight these invaders."

"We cannot fight them. Not to win, anyway. You saw their weapons and what happened at Ghufoor. Not even our walls could stop them."

"I saw us give up. Walk away ashamed from our home. Every man there was willing to fight to the death. The elders and Xauían made us leave. They made us give up Ghufoor to them."

"What would staying have accomplished?"

"We could have killed many of them." Ishpanyan began shouting. "But Xauían would not let us."

"We could have killed many of them. But they would have killed all of us. Leaving Ghufoor was the only way to protect our women and children. Would you have all of them killed or made slaves? There are too many of these strangers."

Ishpanyan tried to walk away, but Poquis grabbed his arm and continued talking. "Our way of fighting is with clubs, but they have more powerful swords, lances, and their guns of lightning and thunder. Also their armor, quilted jackets, and hard leather protect them against our arrows. The men of the other villages now know that Xauían was right about the strangers and they were wrong. All have said they will now follow Xauían. But the time is not right for us to fight them yet."

"When will the time be right? When they have driven us out of our country? As we speak, even more are coming."

"Ishpanyan, listen."

"I am through listening." Ishpanyan yanked his arm away from Poquis's grip. He pulled the buffalo robe off his back and threw it on the ground. "They have forced us out of Ghufoor. When the rest of them come with even more men and their peculiar animals, they will occupy all our towns. Already they have taken some of our women away from us to Ghufoor. Soon they will drive us out of our homeland. Or they will kill all of us."

"We will not let that happen." Poquis bent to pick up the robe, but he held it in his hands instead of wrapping it around himself against the cold. "We are making plans."

Ishpanyan snorted in disgust and began walking toward Puaray's walls. Looking back, he called out. "If Xauían is too afraid, and you are too weak, then it is I who will find warriors willing to fight the strangers."

# 29

Even though the European expeditionaries had moved into the shelter of the commandeered village of Coofor as winter froze the land, they forced their native allies and Africans to live outside. The non-Europeans suffered from the cold in tents and brush shelters a five-minute walk west of the pueblo.

Many Tiwa refugees forced out of Ghufoor tried to put some distance between themselves and the expeditionaries. They moved to villages across the river. When the river froze that December, however, the Spaniards began turning their horses loose into the harvested cornfields on the river's east side. The livestock had consumed the fields of the west side villages.

Winter's frigid temperatures made it more clear to Coronado that he needed to get warmer clothing from the same place he obtained most of his food—the Tiguex Province pueblos.

Angered by Indian leader Juan Alemán's refusal to collect three hundred blankets, Coronado sent his men out to get what they needed. He ordered his captains to sweep the pueblos on both sides of the river with Spaniards and Indian allies.

Castañeda recalled the severity of the collection.

"They did not give the natives a chance to consult about it, but when they came to a village they demanded what they had to give, so that they could proceed at once. Thus these people could do nothing except take off their own [buffalo robes] and give them to make up the number demanded of them. And some of the soldiers who were in these parties, when the collectors gave them some blankets or [buffalo robes] which were not such as they wanted, if they saw any Indian with a better one on, they exchanged with him without more ado, not stopping to find out the rank of the man they were stripping, which caused not a little hard feeling."

—

Panpahlu wiped her eyes, sighed, and sat back on her folded legs upon the floor as she looked toward Poquis.

"I know," Poquis said. The walls in their new room at Puaray seemed too close to hold his mate's spreading anxiety. How could he comfort her? Her face flickered in the firelight as he looked at her. He knew her grief but didn't know what he could do about it.

She motioned toward the fire. "How will any of us heat our homes if the strangers' horses continue to devour our corn stalks? It is the fuel we have always used for winter. Or will you and the other men walk to the mountains each day for wood? We cannot eat bells or keep warm with beads."

Poquis lowered his eyes.

"What will we do, Poquis? These strangers take whatever they want from us. How will we survive the winter? The strangers eat all our stored foods and grab our turkey feather and rabbit fur cloaks, our cotton blankets, deerskins, and buffalo robes off our backs. The strangers no longer even pay us with their worthless trinkets. They just go to each village and take what they want. I have seen them strip robes and blankets off the backs of elders and women."

"Our walls always protected us against our enemies," Poquis said. "I was wrong to think they would protect us against these strangers. We must find a new way to fight them, but I do not know what that will be."

—

Alone, Poquis left the village and walked up through the sand hills undulating in mounds at the base of Turtle Mountain, also called *Kee-bien-ob*. As he entered the mountain foothills, the dry grasses of the prairie along Big River yielded to a landscape thick with junipers and shrubs. Snow-covered cliffs and slopes thousands of feet high towered around him. The temperature dropped as he climbed higher. The landscape changed from junipers to piñon trees and then tall, thick ponderosa pine trees. A deer burst from its cover and bounded away through the snowy forest. Now and then a blue mountain jay would fly from a cedar tree with a sharp cry. Mostly, there was silence.

When Poquis found the mountain shrine at a spring inside shadows of the pines, he lowered himself to one knee. He leaned his feathered and carved prayer stick against a tree. Many other prayer sticks were there, weathered from years of exposure. Only members of the Warrior Society knew of the shrine. It honored the Warrior Twins Maseway and Oyoyeway. Those two katsina spirits lived high on this mountain so they could keep watch over the people and protect them.

Poquis pulled the buffalo robe tighter around him when a cold wind through the trees buffeted him. He had worn his eagle feathers as a member of the Warrior Society so the Warrior Twins would welcome him. The feathers were the badge of a warrior who had killed enemies in battle.

He wondered why the Warrior Twins shrine was at this place. It had always been there for generations beyond counting.

He opened a small leather pouch hanging from his neck. Reaching in, he took out a pinch of corn meal and sprinkled it on the ground as an offering around his prayer stick.

He would build a fire for warmth and stay awake all night. He'd send his prayers into the vast sky overhead, asking the Creator to make him worthy of the trials ahead.

Panpahlu was right. There would be no food or blankets left soon for the villagers. The Tiwas would need to fight to survive. But Poquis had seen the metal people and Aztecs destroy the warriors from the two pueblos who had challenged them on the way up the river to Taos. After the hopeless resistance at Ghufoor, Poquis did not think fighting from the village walls would succeed either. The Tiwas would not be able to prevail in open battle against the strangers' overwhelming numbers and weapons.

So how could his people survive?

# 30

Poquis and Xauían crouched in the knee-deep snow outside Ghufoor's walls and watched the Castilians coming and going on their horses.

Every day patrols of horsemen, accompanied by militiamen and Aztecs, rode out on the trail heading south from Coofor and swept through the twelve Tiwa villages along Big River, demanding clothes and food.

"Why are you watching the horses all the time?" Xauían asked. "I fear no man, but these horses are terrifying. I have never seen anything like them."

Poquis stripped some seeds off a saltbush and tossed them into the wind to blow away with the snowflakes swirling around them. "Perhaps even beasts like these once lived here. Men have forgotten, but the grass would remember."

Xauían clenched his hands. "The sight of these strangers astride their fierce horses, entering with such speed and fury into our country, strikes awe and terror into our hearts. I think they are evil. A Zuni told me that these beasts eat men."

"No. They eat our corn and grass, but they do not eat men. No man can outrun them, and they carry the metal people into battle with lances and swords. They are evil in that way."

Four cavalrymen rode past them on brown horses. Their helmets and armor flashed with daylight, swords clanked at their side, and each carried a metal-pointed lance in his right hand. Xauían and Poquis shuffled backward to let them pass. They backed up to a cross ten feet high that the strangers had erected in front of the pueblo. Tiwas had decorated it with evergreens, pieces of cloth, and small bells that tinkled in the wind. Behind the conquistadors walked twenty militiamen. Bearded young toughs with hard eyes, they carried arquebus muskets and crossbows. All wore the seven-layer elk leather or thick quilted jackets so effective in blocking Tiwa arrows. Some wore chain-mail vests. Every man carried a sword.

Fifty Aztecs followed with their painted leather shields and obsidian-edged maquahuitls. They were adorned with blue and red macaw feathers and quilted cotton armor. Some wore the skins of tropical predators. They were off to demand food and clothing from the villages south of Ghufoor.

Poquis and Xauían knew the Castilians had bribed some Tiwa women to live with them. The Castilians lured them with food and clothing as such goods became scarce in the villages. The women were little better than sex slaves, but at least they were able to survive.

Xauían looked over at three women carrying corn meal in large bowls balanced on yucca fiber rings atop their heads. The women walked from the village walls to the encampment, where the Mexican Indians and Africans stayed. All three were widows from the Ghufoor fighting.

"The metal people say they are looking for rocks they can melt into something they call gold," Xauían said. "But I think they are looking as much for women."

Poquis nodded. He turned his head to watch as the conquistadors rode south on their horses along the trail on the high bluff above the river.

Xauían's voice shook with intensity. "We must fight these metal people before it is too late. Look how they made their dogs attack my friend from Pecos. I am as angry as the people of Pecos about that. These invaders are eating all our corn and other food. Many of our people no longer have any blanket or robe to keep warm this winter. There are no corn stalks to burn for fuel."

Xauían paused. He looked into Poquis' eyes. "We must fight while we still can from our stronghold on the mesa with lichen-covered rocks."

"You are a great war captain," Poquis said to him. "Forgive me when I no longer think we can succeed behind our walls. These invaders are not like the wild desert raiders that we trade and fight with. I have been thinking of how we could fight these enemies differently. To fight from our walls is to be destroyed, for there are too many strangers already, and soon there will be even more."

Xauían looked over at the younger man. If Poquis had not stopped the Castilian on the ladder, that one armored man would have used his sword to kill every warrior on Ghufoor's roof. Poquis had then fought in the most dangerous place beside Xauían. And he had retrieved the maquahuitls from the battlefield so they could be smuggled out of Ghufoor. Xauían would need Poquis and every other fighting man when warfare resumed. Everyone agreed they could not survive much longer like this.

"I respect your judgment as a warrior, Poquis. The Zunis proved we cannot fight them in the open. And we lost Ghufoor. So how do you think we can fight the metal people?"

"These horses." Poquis's voice trailed off as he thought. "If we could capture some of these horses, we could learn to ride them like the metal people. I think we then could go into the mountains and defend ourselves better there."

"Capture the horses? How would we know how to ride them? Go into the mountains in winter. That will never work. Better to go to the mesa and fight from there. The walls there are stronger than any other place."

"That works against the wandering tribes, but it will not work as well against these people. There are so many of them that we cannot hold them out forever. But I am working on a plan. We cannot take saddles without being noticed. I have seen metal people riding on the horses' bare backs, however, so I know we also can. I took one of the leather straps that are called halters. Our women are making copies of them. With halters we could lead the horses into the mountains until we learn how to use them. We would have a few horses. Our enemy would have that many fewer horses."

Xauían thought about that. "Your men are not afraid of the horses?"

"All of us watch the horses. All of us are learning about them. They are just animals. It is our best chance."

Xauían shook his head. He turned toward Poquis, an irritated look on his face. Then he looked away again at another group of horsemen and Aztecs walking out of Ghufoor in single file.

"Even more will be here soon," Poquis said. "Runners say the main force is struggling through the snow toward us from the land of the Zuni. Soon there will be hundreds more metal people and their allies with thousands of their animals. We cannot feed and clothe those already occupying Ghufoor. How can we meet the demands of so many more? We all will starve or perish from the cold."

—

A day later, from their position on the high bank overlooking the river, Poquis and Xauían looked down into the narrow forest of cottonwood trees that grew along both sides of the river. They saw a boy racing between the tree trunks. Poquis stood so the boy could see him and motioned to him. The boy turned toward them. He ran out of the tree line and scrambled up the steep, snowy embankment on hands and knees until he reached the top. Xauían rose to stand beside Poquis. They recognized the boy as the Tiwas' fastest runner. Xauían extended his arm to rest a hand on the boy's shoulder. "What news do you bring us in such a hurry?"

The boy gasped for air before he could speak. "The elders sent me. One of the Castilians who rides a horse raped a woman in our village while taking our food and blankets. Our men are coming with the woman's mate. The elders say you must arrange a meeting with the strangers. Her mate will identify their man who did this."

Xauían turned to Poquis. "This was bound to happen. I must see to this." Then Xauían and the boy began running through the snow toward Ghufoor's walls.

Poquis followed at a distance. By the time Xauían emerged from Ghufoor with Cárdenas and several armed expeditionaries, the delegation of Tiwa men had gathered nearby, shouting angry demands. Poquis knew the strangers called the men's village by a word in their own language: Arenal.

Cárdenas ordered everyone to be silent. "Why have you come from Arenal?" he demanded of the group's leader. He scowled when the Tiwas said one of their women had been raped.

Poquis watched as Cárdenas ordered the expeditionaries who had been requisitioning at that village to line up. The woman's mate became confused, saying all the bearded strangers looked alike to him. He said he would be able to identify the horse. So Cárdenas ordered that all the horses used in the foraging be brought out. The husband identified a peach-colored horse that belonged to Juan de Villegas, but Villegas denied he was the man.

Cárdenas said the accuser must be wrong. He ordered the Tiwas to leave.

Francisca de Hozes, one of the expedition's few women, would later testify, "Their wives, daughters, and other things that the Indians had in their houses were taken by force and against their will." That is why, she concluded, the people of Tiguex rebelled.

—

Any elders from other Tiwa villages who could not make the trip for the meeting that night sent more fit men in their place with instructions. Poquis stood outside the kiva of the village where the woman had been raped. A downcast-looking Xauían emerged from the kiva into the darkness and a wind-churned swirl of snowflakes.

"As I thought, I must talk to you," Xauían said. "You saw what happened. Metal people rapists will not be punished. Now our women are not safe even in our villages."

Xauían told the decision of the elders from all of the Tiwa villages. "We must leave our villages," Xauían concluded. "I told them what you said about the horses and the mountains. They want you to take our people from the villages into the mountains where they will be safe. These strangers bring starvation and brutality. If we wait any longer, so many will be here that it will be impossible to get away."

Poquis betrayed his surprise. "When?"

Xauían looked toward the mountain peaks to the east, now a looming shadow in the darkening night. "Runners already have left for the villages to tell the people to grab what they can for food and warmth. They must go to the mountains tonight while darkness and this snow storm hides them. Not all the women and children will go, but many will. Some warriors will go with them. I need the rest to stay and fight the strangers from our mesa stronghold so our people can escape."

"Good. I will go with you and fight."

"No, Poquis. The elders want you and your men who are not afraid of the horses to capture as many as possible in the cornfields here. Because the strangers are at Ghufoor, it will take a while for them to react. We can do nothing about all the horses on the trade road coming here. But if you could take even the ones here, it would weaken the metal people for at least a little while. They need the horses for war. As you told me, the ones you take will leave fewer for them."

"Several of us have been planning for this. Even so, it will not be possible until close to dawn."

"Do it then. Have some of your men take our people into the mountains. I have seen how the strangers often use the horses to carry supplies. You can do the same. But you must move quickly."

"What are you going to do?"

"I will take warriors to our mesa stronghold among the lichen-covered rocks. The elders will tell the warriors from the villages to join me there. I will also take the women and children who cannot or will not go to the mountains."

"I will join you as soon as I can."

"You do not understand. Ishpanyan is assembling warriors from the other villages to make a stand here. The metal people and their allies will come to this village first when you take their horses. They will not chase you if they see a fight facing them. The resistance by Ishpanyan will give our people time to escape and also give time for me to get ready on the mesa. This Coronado does not know about our stronghold yet. He will find us soon enough. I will make sure of that. When he does, he will not be able to spare fighters to look for you and our people in the mountains."

"Then what am I to do, if I do not fight beside you?"

Xauían grasped Poquis' arms. "I will defend our country on the mesa. Ishpanyan will delay them at the village. Even though you are young, you are the warrior whose judgment I trust the most. You think differently. You might think of new strategies to fight these strangers. Things I would never think to do. Perhaps I can stall the strangers long enough for you to prepare. You might be our tribe's last real chance."

Poquis started to protest, but Xauían gripped the warrior's arms tighter. Xauían's face tensed as he said, "I need you in the mountains to protect our people."

# 31

Coronado kept writing as Alonso Álvarez entered the room at Ghufoor. Alonso bowed in greeting to his general.

"Go find the field master and bring him to me," ordered Coronado, looking up from the report on his table.

"He is already with me, my lord, waiting outside at your command."

Coronado leaned back in his camp chair and grinned. "You often anticipate me, Alonso. Very well, bring him in."

Cárdenas ducked to enter the tent and stood straight and still before the general. He had taken off his breastplate armor but still wore a chain mail vest. "At your orders, captain-general," he said in a determined tone.

"The barbaric Indians killed several horses and mules this morning at Arenal," Coronado said, rising to his feet. "Maybe they even captured some horses. We're missing forty or more. Both you and I have lost some of our mounts, most certainly. What is the cause of this rebellion?"

"They have rebelled of their own accord," Cárdenas said heatedly. "No cause has been given by us, nor any harm done to them."

Coronado scratched his beard. "Because they stole the horses out of their cornfields, perhaps they are angry about the horses grazing there."

"That could not be a problem," Cárdenas said. "Nothing is left but corn stalks, so we have done nothing improper. It has been the law for centuries in Spain that anyone could send livestock into anyone else's field once it was harvested. No, they did this because they have wanted to revolt ever since we arrived."

"The reason does not matter. I want the horses back. I need you to find out if this is an uprising or an isolated incident. Retrieve our horses. Report back to me as soon as possible."

"The news is spreading through Coofor already," Cárdenas replied. "I will take Diego López and his horsemen and be at Arenal within the hour." Cárdenas bowed, turned on his heels, and ducked through the room's hide-covered doorway.

—

Cárdenas and the eight lancers proceeded from Coofor to Arenal. All the ladders were drawn up, and Tiwas shrieked at them from the rooftops. Several horses and mules lay dead all around. A palisade of logs blocked Arenal's narrow entrance. The Spaniards could hear horses running in the interior plaza amid the shouting of Indians.

"Listen to that," López said. "The Indians are shooting our horses with arrows. They are killing them."

The pueblo stood on a rise of land in a flat desert with grasses and small shrubs. Lumpy sand hills close to one another extended east on rising ground white with snow toward the mountains. The bare branches of cottonwood trees twisted like broken bones along the nearby river.

Cárdenas and López galloped their horses to the walls. Indians lined the rooftops. Several shook their fists and shouted Tiwa curses. Others sang defiant war chants. López drew his sword and slashed the air. A rumble of hooves thundered inside as horses ran around the plaza on the other side of the wall. Cárdenas recognized an Indian on the wall named Ishpanyan. He shouted in angry Spanish. Ishpanyan shouted back in Tiwa. The argument raged for a full minute with neither man understanding what the other was shouting.

Cárdenas then tried to tell the Tiwas with sign language that he did not care about the horses they killed because he had many more. He promised he would pardon the Tiwas if they would come out and be friends. The Tiwas at the wall continued to shout insults at him. Cárdenas tried to read the requerimiento, ordering the Indians to submit to the obedience of king and pope. He could not make himself heard above the shouting, war chants, and whinnying of horses inside the pueblo. No one there understood his Spanish anyway.

He turned to López. "Let us go back to Coofor and tell the general that the barbaric Indians have rebelled for no reason. They have killed many horses. For that they must be punished."

—

Coronado's eyes narrowed and his jaw muscles tightened as he stepped out of Coofor the next morning. He saw Field Master Cárdenas waiting for him on the snowy plain. Coronado always consulted his council of nobles and captains, royal financial officers, and friars before making major decisions. They had made the course of action clear in the previous night's meeting.

War.

His most important permission had come from the Franciscans. Friar Padilla said Coronado was justified to wage war in the Tiguex Province over the horses.

With Alonso Álvarez at his side carrying his banners, Coronado approached Cárdenas. He saw sixty horsemen saddled on their mounts in formation in the snow, their long lances pointed skyward. Off to one side were rows of militia standing with their crossbows, arquebuses, shields, and swords. Banners flapped in the cold wind. An occasional cough could be heard. There was a clinking of metal weaponry and the snorting and pawing of the horses. Behind the militia ranks stood hundreds of Mexican Indian warriors with their shields and feathers. They brandished Native weapons and wore small blankets tied like capes over their backs. The most elite fighters were dressed in jaguar skins or festooned with eagle feathers.

"Remember what the friars told us last night," Coronado said. "Read the requerimiento to the rebels. If they refuse to come to peace and submit to obedience to the king and the church, then your attack will be just. It must be a war of fire and blood. To set an example for the other barbaric Indians, everyone who defies us must die. Go into battle with St. James to protect you."

They agreed to send messengers back and forth every hour so Coronado could be kept informed while he stayed behind at the Coofor headquarters.

Cárdenas walked forward to stand before the riders and their horses. "Listen to me," he said in a loud voice. "Your captains have their orders on how we will proceed. I know every man will do his duty if the savages do not come to obedience."

Some horses shuffled restlessly as the riders reined them tighter. The men's lances waved about with the horses' movements.

"One last thing." Cárdenas pointed to a horseman. "Even though you were trained better, I saw Antonio de Ribero make a foolish error at Cíbola. Tell them what you did, Antonio."

The horseman grimaced. He hoisted his lance. "I lanced a savage in the chest."

Cárdenas placed his hands on his hips. "And then what happened?"

"Even though I drove it through his chest, the son of a whore grabbed my lance with his hands and pulled me off my horse."

The other horsemen laughed as Antonio's face flushed at the recollection. The laughter ended when the men realized Cárdenas's anger. "It is not funny," he shouted in an even louder voice. "Antonio is nineteen. But I've seen many older men who should know better do the same. I should never see anyone else lancing an Indian improperly. Whatever we think of them, the Indians have courage and a fierce will to fight. That is why we train you to lance them in the head or neck."

He stepped over to the infantry. "I expect the arquebusiers and crossbow men to shoot the Indians off the walls from a distance. A few will go with the swordsmen. When they reach the rooftop, the rest of you will follow them for close combat. I will punish any man who does not follow orders."

The men stared straight ahead. No one spoke. Punishment could mean only one thing. They would be hanged.

The Aztec war captain Quauhtli stepped forward when Cárdenas motioned to him. The man was taller than any of the Spaniards or other Mexican Indian allies. He had a muscular chest and arms. His eyes looked like dark stones against his caramel-colored face. The lower jaw of a bear hung from his chin, the fangs pointed upward. He had tied his black hair in a bun on top of his head with a cloth as red as blood. He wore a tall staff affixed to his back, decorated with a pennant of green and red stripes, which ended two feet above his head in a swirl of long green feathers. The staff was intended to make him more visible to his warriors in the confusion of battle. He had necklaces made up of scores of human teeth around his neck. Tattoos and scars patterned his chest, arms, and legs. Two human lower jaws hung by leather straps from each leg. In his left hand, he carried a round shield decorated in geometric lines, an array of eagle feathers dangling along its bottom edge. In his right hand, he carried a maquahuitl club, its sharp, black obsidian blades so shiny they reflected the sunlight.

Cárdenas glared at the Aztec war captain. "Are your warriors ready?"

There was no expression on the Aztec's face as he replied in perfect Spanish, "We are thirsty for the blood of your enemies, my lord."

# PART V – FIRE AND BLOOD
## December 1540 to April 1541
### 32

Ishpanyan stood behind a low wall on the surrounded village's second-story rooftop. He watched as three of the metal people rode their horses across the desert toward the west wall. All three wore steel helmets and breastplates. Even their horses were protected with multi-layered coats of hard leather. In the distance, on every side, other metal people sat on horses. There were a great many invaders on foot. They had no metal armor, but they carried swords, the guns of lightning, and crossbows. Foreign warriors ringed the entire area. Ishpanyan estimated the Tiwas were outnumbered five to one.

The pair of horsemen flanking Cárdenas held their lances upward. Cárdenas carried a large sheet, like a roll of bark. The words on it spoke to him, and he recited them in a loud voice to the Tiwas. None of the Tiwas could understand him, but they recognized the threat in Cárdenas's voice. For a moment, Ishpanyan wished Poquis were with him. Poquis would know some of the words. What was this madman saying?

Poquis was right about one thing. The metal people had come to fight him instead of chasing after the Tiwas escaping to the mountains.

Ishpanyan understood everything he needed to know about these strangers. They wanted to take over the Tiwa homeland. They even renamed this village as Arenal, as if it already belonged to them. Two elders wanted to negotiate, but Ishpanyan felt it was time to stop the strangers before they became even stronger.

Cárdenas and the other two strangers turned their horses around and trotted back to the others. Ishpanyan led his warriors in shouting their defiance.

# 33

"We've read them the requerimiento, so they've been given their chance to come to peace," Cárdenas said to the horsemen. "Now the sword will bring them to obedience." He turned in his saddle. "Bring up the ladders," he told one officer. To the German Juan Fioz holding a trumpet, he said, "On my command."

"The Cíbola town was larger than this," one captain said. "We shall kill them all within an hour."

Cárdenas held up his hand. Two Tiwa elders had come out of Arenal. They carried no weapons as they walked toward Cárdenas and the other horsemen.

"They want to parley," said a horseman, struggling to control his excited horse.

"Too late for that now," Cárdenas said. He walked his horse over to a pair of horsemen and gave them their orders. The horsemen rode out and circled behind the two Tiwas. The elders glanced back at the horsemen before they resumed walking toward the Spanish lines.

When the Tiwas were a crossbow shot from Cárdenas, the two horsemen spurred their horses into a gallop. They lowered their lances and drove them through the heads of the two elders from behind. The bodies fell into the snow. Rage erupted from the village's walls as arrows pursued the two horsemen racing back to the Spanish lines.

Killing the emissaries also disturbed several Spaniards. "They could have taken them alive without any risk," complained Juan Troyano to others around him.

When the trumpet sounded, everyone charged into a hail of arrows. Coronado's officers had learned from fighting at Cíbola and Coofor. They brought so many ladders this time that men with swords and lances reached the first rooftop within minutes. There they engaged Tiwas in hand-to-hand combat. A few arquebusiers and crossbow men were in the first wave onto the roof. The rest hurried across the desert to join them.

Atop the roof, Juan de Zaldívar slashed and stabbed with his bloody sword, making his way into a room where Indians had surrounded two Castilians. Zaldívar no sooner had broke the melee apart when he spotted Ishpanyan and two other Indians enter through a doorway from an adjacent room. As they drew on their bows, Zaldívar backed away. One arrow tore through his nose and two others struck him in the temple. The men he'd rescued dragged him unconscious into another room and carried him away.

Several Tiwas on the first roof were killed before the rest scrambled up ladders to a second roof, pulling the ladders up after them. They dropped into the rooms, and from inside the towers they continued firing arrows through loopholes.

The arquebusiers and crossbow men exchanged shots with the Tiwa archers. But the Castilians and Mexican Indian allies were exposed while the Tiwas were protected behind the walls. Several expeditionaries and their Mexican Indian allies were wounded or killed as the fighting continued.

Fighting ceased when night's darkness enveloped everything. The expeditionaries remained on the roof of the first terrace but not in control of the pueblo.

—

Uhlaíto felt confused when he regained consciousness inside a dark room. Then he remembered seeing the flash of fire and smoke from the bearded man's gun. He gritted his teeth, bearing down on the pain that burned from bleeding holes in his stomach and back. Pain rolled in waves across his abdomen. He gasped involuntarily. At the sound, a man beside him placed a hand over Uhlaíto's mouth. Even in the low whisper, Uhlaíto recognized the voice of his best friend. But Uhlaíto couldn't remember his friend's name.

"I know you suffer, Uhlaíto, but you must not make a sound. Our enemies are nearby. Can you hear them outside?"

Uhlaíto opened his eyes. He heard low voices outside speaking words he could not understand. The voices were muffled, as if wrapped in cotton. Hard objects bumped together outside like dull rocks sometimes but with sharp sounds other times. He shivered, but he was not cold. He felt only pain. He clenched his teeth and looked around the room. The room smelled of bowels, like a gutted deer. He could make out a form nearby in the darkness on the floor. The room he was in was barely large enough for the three of them.

"It is a warrior from Kuaua," his friend whispered. "I do not know him. I carried you both in here. He has died."

Uhlaíto closed his eyes. He had been trained since a boy to withstand pain, to ignore hunger, to endure hardship. He bore down with all his will power against the pain.

His parents had counted back the seasons once. He was fifteen cycles in age. This was his first combat, and he'd prayed to the Warrior Twins for courage. When he'd looked down at the plain, the enemies were so numerous that it seemed like a black mass moving across the grass toward the village walls. He found himself beside others on the first roof terrace, pumping arrows down at the attackers. The invaders had brought so many ladders that they poured onto the ground-level rooms' roof terrace. Other warriors charged forward. Then Uhlaíto dropped his bow, threw off his empty quiver, pulled his club from his waistband, and ran to join the fight. It was terrifying to be amid the crashing weapons, shouts, and grunts of strong men fighting hand-to-hand. Death raged all around him in the strangers' onslaught—but he had never felt so alive. He wondered now, how could it be both? He saw a helmeted Spaniard with a red sword blade and wearing a shirt of metal links. Uhlaíto lunged at the man, pushing with his shield until the Spaniard fell off the roof backward with his arms flailing. Uhlaíto regained his balance in time. Then the gun's blast knocked the breath out of him, and he fell onto the roof. He tried to get up, but he couldn't move. It was as if a hundred buffalo robes were piled on him.

He remembered his friend grabbing him and carrying him down the ladder of a rooftop entrance into the beehive maze of the ground floor rooms. His friend had dragged and carried him through small doorways from room to room. The pain had been agonizing. He must have passed out.

He forced his eyes open again to look at his friend. That's when he saw his friend's right arm was missing from the elbow down. Someone else must have tied the headband above the amputation to stop the bleeding. Someone else who must be dead now, Uhlaíto thought. His friend's head also was bloody and bleeding through his headband. Uhlaíto could hear his friend's heavy breathing. His friend always had been as strong as a bear. He would need such strength to survive.

His friend, who had been kneeling on the floor, lay down beside Uhlaíto.

"They have stopped searching the lower rooms," his friend whispered, his breath blowing warm against Uhlaíto's ear from being so close. "The Warrior Twins protect us. The strangers missed this room." His friend paused, struggling against his own pain.

Strength of a bear, my friend, Uhlaíto thought. Keep the strength. We must fight on.

"You are wounded," Uhlaíto managed to say.

"Not as badly as you," his friend whispered. "And not as badly as the Kuaua warrior. Be quiet. I hear footsteps."

Uhlaíto held his breath, struggling to hold back a cough. Through the room's small door, the next room brightened. A torch must have been thrust through the ceiling's smoke hole. The footsteps paced away.

"I hope they do not bring a ladder to check the rooms better," his friend said.

Uhlaíto's body began shaking. He couldn't stop it. His abdomen was on fire.

His friend struggled to his feet. Don't leave, Uhlaíto thought. When his friend returned, he carried a pottery canteen he'd found in another room. Resting Uhlaíto's head on his leg, he held the canteen to Uhlaíto's lips so Uhlaíto could drink. Then he drank the rest.

"I will pray for both of us," his friend said. And he began whispering a prayer. He asked the katsinas to help them and the other Tiwas above them in the second-story rooms. The others would continue the fight again in the morning. His friend prayed for a long time. Uhlaíto repeated the words in his mind, but he was too weak to talk. His body kept shaking. The never-ending pain drained his strength.

Uhlaíto was afraid. He was afraid of the torch. Of the ladder. Of the night.

And then the pain disappeared and he dreamed. He was a boy again playing by Big River. That bothered him, because even while dreaming he knew he was not a little boy any more. The appearance of his grandmother calmed him. She had gone to the ancestors so long ago, but now she kneeled beside him. She pulled him into her arms. It was so warm in grandmother's arms. So peaceful.

# 34

As dawn arrived, Coronado's Indian allies began smashing holes in the adobe walls of the second floor with battering rams. They threw in brush for fires. Smoke poured through Arenal's upper rooms.

Melchior Pérez was on the roof beside Cárdenas when the first Indians emerged from a smoky rooftop entrance. The Indians, racked with coughing, dropped their weapons and crossed their hands in the shape of a cross. Cárdenas lowered his sword and made the sign of the cross back to them, urging them to come forward.

"Lord, do not show them the cross unless you intend to fulfill your promise," Pérez said, unable to believe the field master would pledge safe passage to the Indians. Cárdenas said he'd made the sign of the cross incorrectly.

More Indians came out choking and gasping after they saw the first ones were not cut down. One threw a blanket across Cárdenas's shoulders as a further sign of peace. Those who came out under the sign of the cross were taken to a large tent that had been erected for Cárdenas on the plain outside Arenal. Lancers on horseback and militiamen with swords surrounded the tent's captives.

Meanwhile, several Tiwas were yanked from smoke-filled rooms by their hair and stabbed or clubbed. Their bodies were thrown back into the fires. Other Tiwas emerged staggering and choking from the smoke but still firing arrows or swinging clubs. Ishpanyan was one of those men. Three Aztecs overpowered him and knocked him unconscious. They carried him to the tent with the other captives.

When the battle ended, Cárdenas sent a messenger on a fast horse to Coronado to report that Arenal had been conquered. Alonso introduced the messenger to Coronado in the general's quarters at Coofor. Coronado slid his chair back from the camp table and beckoned for the messenger to report.

"Field Master Cárdenas has pacified Arenal," the man told Coronado. "Now he needs to know how the general wants to punish more than a hundred captives in his tent."

Coronado already had decided the war would be fought without mercy. He gave the messenger his order. Cárdenas was to burn the captives alive at the stake.

"At your orders, my general," the messenger said as he bowed.

"Wait," Coronado said, stopping the messenger. Coronado turned to his groomsman, Juan de Contreras, who was also in the room. "You go with the messenger," he told Contreras. "Tell don García not to execute the Indian captives until I've sent Turk and Ysopete to Arenal. Make them see our punishment for any who rebel against us."

Alonso left Coronado's room in a daze. He felt relieved Coronado had not required him to go to Arenal. He didn't want to witness the burnings. He feared Coronado would tell him to do so if he stayed in the room.

—

Some men chortled at the sight. While waiting for Coronado's reply, expeditionaries had pulled scores of poles out of the pueblo's ceilings. They set them into holes they dug in the flat desert plain around Arenal. Upon arrival of Turk and Ysopete under guard, several expeditionaries went into the tent and escorted about thirty Indians out and tied them to the stakes. Mexican Indians then dropped armfuls of dry willow canes at each stake. The willow canes were piled around the Tiwas, covering them up to their chests, and set ablaze.

When Indians in the tent heard the screams of pain and saw through the tent opening their friends being burned alive at the stake, they realized their fate. Men who had surrendered hours earlier began fighting now with bare hands against steel swords trying to get out of the tent.

Expeditionaries thrust their lances and swords through the tent sides, killing Tiwas around the edges. Other Tiwas surged toward the tent entrance and other openings that had been slashed in the sides, trying to escape in a turmoil of screams and groans. Heads, arms, legs, and disemboweled torsos lay in pools of blood in and around the tent. Some Tiwas made it past the tent's furious slaughter. Horsemen then chased them down on the level countryside and drove lances through them.

After all who had escaped the tent had been killed, the horsemen returned to the pueblo's smoking ruin. Expeditionaries set fire to the brush piles around the remaining Indians tied to the stakes.

When those who were at Arenal told Alonso about the killings in gruesome detail, the boy never forgot the horror.

—

At one point, a warrior, whose bindings had burned through, leaped away from his stake and picked up a burning branch. Expeditionaries ran at the sight of the Tiwa, blackened by flames, charging them.

After he had struck several of his tormentors, Ishpanyan returned to the flames. His final remaining duty was to die with his companions.

## 35

In the mountains where he and other warriors had led Tiwa elders, women, and children to safety, Poquis climbed the first ridge overlooking the valley of Big River.

It bothered Poquis how metal people referred to Tuf Sheur Teui as Sandia Pueblo. They'd also renamed Turtle Mountain as Sandia Mountain, the burned pueblo as Arenal, and his home village as Coofor. They refused to call Xauían anything except the alien-sounding name of Juan Alemán. They were naming everything in the Tiguex Province with Spanish words.

Cresting the ridge, Poquis looked between the junipers and rocks. Straight ahead toward the river was the town of Tuf Sheur Teui, now abandoned like all the rest. People from other villages had streamed across the desert toward the mountains or toward the mesa-top stronghold in the safety of darkness and a winter storm. Falling snow obliterated their tracks, and the desert lay white and smooth far below.

Poquis groaned as he looked at a distant haze of smoke still rising from the ruined village the strangers had attacked. Seven warriors gathered around him, dismayed by the sight.

Poquis looked at his men. "The strangers will kill us just like that unless we find a better way to fight them."

All of them knew now. A wounded man who had hidden in one of the burned village's rooms had escaped into the mountains after the second night. He told how the strangers had killed the men who surrendered or were captured, burning many alive at the stake.

While drinking water and eating, the escapee described how he'd hid in a room after losing an arm in the fighting. From the village, he'd watched Friar Padilla walk up to each of the men tied to stakes. Through an interpreter, the Franciscan offered to baptize them so they would not go to hell. The men at the stakes had stared straight ahead, their mouths set firm, ignoring the priest.

Once the wounded survivor was safe on the mountain, women had hurried forward to care for him.

Shiw-tu, a muscular warrior from Tuf Sheur Teui, joined Poquis at the crest and looked out over the valley with him.

"I am sorry for the foolishness of the men in the villages," he said, gritting his teeth. "They would let us keep only two horses and killed all the rest."

Poquis shrugged. He'd already vented all the anger he could muster when he'd first heard about the slaughter of horses he'd wanted to take into the mountains. Nothing could be done about it now. "You and I hoped for more, but we must understand," he told Shiw-tu. "Our people feared the horses as much as they hated the strangers. At least we were able to lead away two. I must think of another way to fight the strangers. We will see what we can do."

"I feel we have lost an opportunity for a great advantage," Shiw-tu said.

Captured Tiwa women at Ghufoor had sent word earlier that the expeditionaries were preparing to track them down in the mountains. But Xauían also had sent a runner to say he would keep the metal people and their Indian allies from Mexico tied down for as long as possible on the mesa. If he could resist them long enough, Xauían said, the people in the mountains would be safe from attack during the winter, when they were most vulnerable for lack of shelter, food, and clothing.

Poquis picked a man to leave with the runner that night to report to Xauían how the burned village's defenders had fought and died.

Poquis gathered scores of his warriors in the dark, in the midst of a blowing snowstorm, around a campfire in the mountaintop forest. They could hear the women and children crying for the warriors who'd died in the burned village. The women's wails echoed through the canyons.

Until they could return to their villages, it would be impossible to hold a gourd dance to honor the slain warriors. Instead, the sun priest led the men in an honor ceremony, praying for the warriors' spirit journeys. Their sacrifice had given time for the people's escape to the mountains.

The sun priest brought out figures of the Warrior Twins Maseway and Oyoyeway. He tied feathers to the carvings. The feathers would lift their prayers into the sky, asking the Warrior Twins to avenge the men who died in the burned village.

At the end of the ceremony, Poquis and his men formed a circle and took up the pledge Xauían had sent from his fortress. From that day forth, they would battle to the death or withdraw in fighting retreats.

There would never be another Tiwa surrender.

# 36

Tlecanen cared for the Tiwa warrior he'd captured in hand-to-hand combat at Arenal as he would treat an injured son. He'd stitched the wound he'd inflicted with his maquahuitl. He treated it with herbs he'd brought from Mexico City. They were warm now beside the fire in Tlecanen's brush shelter outside the walls of Coofor even as snow whitened the outside.

The Aztec leader smiled when he saw the pleasure on the captive's face as the wounded Puebloan tasted the chocolate Tlecanen had brought all this way. From now until they returned to Mexico City, Tlecanen would bestow kindness on his Tiwa captive. Tlecanen would give the man his own food and water if necessary. He would protect the captive against anyone who might do harm. He would nurse the man back to health.

At forty-nine, Tlecanen was the expedition's oldest fighter. But he still had the physique of a man much younger. As a jaguar knight in his late twenties, he'd fought Cortés's army of Spaniards and their Tlaxcalan allies in the doomed defense of Tenochtitlán. Luckier than most, he'd survived his wounds to live into Spanish rule. Because his heroism and fighting ability made him a leader, he didn't need to submit himself to forced labor. Instead, he assigned his group of Aztecs to work like slaves for Viceroy Mendoza and other Spanish overlords. Tlecanen also was a leader of the hundreds of Aztecs who'd volunteered for the expedition. Mendoza had paid for their service as mercenaries by reducing their tribe's tribute payments and forced-labor requirements.

Tlecanen felt a mixture of joy at his capture of the Tiwa and regret that fourteen of his own warriors died in the Arenal battle. Taking a captive at his advanced age, however, would move him higher in status and respect in what was left of Aztec society. He'd dressed his captive in the clothes of a fallen Aztec—a warrior his own captive had killed—to disguise the Tiwa from the Spaniards. He would never let the man out of his sight.

Tlecanen's warriors had pulled wood poles out of the ceiling of one of Arenal's rooms and carried them to Tlecanen's brush shelter. Tlecanen fed more of the wood to the fire to keep his captive warm. He looked up to see the Aztec named Meztli approaching through the falling snow. The visitor crouched to enter the low entrance. He gave a greeting in Tiwa to the captive to reassure him, then sat cross-legged beside Tlecanen.

"I congratulate you, Juan," Meztli said in Nahuatl.

Tlecanen bristled. "Do not call me by my Christian name when I am at war. I let the friars baptize me, but I have not abandoned our Mexica gods for Christian gods." His lips curled into a sneer.

Meztli bowed his head. "I did not mean to offend Tlecanen, who is a great warrior. It is good to feel like a man again now that I am at war like you. That is why both of us came with these gold-hungry murderers. To be men again in war and no longer a slave. Our broken spears are whole again, at least for a season. I am pleased you have won a captive in battle. Our people will honor you with flowers, quetzal feathers, and songs."

"Do you have any cocoa beans left? My captive likes the chocolate, but I do not have many beans left."

"I do. But I want to keep them. I might have the good fortune to also capture an enemy."

"Keep your beans then. I wish you success."

Continuing to speak in Nahuatl so the captive would not understand, Meztli said that other Aztec leaders such as Coavis and Yaotl would be envious. "Where will your ceremony be when you return? The Christians must not find out."

"There are places where our gods are still honored. When it is time, my brave captive's heart will be offered on a stone altar to our god Huitzilopochtli."

Tlecanen turned back to his captive and offered a second cup of frothy chocolate.

# 37

By the time Captain Tristán de Luna y Arellano could start the bulk of the expedition's departure from Cíbola, winter struck the countryside in freezing storms. Even twenty years later, the ordeal of traveling to Tiguex Province with the main part of the expedition remained vivid to Pedro de Castañeda. He wrote one of his longest single-event passages to describe the severe weather.

"The army continued its march from [Cíbola] after it stopped snowing," Castañeda recalled. "And as the season had already advanced into December, during the ten days that the army was delayed, it did not fail to snow during the evenings and nearly every night, so that they had to clear away a large amount of snow when they came to where they wanted to make a camp. The road could not be seen, but the guides managed to find it, as they knew the country. There are junipers and pine trees all over the country, which they used in making large brushwood fires, the smoke and heat of which melted the snow from two to four yards all around the fire. It was a dry snow, so that although it fell on the baggage and covered it for half a man's height, it did not hurt it. It fell all night long, covering the baggage and the soldiers and their beds, piling up in the air, so that if anyone had suddenly come upon the army nothing would have been seen but the mountains of snow. The horses stood half buried in it. It kept those who were underneath warm instead of cold."

Arellano reached Coofor the day after the fall of Arenal. He brought the rest of the expedition's men, women, children, servants, and slaves, hundreds of more Mexican Indian allies, and thousands of sheep and horses.

—

Velasco de Barrionuevo entered the doorway into Coronado's office at Coofor. A Spanish-built fireplace poured heat and light into the room. Barrionuevo stomped the snow off his boots.

Coronado rose from a chair and invited Barrionuevo to join him at a table where a half-completed game of chess laid waiting. Before sitting behind the table, Coronado lined up his bishop on the same rook already targeted by his remaining knight. "Come, Captain, and let us see you get out of this trap," he said.

Velasco and his young brother Rodrigo shared the Barrionuevo name with one of Coronado's heroes, Francisco de Barrionuevo, a conquistador famed throughout the Indies. Recognizing Coronado's interest, Velasco had become an expert in his famous namesake's career. He also grew closer with Coronado because he was Coronado's equal in chess. He made sure to lose more games than he won.

After a few polite pleasantries, Barrionuevo moved his rook out of danger and voiced the concern that had driven him to ask for a meeting.

"Perhaps, my esteemed general, we should tell Field Master Cárdenas to announce that all the horses were killed or recovered. Write that into your records. If the viceroy and the king learn that these Indians might have taken any horses into the mountains, as Enriquillo did a few years ago on Hispaniola, there will be much trouble for all of us."

Coronado looked up in surprise. Barrionuevo would never dare speak so frankly to Coronado if others had been present. In their private meetings, however, Coronado encouraged Barrionuevo's advice.

"Captain, it is a few horses at most we might not be able to account for. The Indians do not have them. They are terrified of them."

"As you say, my lord. But the Indians see us ride horses. It will not take much imagination for them to realize they could ride them too. I humbly remind you again of Enriquillo. Because he had horses and Spanish arms, he fought us for fourteen years in the mountains of Hispaniola." Barrionuevo swept his hand toward the east, where the rugged mountains they called Sandia rose a mile above the river valley.

Coronado scoffed. "I am aware of how well informed you are about our famous conquistador, captain, especially in Hispaniola. However, Francisco de Barrionuevo forced Enriquillo's surrender with two hundred Spanish soldiers. Our force is more than ten times that size."

Barrionuevo bowed to hide a frown on his face. "With your permission, my distinguished general. You have greater numbers. But almost all these men with us are militia at best, with little or no military training. And our thousands of Indian allies from Mexico often act on their own. Enriquillo took away our advantages when he went into the mountains. These Tiwas could do the same to us."

Coronado stared. "These barbaric Indians are no match for Spanish arms."

Barrionuevo grimaced. "It is not well known from that time that our king's orders were to grant Enriquillo's demands and obtain a peace. Another military expedition was to be launched only as a last resort. If Enriquillo had not come to terms just seven years ago and pardoned by the king, perhaps his rebellion would still be going on."

Coronado stroked his goatee and set his quill down. Every conquistador knew how Enriquillo had won freedom for Taino Indians on Hispaniola. Enriquillo had fought the Spaniards to a deadlock at great cost to the crown. The humiliation still burned. Viceroy Mendoza would fear the worst if he heard there was any possibility Tiwas had fled to the mountains with horses as Enriquillo had done.

Barrionuevo pointed to Coronado's half-finished message to the viceroy on another table. "I humbly advise you to say nothing about even the possibility any horses are unaccounted for."

Coronado nodded. "Perhaps you are right." He adjourned their game again. He sent Barrionuevo away with orders to triple the guard on the remaining horses.

—

For the next week, everything was quiet in the Tiguex Province. Too quiet. Tiwas had disappeared. They had abandoned all their pueblos just before Arenal's destruction. Occasional tracks through snow made it clear they'd fled to the mountains.

Coronado had been preparing to order a force to go after the Tiwas in the mountains when the Arenal fight intervened. Now Field Master Cárdenas reported a more immediate threat.

Three Tarascan scouts had brought the news. The fall of Arenal and slaughter of its defenders had not terrorized the Tiwas, as Coronado had hoped. Instead, hundreds of Tiwas had gathered in another pueblo atop a high cliff to the north. When the Tarascans had approached, Tiwa warriors attacked them.

"They spotted Juan Alemán on the walls," Cárdenas said as Coronado leaned back in his camp chair to listen. "I wish we had burned him at the stake with the other barbarian Indians at Arenal."

Coronado chuckled at his field master's remark. He turned solemn again as they both thought about the Tiwas' continued defiance, now in a fortified pueblo on a high mesa.

He would need to overcome them before going after the mountain escapees. He felt there was plenty of time to deal with both. Coronado and his officers had made plans to go to the buffalo plains in the spring to find Quivira and the riches Turk promised. But he could not leave the Tiguex Province in revolt.

He knew who to send to deal with the rebels on the mesa. He motioned to Alonso, standing against a wall of the room and holding a staff from which draped Coronado's pennons and standard. "Bring me Captain Rodrigo de Maldonado."

A few minutes later the cavalry captain appeared in the doorway, bowed, and stepped into the room. He knuckle-tapped his chain mail vest. "I am at your orders, my general," he said.

# 38

Xauían waited with warriors, along with women and children who wouldn't leave their men, in the fortified pueblo. From their perch atop a high and steep-banked mesa, they could look down and see Big River. Xauían wondered if he could defend his mesa-top stronghold long enough so the strangers couldn't attack the Tiwas during winter in the mountains.

The stronghold was built to withstand a siege as the Tiwas' ultimate defensive position against enemies. There was storage capacity for food and water. The fortifications had taken years to complete. The building had a high wall with several sections of an additional story, and it was built on the edge of the mesa's eastern vertical cliff. Unlike other villages, where a person on the first terrace could walk around the entire village, the stronghold's roofs had gaps between sections. Attackers could reach one section of roof but could not cross to other parts. At the same time they would be exposed to arrows fired from loopholes. Rocks could be dropped on attackers from the tops of the towers.

The outward walls were unlike anything the strangers had encountered before. Over the years, teams of men had carried tree trunks from the mountains and hauled them up to the mesa's top. The thick pine logs were anchored into the ground to reinforce the walls. Woven branches bound the logs together. The outside was coated with dried mud so it appeared to be like any other adobe village wall. The stronghold's outer wall was honeycombed with firing loopholes. Warriors could fire arrows from inside the rooms with impunity.

Other Tiwa men and women walked to a similar stronghold not far away.

Xauían looked down into the valley. In the distance, he could see several strangers coming on horses, leaving a long track behind them in the snow. Sunlight flashed off their metal weapons as they rode.

—

More dispossessed Tiwas kept straggling into Poquis' mountain hideout every day, led by guides he posted at the mountain base. The snow was deep and the people were cold. He'd spent his first week building shelters, assigning warriors as lookouts along mountain passes, and organizing the sanctuary. At the same time, he and his men spent time getting used to the two stallions and letting the horses get used to them. He kept the stallions inside corrals or tied with a strap to trees, as he'd seen the strangers do. A mountain lion had already threatened the horses. Poquis now kept a ring of men around the camp and horses, alert for strangers or lions alike.

The first week in the mountains was the hardest because food was scarce. Every night Poquis sent men to the abandoned villages to gather whatever corn and other food the strangers had not already taken or destroyed. But there was never enough. Many old men and women began giving their portions to the younger women, warriors, and children. The sun priest continued eating, for the Tiwas would be imperiled without their religious leader. But other elders fasted into oblivion.

When Eye-Black Leader became too weak to stand, Panpahlu asked Poquis to carry the elder into their bark-and-stick shelter. She knew of Eye-Black Leader's efforts to convince Poquis to leave her when she didn't have children. She disregarded all of that now to care for the old man. Panpahlu wrapped him in a buffalo robe, trying to make him comfortable, giving him sips of water. He continued to refuse the food she offered him.

"It is the tribe that must survive, and my heart tells me my time has run out," he said. "Give my food to the others. I am old and not well. I have lived a long time."

On his last night, Panpahlu stroked his hair to comfort him. "You do not belong here any more," she whispered to him. "When you become a cloud being, tell our ancestors of our suffering. Come back to help our people."

The old man's eyes fluttered open, and he looked at her. "I will send you rain for your corn," he promised.

Later that night, Eye-Black Leader fell into a sleep from which he never awoke. The winter ceremonial people had lost their treasured elder.

—

In the morning, a Tiwa runner scrambled up the long, steep slope toward the camp.

He gasped out the words to Poquis and others who assembled at the top of the ridge to meet him. "The strangers have found the mesa stronghold."

# 39

Captain Rodrigo de Maldonado and his lancers rode more than twelve miles up the river. Then they saw the pueblo perched on the high mesa's edge. As horsemen rode forward, they looked up a sheer cliff of volcanic rock rising two hundred feet.

"Rest," ordered Maldonado. Some horsemen rode the hundred or so feet to the river so they could look back and see the stronghold better. From there, it looked like any of the valley pueblos, except it was one high story with other compartments rising like towers around the enclosed sides.

Maldonado wondered why the pueblo was so special that Juan Alemán would choose to fight from there. The pueblo was built on a great height, like European castles. On the way, however, Maldonado had found an eroded area like a ramp where men and horses could ascend to the top.

Maldonado began thinking of what he would say in his report to the general. Give me ladders and brave men, he thought. I will kill everyone inside these rebels' feeble fort within a day. He had orders to read the requerimiento to them, although he couldn't understand why he should bother.

Once everyone was rested, the Castilians remounted their horses in a clanking of metal and creaking of leather. They rode in formation, their lances pointing up above the snorting horses' bobbing heads. Alonso Álvarez lifted the expedition's banner so the winter wind would fill it out. They stopped near the mesa base, the pueblo high above them.

As the horsemen approached, Indians lined the tops of the stronghold's walls. Their faces twisted in scowls and were colored with painted designs.

Maldonado looked up and recognized Juan Alemán, who motioned for him and his men to ride closer.

Turning in his saddle to look down at Bartolomé standing on the ground beside him, Maldonado told the interpreter to step forward so the Tiwas could see him better. "Tell them that if they come out," Maldonado said, "there will be peace. Tell them that the Indians at Arenal who killed the horses have been punished. Tell them we have no quarrel with them here. They must give their obedience to the king and the pope."

Bartolomé looked up toward Juan Alemán. In a combination of common Nahuatl words and some Tiwa he'd picked up, he shouted as loud as he could. His voice carried up to the Tiwa leader through the cold, thin air. He hoped they would be able to see his sign language filling in gaps when he could not think of words he needed. Tiwas along the wall started shouting, but Alemán ordered them into silence. Then the Tiwa spoke back to Bartolomé in sign language and a mix of Nahuatl, Tiwa, and Zuni.

Maldonado tightened the chin strap of his metal helmet. He didn't like the tone of the Indian leader's voice. "What did he say?"

Bartolomé stepped back beside Maldonado's horse. In halting Spanish, which he'd improved on over the past few months, Bartolomé replied. "He says that Castilians are not to be trusted. He says we betrayed the Pecos Indians when we took Bigotes and their elder captive. He says we promised safety to the Tiwas at the burned village. Then we broke our word and murdered everyone. He says they do not trust those who do not know how to keep good faith after they have given it."

Maldonado sneered and looked around at the other horsemen before turning back to Bartolomé. "He does not need to trust us. He just needs to do what I tell him. Translate what I read to them as best as you can. I will go slowly."

He unfolded the requerimiento and began reading it, pausing after each sentence for the interpreter to repeat and catch up. Reading the paper, he promised the Indians clemency and peace if they would surrender. He vowed ruinous warfare if they did not. He rolled the paper back up after reading the final sentence, which warned what would happen if the Tiwas refused to agree to Spanish terms. Bartolomé, who had again moved several feet in front of the horsemen so the Tiwas could hear him better, relayed the requerimiento's closing threats in a shaky voice.

"If the Tiwas do not surrender, the Spaniards will make slaves of you all, take your women and children, and do with them what they wish," Bartolomé said in his translation, rephrasing as little as possible in his combination of languages and signs. "And the Spaniards will take away everything the Tiwas own and harm them as much as they can. And if the Tiwas do not obey their lords, the pope and the holy Roman emperor and king of Spain, then they will be killed. Their deaths will be their own fault."

Bartolomé continued interpreting into a rising roar of anger along the top of the wall. When the final threat of the requerimiento was interpreted, warriors raised their bows and a volley of arrows swept down from the height into the Spanish ranks. Horses reared, and men screamed curses. Maldonado's men spun their horses around in a swirl of dirt and snow dust to gallop out of range. Bartolomé sprinted on foot behind them. Arrows wounded several men and horses. Maldonado's men began shouting their outrage as they regrouped beside the river. Maldonado looked back at the jeering Tiwas atop their wall.

"We offered peace, and they have replied with war," he shouted to the lancers around him. His men were still trying to rein in their frightened horses. "We will report to the general this Indian treachery."

# 40

Even before Maldonado had arrived, Poquis's runner had told the mesa-top defenders how Cárdenas had burned warriors alive at the stake at the village Ishpanyan had been defending. He told how Cárdenas had the rest butchered in the tent and on the adjoining prairie.

A few days after Maldonado left, Xauían looked down from the stronghold's rooftop to see Cárdenas leading a second group of horsemen and Indian allies toward them. Cárdenas, the hated man who had burned the first village's warriors. His men recognized Cárdenas as well. They began shouting Tiwa curses at him, vowing to avenge their friends who'd died at the burned village. Xauían fixated on Cárdenas's face. He felt he was looking at the greatest evil he'd ever known.

Xauían watched as the enemy milled around at the mesa base. Then he descended a ladder into the courtyard inside the walls. He signaled to some warriors to meet him.

He told them his plan.

Cárdenas read the requerimiento in Spanish. All the Spaniards stayed out of arrow range.

Instead of a volley of arrows in response, however, Xauían reappeared on the roof and lowered a ladder outside. Seeing arquebuses pointed in his direction, he raised his hand, indicating he wanted to talk. He and two warriors began walking down a narrow, rough pathway cut into the cliff's side.

Cárdenas shouted at the arquebusiers, reassuring the Indian delegation they would not be fired upon.

Xauían was halfway down the path when he called to the interpreter Bartolomé. "Perhaps it would be best," he said, "if we could settle our difference without war. I wish to talk, but only with García López de Cárdenas."

# 41

Cárdenas ordered his men to stay back. He rode his horse forward and stopped a short distance from the cliff. He watched the Tiwa war chief warily as the man descended the path farther. He knew the man's name was Xauían. Nevertheless, to show his disrespect, he referred to him as Juan Alemán like other Spaniards did.

"If you wish to talk," the Indian war captain said through Bartolomé, "then leave your horse, for I fear it. Come forward to meet me without your sword or lance." The Indian leader held out his hands to show he was unarmed. Cárdenas trotted his horse back to his men. He swung out of his saddle and handed his reins and weapons to Alonso Álvarez, along with his lance and sword. Alonso passed the lance and sword to the nearest infantryman, the red-bearded Juan Galiveer.

"I do not like this, sir," said Galiveer, taking Cárdenas's weapons.

Cárdenas glared at him. "I must talk to this savage if it is a chance to bring them to peace. We can hang him after the rebels surrender." He began walking toward the Indian leader.

Captain Rodrigo de Maldonado leaned from his horse toward Galiveer. "Never again question the field master, Englishman," he snarled.

Then Maldonado motioned to another horseman, who moved his horse forward to stop beside the captain. "Now listen," Maldonado told the horseman. "The rest will fall back, but you and I will hold our positions. We will see what happens."

Another horseman wrote years later:

"When [Cárdenas] met them, Juan Alemán approached and embraced him vigorously, while the other two who had come with him drew two small clubs which they had hidden behind their backs and gave [Cárdenas] two such blows over his helmet that they almost knocked him senseless. Two men-at-arms on horseback had been unwilling to go very far off, even when he ordered them, and so they were nearby and rode up so quickly that they rescued him from their hands. The horsemen were unable to harm their enemies, though, because the Indians had a refuge nearby. Of the great shower of arrows that were shot at

them, one arrow hit a horse and went through his nose. The horsemen all rode up together and hurriedly carried off their captain ... while many of our men were dangerously wounded."
—

Mounted on his favorite gray horse, Coronado led the third force through deep snow out of Coofor a few days later. He left some men-at-arms along with about half his Indian allies behind to guard the livestock and expeditionaries' family members. He took the rest of the expedition in a fighting column a half-mile long. There were three hundred horsemen and footmen as well as more than a thousand Aztecs and Tarascans. Since the barbaric Indians want a fight, he told his officers, he would overwhelm them quickly with a large force and wipe them out.

As he rode, Coronado seethed at the memory of Cárdenas's report. Cárdenas had told how he had been able to escape Juan Alemán's trap because of a dagger he'd concealed. Two horsemen also had come to his rescue. Afterward, Cárdenas had also read the requerimiento to a second fortified pueblo, *Pueblo de la Cruz*— Town of the Cross—on a mesa about a mile away. He was defied there as well.

Cárdenas told Coronado there had been one victory. When Cárdenas returned to Juan Alemán's stronghold, he'd lured several Tiwas out on the plain at the mesa's base by having his men pretend to retreat. Then his cavalry turned their horses and charged, lancing several Indians before the rest fled back to the stronghold.

Coronado sent Rodrigo de Maldonado ahead with several horsemen to guard the base of the mesa and block any attempt by Tiwas to escape. Once the attack began, Maldonado's men with swords were to race up the stepped pathway the Indians had cut into the cliff and attack from that side.

Coronado led the rest of the expeditionaries up a natural eroded ramp. The Europeans reached the mesa top with much difficulty by foot and horseback, followed by the Mexican Indian allies.

Black basalt rock from an ancient lava flow had formed the mesa. The rock paved the exposed mesa top, interspersed with clumps of grass poking up through snow. Coronado settled on the word *Moho* for the stronghold, because that was the Spanish word for the lichens seen on the mesa's rocks but not in the valley. The freezing wind that thinned the snow by blowing it off the surface also whipped Alonso's banner and pennons. They could see the whole width of the river valley from the top, sloping up to the mountains where the rest of the Tiwas had fled. Well, Coronado thought, he would deal with them soon too.

The expedition's fighting men moved across the mesa. In the distance they could see the Moho stronghold perched like a rectangular box on the cliff's edge.

The following dawn, Coronado told his officers the time had come to teach these heathen Indians the power of Holy Roman Emperor Carlos V's legions.

Coronado once again had the requerimiento announced in Spanish to the Indians.

But Xauían stood at the top of the wall facing the Spaniards and gave the reply of all in the stronghold. "We cannot trust people who do not know how to keep their word," came his words interpreted to Coronado. "We remember that you are still holding Bigotes prisoner, and we remember you did not keep your word when you burned those who surrendered in the valley village."

With that, Coronado motioned to his forces around him. He called out the Santiago battle cry, the German trumpeter Juan Fioz pealed the notes for an attack, and fourteen-hundred expeditionaries and Mexican Indian allies charged the Moho fortress with battering rams and scaling ladders.

# 42

A twelve-year-old boy showed them how.

For the first five days in the mountains, the Tiwas had fed and watered the two stallions as they'd seen the strangers do, keeping them tied to pine trees. On the flight to the mountains, Poquis and his men had loaded buffalo hides full of corn meal and other supplies on the horses' backs, also as they'd seen done. Poquis sensed that survival of the Tiwas depended on having the horses and Tiwas getting used to each other.

On the sixth day, the boy untied a horse when no one was watching. He improvised the reins and bridle he'd seen the expeditionaries use. Holding both ends of his yucca rope, the boy made a loop around the horse's bottom jaw into its mouth. He climbed onto the horse's back, gripping the animal with pressed knees, and rode it into camp to the adults' astonishment.

That afternoon warriors began learning to ride the horses. The men took turns every day.

—

Although the river villages were abandoned, armed men of both sides continued to visit them.

Expeditionaries ranged up and down the valley during the days, further dismantling the villages by pulling beams out of the room ceilings. Using ropes, they dragged the logs behind their horses back to Coronado's forces at Moho for firewood.

At night, Poquis sent armed sorties to the same crumbled villages, salvaging hidden caches of corn and other food.

Poquis also sent warriors to the Keres, Tewa, and Towa villages. All carried the same message: "Even though we have had differences in the past, the strangers are the enemy of us all. You know their cruelty at the burned village. Now they are attacking our mesa strongholds. They have driven the rest of us into the mountains to starve and freeze. Will you send us blankets and corn in the night? We do not ask that you fight the invaders. If you cannot help us because of the danger, we understand and pledge our peace with you."

After the first weeks' deaths, and as winter progressed, many women, children, and elderly left. They moved in as refugees with their linguistic cousins in the Piro and Tompiro villages on the east side of the mountains. They also scattered among the Keres, Tewa, and Towa villages up the valley where some had relatives. The warriors remained in the mountain sanctuary. Panpahlu and some other women also remained, unwilling to leave their men. Despite winter hardship, in the mountains they at least lived in a vast pine forest, had plentiful game to hunt, and never lacked for firewood.

—

The storm howled like a wounded animal as it blasted wind and snow into the forest. Looking outside his small shelter of tree limbs and packed dirt, Poquis saw a form moving toward him, blurred by the snowstorm. The form became the outline of a man struggling through knee-deep snow and being staggered by gusts of wind. Not until the figure was almost to the shelter did Poquis see who it was. Poquis leaped to his feet and rushed into the storm.

He gasped when he turned his face back into the wind's force. He wrapped his right arm around the sun priest. He picked the old man up and rushed him toward shelter.

Poquis shouted over the roar of the storm as he maneuvered their religious leader toward the campfire. "Panpahlu, more wood for the fire." He grabbed a buffalo robe and threw it around the old man's shoulders. The sun priest stumbled, unbalanced by the weight.

Out of breath from fighting his way through the storm, the sun priest sat and pushed aside strands of white hair blown across his face. He held out his hands to warm them. Panpahlu and Poquis worked together to build the fire hotter.

"Grandfather," Poquis said when the old man seemed to have recovered. "Why did you walk through the storm? You could have sent someone to me. I would have gone to your shelter."

The old man lowered the buffalo robe and shook his own blanket off his head, sending a layer of snow falling into the fire and onto the ground. "It wasn't that far," he said with a smile, still breathing heavily. "I love the mountain storms. I used to come up here when I was a young man like you." He brushed the snow caked against his legs and gazed into the fire.

Poquis waited a while before asking, "Why do you visit us, Grandfather?"

"I hear things," the sun priest replied. "Even the wind shouted it to me as I walked here. I hear that you think you should join Xauían and fight from his stronghold there."

"I am preparing to do so."

They sat in silence for a while before the sun priest spoke again. "Xauían and I agreed that he needed to make a stand at the stronghold against the strangers so they would not come after the rest of our people."

Then the sun priest looked into Poquis's eyes. "We need you to take care of our people here," he said.

# 43

With the battle cry of "Santiago!" echoing across the mesa, Coronado's forces raced toward the Moho fortress.

Coronado planned a two-pronged attack. Some armored swordsmen would climb the ladders and kill the rebels on the rooftops. Others would charge into Moho at ground level through holes the battering rams broke through the pueblo's sides. That would let in the thousand Mexican Indian allies in what would be a massacre of outnumbered defenders. Fires also could be set inside the walls through the holes, smoking the Tiwas out as Cárdenas had done at Arenal.

Coronado committed his entire force to the attack so the pueblo's defenders would be overwhelmed in the first rush. It was already into January. Coronado didn't want to spend any more time than necessary on the windswept, frozen mesa.

Several Aztecs and Tarascans were killed or wounded running toward Moho across the mesa's bunch-grass prairie. Volleys of Tiwa arrows slashed into their onrushing ranks. Others jumped over the first bodies and ran on. To hesitate or turn back now could be fatal.

The din of battle, punctuated by shouts of anger from both sides and cries of pain on the battlefield, intensified as the attackers ran up to Moho's walls.

Several men protected themselves from dropped rocks by holding wooden platforms over their heads. That exposed them to arrows fired at their faces, arms, and legs from ground-floor loopholes.

White, sulfurous clouds burst from points on the field where all twenty-one arquebuses thundered again and again from a distance out of arrow range. Maneuvering closer to the pueblo, the expedition's nineteen crossbowmen used their more accurate weapons to pick off Indians firing arrows from the first terrace roof.

Men threw ladders against the pueblo's sides at numerous places. Sword-wielding Castilians clambered up. Arrows broke against their breastplates and chain mail or became stuck in their quilted jackets.

Fifty made it to the roofs, but they found they had nowhere to go. At Arenal, they had been able to stride around the pueblo walls, using their swords to cut down every bare-chested Tiwa who challenged them. But here they found themselves standing on isolated, small areas. Men on the roofs were exposed to a whistling crossfire of arrows from nearby loopholes and from archers firing across gaps between roofs at the same level. Rock slabs fell on them from towers another story above them. The Europeans began falling from wounds to their limbs and faces not protected by metal or quilted armor.

On the ground, the attack shuddered to a standstill. The pueblo reverberated from the impacts of Indian allies smashing battering rams into the pueblo's sides. Unlike the valley pueblos, however, Moho was built of blocks of basalt. The sole result was to chip off large sections of mud plaster revealing the thick rock beneath. Other parts of the walls were reinforced with logs far stronger than the battering rams. The Indian allies and Europeans clustered at the base of the wall. There, they often were inches from Tiwas firing arrows through loopholes into the attackers' ranks.

At the wall, Francisco Pobares tried to use mud to plug a man-high loophole through which arrows were being fired. Pobares pushed a double handful of mud into one loophole. An arrow erupted through the mud, striking an eye, penetrating his brain, and killing him instantly.

Coronado saw his men rush up to the pueblo but then splinter and fall back, like a giant wave striking a cliff. He watched as his force retreated down the ladders. Some carried dead or unconscious comrades. Others half-descended, half-fell down the ladders with arrows sticking out of their arms and legs. In disbelief, he saw the rock and log wall materialize as the battering rams knocked off the exterior coating of plaster. The Tiwas continued firing arrows through loopholes. Bodies piled up at the base of the wall from men being hit by arrows or laid out by plunging rocks.

Furious, Coronado turned to the German trumpeter. "Call them back!"

———

Three Europeans and numerous Mexican Indian allies were killed in the first attack. Arrows and rocks wounded more than a hundred so severely that they needed the care of Doctor Juan Ramos, the expedition's surgeon. Men treated each other for less serious but still painful and often debilitating wounds. Casualties amounting to a tenth of his attacking force shocked Coronado.

But even more horror was revealed within a day. Some arrow wounds festered, spreading infections through the wounded.

When men began dying under the surgeon's treatment, Coronado summoned Ramos to his campaign tent, which shook from winter's constant wind.

"It is like the poisoned arrows the Indians use on the Sonora River," Ramos insisted. "But not exactly the same. Here I think they coat their arrowheads with rattlesnake venom. I have found arrows that have a crystallized substance on their stone points."

Coronado slammed his fist on his camp table. He bellowed, "Poison or your incompetence?" He ordered Ramos back to the hospital tent. He shook his head in frustration.

Field Master Cárdenas hesitated, then stepped forward and addressed his general, whose face had reddened with anger. "We must lay siege to this *Pueblo del Cerco*," he said. The Spanish term had a double meaning of "Town of the Surrounded Wall" as well as "Town of the Siege."

Coronado looked up at him. The muscles tensed in his face.

"Truth. You name this hellish place well, don García. Do we have a choice with that rock and log wall? We can't even set fire to the logs because of the enfilading fire from the pueblo's loopholes. Even a man in armor with a shield is not safe at such point-blank range."

The frontal assault had been costly. And not a single expeditionary had been able to climb up the eastern cliff side because the Tiwas hurled rocks down on them as they tried to climb the narrow path.

"We control the water," Cárdenas noted. "They cannot hold out forever. They will surrender when they see they have no other choice. How long can they last on the water they have stored inside?"

"We will find out. I do not want to waste our men in hopeless attacks. We must keep probing for some weakness somewhere. If we do not find a way in, then yes, we will conduct a siege. We will conquer this Moho, or Pueblo del Cerco, as you say."

Ten days. Just when the expeditionaries felt the Tiwas' water must be exhausted, heavy snowfalls began, replenishing supplies inside Moho. The Castilians whispered around the campfires. God is punishing us for our overconfidence, they said.

Coronado kept having the requerimiento proclaimed. And every time the Tiwas paid no attention to Spanish demands except to shoot arrows from Moho's roof and loopholes. They dared the expeditionaries to attack again.

Twenty days. Battering rams were hung from frames with swings, like those used in Europe before gunpowder. They were moved into position at great cost in Indian allies being killed and wounded. But even they could not break through the pueblo's rock and log wall. The expeditionaries tried to attack from a safe distance by catapulting rocks. They even lashed together wood tubes to launch rockets. All failed to dent the Tiwa defenses. It took an all-but-impossible shot for arquebusiers and crossbowmen like Alonso Álvarez and his father Rodrigo to hit anyone behind the loopholes.

Thirty days. When three warriors were captured outside the besieged pueblo one night, they were taken to Coronado's tent outside Moho. In front of Juan de Contreras, his groomsman, and Alonso Álvarez, his standard-bearer, Coronado told his officers to execute the Indians by setting Pedro de Tovar's dogs on them.

Contreras would later testify that, under Coronado's order, "This witness saw them unleash the dogs and kill the Indians." He said the men turning the dogs loose on the captives included Tovar, Cárdenas, and Alvarado.

More snow fell. As the weeks went by, Coronado returned to the comfort of Coofor while his captains maintained the siege. The expedition's members huddled in shivering misery around fires fed with ceiling beams and other wood pulled out of the river valley's abandoned pueblos.

Forty days. Another in the series of assaults was concentrated on a narrow opening that the expeditionaries had managed to make. Frustrated by the inability to break into the village, Captain Francisco de Ovando raced through the hurled rocks and whizzing arrows. When Ovando squeezed on his hands and knees through a narrow and low opening, warriors seized him, dragged him inside, and blocked the opening. Ovando and two other Spaniards were killed in the assault as well as several Indian allies.

"I wish we had field cannons," Coronado said at one council of the royal financial officers, nobles, friars, and captains. "Our small cannons are worthless against that rock and log wall."

"Those accursed Pecos people," Rodrigo de Maldonado interjected. He turned to the others. They had not yet heard a report about Coronado's trip to Pecos because he'd just returned the night before. "They were glad to get their cacique back when the general returned him, but then all they would do was plead for the return of Bigotes. The general asked them to show their gratitude for restoring the cacique to them by sending us men to fight their enemies here. They said they had to prepare their cornfields for planting."

Another officer scoffed. "In February?"

"There was no sense insisting," Coronado said. "We don't need another pueblo to fight. That's why I told Cárdenas to also be patient with the Keres Indians at Zia. They refused his request for fighting men. They only gave us a little corn and some blankets. The same thing happened at the other river pueblos."

"We will remember this disobedience after this Pueblo del Cerco falls," vowed Hernando de Alvarado.

"Not then," Coronado said. "Once we pacify Tiguex Province, all of us will leave for the buffalo plains to find Quivira. I've already ordered our sheep and horses moved to the east side while the river is still frozen. When we have subdued these rebels, and the weather breaks, we will leave with everyone. We will even take our captives. Our gamble in investments will be repaid and more at Quivira. From what Turk says, we will need wagons to bring back all the gold."

Fifty days. At the end of February, a high-pitched trilling and warbling sound drew Alonso Álvarez's eyes to the sky. The sound echoed from high above. He could see large birds circling overhead. Their long, slim wings alternately beat and glided as the birds climbed on air currents. Once they spiraled high enough, the birds arranged themselves into V-formations and headed north. Wave after wave of the birds crossed the sky.

His friend Juan Pastor rode up on a horse. He nodded to Alonso and looked skyward with him. "What are they?"

"Cranes," said Galiveer as he walked by. He paused to look upward at the spectacle himself. "I grew up near the Norfolk wetlands in England. One of my thrills as a boy was to watch migrations of cranes every year."

Juan started to turn his horse away, but Galiveer grabbed the reins. "All we footmen hear are rumors. You cavaliers know what's going on. Is there to be another assault soon?"

Juan snorted. "Listen to me. How many times have we charged that pueblo? What is the use of doing it again? It is best to let them run out of water."

Sixty days. The expeditionaries used snipers with crossbows and arquebuses. They kept Moho surrounded, with men both on the mesa and at the mesa base. Coronado's hope that the Indians would run out of water continued to be frustrated with snowstorms replenishing the defenders.

Sixty-five days. Juan Alemán called down from the top of the wall to the interpreter Bartolomé after Cárdenas had once again read the requerimiento. "Because we believe you will not harm the children, we will give them up to you. The rest of us will not surrender, because we know you will not keep any promise you make to us."

"We will accept the children," Cárdenas replied.

Maldonado, on horseback next to Cárdenas, gave a surprised look at the field master.

"I know," said Cárdenas, acknowledging Maldonado's expression. "The rebels are handing their children and some of their mothers over as a way to conserve their water. But we will accept them anyway." Cárdenas grinned. "The men could use more servants."

More than a hundred women and children descended ladders, many of them crying. Other women appeared at the top of the walls, refusing to leave their men.

—

Town of the Cross, the second fortified pueblo a short distance from Moho, could resist no longer. Without Xauían's leadership, the defenders felt overcome by thirst rather than force of arms.

Coronado had sent captains Diego de Guevara and Juan de Zaldívar to attack Town of the Cross with the same orders he'd given Field Master Cárdenas at Moho. "There is to be no council held with the Indians nor any talks. The men are to be slain whenever and wherever they can be found. The women and children may be taken as prisoners."

Officers would read the requerimiento. The sole acceptable response was capitulation on Spanish terms. Refusing to surrender, but made desperate by lack of water, and knowing how all males had been killed at the valley's burned pueblo, the men decided their only chance for survival was to escape. Women and children were left behind in the hope they would not be harmed.

Guevara and Zaldívar's men spotted the Tiwas trying to leave. Horsemen chased and lanced scores of warriors. They found only the bodies of men on the escape route.

When expeditionaries entered the pueblo, they captured about one hundred women and children inside. Everyone would be forced to work for the expedition. The younger women would suffer a year-long nightmare of hardship and sexual abuse.

## 44

Xauían mourned. The cavity they had quarried out of the rock to build the stronghold had been serving as a reservoir. It had collapsed when warriors tried to dig it deeper in hopes of finding a spring or underground stream. Some men had suffocated when buried by the collapsing sides.

The Tiwas had held off the strangers for about eighty days. By giving up the children and their mothers fifteen days earlier, they had been able to stretch their water supplies. But now it was near the end of Strong Wind Moon. Although they still had plenty of food, there was no more water. A cloudless, bright, and blue sky came with each sun. Xauían knew there would be no snow or rain. Down at the mesa base, everyone could see the flooding spring-melt river. Finally free of ice, it still was bitterly cold. Most bitter to the Tiwas, however, was the sight of water out of their reach.

Xauían looked at the men from several villages gathered around him. His fighters were no longer just warriors. There also were elderly men, proud of their return to warrior status. There were boys as good with a bow as any man. Younger women had picked up the bows of fallen warriors and fired arrows at the invaders. Everyone's stern faces told him all he needed to know. They preferred death to captivity. If necessary, they would go down fighting.

They reaffirmed their pledge to never surrender.

"Bring all the clothing, blankets, jewelry, and whatever else you cannot carry out with you," said Xauían, turning as he addressed everyone crouching in a circle around him. "We will burn everything. The strangers will enter this place with empty hands and leave the same way."

Then he told them the plan of escape. "Tonight, Moon Mother will die and turn the night to black before being reborn. Our men will form a circle around the women for their protection and leave in darkness. After we cross the river, we will head for the mountains and join Poquis and the others there."

Xauían held his wife's hand all the way descending the mesa's steep cliff. He and his warriors formed a defensive line around the women when they reached the bottom and began running for the river not far ahead.

—

It was in the fourth watch, when sentinels are the most tired, that a Spaniard at the base of the mesa drew his sword. He'd heard a slight noise in the coal blackness of a new-moon night. He peered intently, squinting his eyes. He thought he could hear people in front of him moving toward the river. He called out that the Indians were escaping. Rodrigo de Maldonado shouted for his cavalrymen to mount their horses. With their lances pointed into the darkness, forty horsemen charged toward the sound of people running.

The Tiwas raced for the nearby river as they heard the shouted alarms in Spanish and the pounding of horses' hooves.

Then the horsemen were upon them, stabbing with lances and cutting people down with swords. Fleeing Tiwa men and women groaned in shock and pain as they fell under the attack.

The shadow of a Castilian and his horse loomed before Xauían. The war captain shoved his wife forward, shouting at her to run. Grasping his war club, Xauían tried to dodge the lance. But death rushed at him too fast, too remorseless.

Most Tiwas never reached the river. Bodies of dead men and women mounded along the retreat path. Horsemen who waded in after them killed some Tiwas even in the river. The water turned darker with blood from bodies that floated away on the current.

Pedro de Castañeda would later recall that night. "The enemies knocked one Spaniard and one horse down dead and wounded others. But they were driven back with great slaughter until they came to the river, where the water flowed swiftly and very cold ... There were few who escaped being killed or wounded."

—

Banqín, a warrior from Ghufoor, was among the few Tiwas to make it to the river's other side. They crawled up the riverbank and into the cottonwoods. Most collapsed there from exposure to the river's near-freezing water, the frigid night winds, and their wounds.

Banqín ran among the prostrate forms, urging them to get up. "We will join Poquis in the mountain sanctuary," he shouted to one half-conscious man, bleeding from a sword wound to his side. "We must hurry before they come across the river after us." The man groaned, gritted his teeth, and closed his eyes.

Gripping and waving Francisco de Ovando's sword he'd taken when Ovando had managed to enter the stronghold, Banqín was able to rally the strongest —sixteen men and four women. They gathered around him.

Banqín looked toward the river. The moonless night made it impossible to see, but he could not hear any horses splashing in the river. Perhaps the Spaniards were reluctant to swim their horses across the river and ride into the trees in the dark. Perhaps it might still be possible to get away.

"Follow me," he said to them. "We cannot help the others. Most are too wounded to push on. We need to reach the mountains to let our people know what happened here."

They stumbled across the winter-dead land, heading by memory for the dark mountains in the distance.

—

The inability of a Spanish-led force as large as Coronado's to defeat Indians fighting from fortified positions for nearly three months was unprecedented. A later Spanish historian expressed disgust that his countrymen of that time had been unable to storm fortresses manned by what he considered primitive inferiors. He decided Coronado was unworthy of victory because he'd burned Indians at the stake at Arenal.

"And thus, one night the besieged went forth in flight, leaving our people fooled and with no gain except the poor plunder of the besieged place," wrote Matías de la Mota y Padilla of the mesa-top stronghold. "And the Indians went out valorously."

# 45

Spaniards entered the abandoned Moho as soon as dawn revealed the bodies along the escape route to the river.

Castañeda was among those who entered the eerily silent pueblo that morning. He never forgot the strange sight of Francisco de Ovando's naked body lying in the plaza. In contrast to the maiming slaughter outside, Ovando lay untouched. His body showed only the wound that had slain him forty days earlier and a finger cut off to take his gold ring. Ovando's body was white as snow and without any odor because of the cold weather, as were the bodies of many Indians.

While Castañeda and others explored the pueblo, appearing to be empty except for corpses, other expeditionaries crossed the river. They brought back Tiwas unable to resist because of hypothermia or wounds.

Women survivors were treated and kept as captives.

As for the men, none would surrender. The ones taken prisoner were a few who were overpowered, too wounded to fight on, or comatose from the cold on the opposite river bank. The prisoners with the worst wounds were thrown to war dogs, which were trained to kill humans by ripping open bellies and tearing out throats. Lances and swords were used to kill many others.

Some Tiwa men and women remained in Moho's rooms. Coronado ordered that they be burned inside. Expeditionaries began stuffing burning wood and grasses into the rooms. Unlike Arenal, the Tiwas refused to come out and died in the flames and smoke.

Alonso Álvarez stood in the plaza, his face contorted in shock. He held Coronado's standard with its colored streamers and pennons. Castañeda rode up on his brown horse and stopped beside him.

"The field master told me to hold the colors so you can help burn the rooms," Castañeda said.

Alonso looked toward the expeditionaries setting fires throughout the pueblo. Indian screams and choking coughs echoed through Moho. "Look at this," Alonso said to Castañeda. "They fought as hard as they could. Now they refuse to surrender. These are worthy people."

"Yes. But they killed and wounded many of us. They killed even more of our Indian allies. They defied the requerimiento. They must be punished so the other pueblos will fear and obey us. Then the province will be at peace."

Alonso felt ill. He'd been tormented by the reports he'd heard of the stake burnings at Arenal. Now the field master wanted him to help with the burnings here. How could he do it? He would not do it. He knew everything Castañeda said was true. As standard-bearer, Alonso was a member of Coronado's personal household. He had been present when the general ordered Alvarado to set the dogs on Bigotes in an attempt to make Bigotes admit to having Turk's gold. It had distressed him to see how Bigotes was so bitten by the dogs that it took a long time for him to heal. Villegas had raped the Arenal woman and not been punished. Clothing and food had been taken from villages by force. Spanish livestock had been turned into the Indian cornfields. Alonso felt that the Tiwas rose in revolt for all those reasons.

Alonso understood better than most, because he was almost always at Coronado's side during meetings with his officers. Alonso had heard Coronado order the abandoned pueblos destroyed, and he'd heard the general order the male prisoners executed by dogs. He was beside Coronado when the captain-general gave the order to burn Tiwas at the stake at Arenal and in their rooms after Moho fell.

Alonso also was among the few who knew what Coronado had ordered Cárdenas to do to the ten Indians in iron shackles sitting off to one side.

Could he bear this any longer? He was loyal, but he could not bring himself to participate in this.

He understood everything, even though he had just turned sixteen.

Castañeda reached down from his horse and gripped the standard's pole. Alonso pulled it away. "You must obey the field master's order," Castañeda said.

Alonso shook his head. "He did not order me to do anything. He asked you to come over and hold the standard so I could help burn the Indians. But I do not wish to help, so there is no need for you here."

Castañeda arched his eyebrows so high that they disappeared under the rim of his tall, peaked hat. He started at Alonso with wide eyes.

Alonso studied Castañeda. "I know that even you do not approve of all we do," he said to the horseman. "Against brave people like these, you think as I do. Such punishments cause anger, not fear."

Castañeda frowned. "I agree this war could have been avoided and is a great misfortune," he said. "If the collection of food and clothing had not been done so clumsily, and if the general had punished Juan de Villegas for the rape, the Indians would not have risen in rebellion. Truth, burning the Indians who surrendered at Arenal angered rather than terrorized the other Indians. They refused to believe we would not do the same thing to them. That is why they fought us for nearly three months." Castañeda said no more. He sat on his horse with Alonso standing alongside. They watched as fires were set in rooms.

As the final measure of conquering Moho, Coronado had reserved a special punishment for ten Indians. Turk and Ysopete were brought from Coofor and forced to watch.

While the smell of smoke still thickened the air, the field master strode over to the last ten male prisoners. Expeditionaries pulled them to their feet. With an expeditionary holding each arm, and another clasping each man's head from behind, García López de Cárdenas clutched each man in turn by the throat. He sliced off each man's nose with a dagger. Then each captive was taken to a block, where expeditionaries hacked off both hands with swords. Expeditionaries used torches to cauterize the wrist stumps so the captives would not bleed to death.

Then Cárdenas told a captain to have horsemen escort the maimed men to the mountains. Coronado had said he wanted the sight of them to terrorize Tiwas hiding in the heights.

# 46

A sentry left his post so he could run to Poquis with the news that Tiwa escapees from Moho were approaching the mountain at dawn. Poquis and Shiw-tu mounted the two horses and rode down the snow-choked trail. They rode past the pre-selected ambush sites, and then past the boulders ready to be toppled onto the narrow trail to prevent horses from coming up. They saw the mountain base sentry leading the few refugees who'd swam across the river after the fall of Xauían's stronghold.

Poquis's fear had been confirmed. Xauían had resisted for as long as he could. However, the traditional defenses that had served Tiwas so well for centuries were futile against these new enemies. A few stragglers from the other besieged mesa pueblo had arrived earlier. Now even the mightiest Tiwa stronghold had fallen.

"We must be ready to fight them next," Poquis said to Shiw-tu. "But we will fight them in ambushes, with stealth and raids, not massive resistance."

Shiw-tu shifted his weight on the back of his horse. "I wish Ishpanyan were here. He would be the first to admit that the old ways no longer worked. He would have said you were right to fight these strangers in a different way. He would have stood shoulder-to-shoulder with us."

"He and the others gave their lives so we could have three months to prepare. Otherwise, we would not have had time to strengthen our hand here and fight a different way. I grieve for him always. Ishpanyan, Xauían, and the men who died with them are the people's heroes."

The fourteen men and six women escapees stopped in the trail, astonished at the sight of Poquis and Shiw-tu riding horses toward them. Even though their escort had alerted them, they had trouble believing what they were seeing.

Poquis fastened his eyes on the survivor walking beside the sentry. The man carried a sword in his right hand. He recognized Banqín, his friend from Ghufoor who had volunteered to fight with Xauían.

Banqín raised the Spanish sword above his head and waved it in the air when he saw Poquis and Shiw-tu approaching on horseback. "Poquis and Shiw-tu show me we have a chance," he shouted, turning to the escapees. "Once it was I who always could out-wrestle either of them. Oh, how they used to fear me." He looked around with a grin. "But now it is I who am afraid of them on their horses."

In answer, Shiw-tu laughed. "Even my little son can ride a horse. I might be able to teach you as well."

Banqín jammed the point of the sword into the ground beside him. "You have been busy up here. Taking the metal people's horses and learning to ride them. Not hiding like rabbits as we thought. So, we will not surrender?"

Poquis, Shiw-tu, and the sentry replied as one. "Never."

"Only one of the metal people managed to get inside our walls," Banqín said. "Because I fought and killed him, Xauían let me keep the invader's sword. I cut down another Castilian in our escape. I lost the sword's holder in the river."

"We can use you and those you brought out with you," Poquis said. He dismounted and clasped his hands on the shoulders of each man and woman.

No one needed to ask about everyone else's fate at the stronghold. The burned village had already taught them about Spanish warfare.

—

The next day, twenty horsemen escorted ten Tiwa men in collars and chains to the base of the mountain. They set the prisoners free at the entrance to a canyon cut between the front ridge of the mountains and the main bulk rising high into the sky.

After the Castilians rode away, Poquis's sentries went to the released men. When they saw them, they stopped, stunned. The men's faces were gory with blood where their noses had been cut off. Their arms ended in blackened and blistered stumps.

The sentries fed the men and let them rest before taking them up the steep trail to Poquis' camp. There the women fed the men again, heating up corn cakes and game meat. Anger burned through the crowd as the Tiwas listened to the men tell of Xauían's last stand.

Late that afternoon, the men said they refused to be a burden on the tribe. Without hands, they said, they would be of no use. They would need to be fed and cared for like babies. They refused all attempts to talk them out of their decision.

The camp of a hundred people followed the men to the edge of a cliff that faced west. Panpahlu and other women stepped forward and painted sacred symbols on the men's faces so the ancestors would recognize them. The men placed their feet at the edge of an abyss that plunged so far the boulders below looked like pebbles. There the ten maimed men sang their death song:

*Great Creator, we are ready.*
*Guide us on our spirit journey*
*To the west.*
*A man uses up his life,*
*And his time has come.*

They sang the song four times, because anything repeated four times is done properly. Then the ten men linked their arms together and took a step forward as one. They disappeared without a sound over the edge.

Panpahlu and the other women wailed and wept, holding children close to them. Poquis, Shiw-tu, and Banqín stood with the other warriors. Every man remained silent and still, gazing toward the western horizon as the sun turned red and colored the soft clouds. Then the sun set and the red glow faded, the light failed, and darkness covered the world.

# 47

Since his return to Coofor two days earlier from the carnage of the mesa strongholds, Coronado had much time to reflect on his lack of success so far on the expedition. He sat alone in his room at Coofor. He stared at the fire in the fireplace his men had built for him, absorbing its warmth through this still-freezing night of late March 1541.

He knew now, in hindsight, that the Zuni warriors who'd confronted his forces at Cíbola had meant to delay him. Many had sacrificed themselves to give their women, children, and elders time to escape to their mesa-top refuge. Afterward, he realized he could not reach them atop the towering sandstone cliffs. They refused to come down.

The Franciscan friars had wanted to climb to the top alone, but that would have been a suicidal missionary effort. These Franciscans were always so eager for martyrdom, Coronado thought, and its sure heavenly reward. They would sacrifice themselves even if it meant his men would be demoralized by their deaths and lose any chance for spiritual comfort in Mass and confession.

Then in the months of besieging the two Tiguex strongholds, he had become frantic at times. He knew he should pursue the Tiwas who had fled to the snowy mountains to the east while they were still disorganized and weak. But it took all of his forces to attack the two strongholds and also forage for food and firewood for up to three thousand expedition members, counting the spouses, slaves, and servants.

Once again, he suspected the Indians had outmaneuvered him. They'd done it this time by tying down the expedition to keep him away from the mountain sanctuary.

He had to admit the Puebloans in the strongholds had fought like lions. No matter how outnumbered or trapped, no matter how inferior their weapons, they fought to the death.

Although he would not admit his doubts to anyone else, he had begun to think he had been wrong to execute the warriors at Arenal. Rather than terrifying them with the executions, he'd strengthened their resolve. He decided he should have cut off the survivors' noses and hands and sent them back to their people, as he'd done at Moho. He was sure that would have frightened them into obedience.

What would the viceroy think once he learned that for almost three months Pueblo Indians had prevented Coronado's massive force from conquering them? Spain's history for its half century in the New World had been quick and total annihilation of all Indians they encountered. Yes, it had taken Hernán Cortés a year to defeat the Aztecs. But he'd faced a warrior cult that had many times more fighters than these desert Puebloans.

After defeating the Aztecs, Spanish arms had swept through Mexico and everywhere to the south, conquering tribe after tribe. By 1540 the only remaining major opposition was from the Incas, several Mayan tribes, and the Guaymí in Panama.

Now he'd been brought to frustration in a country entered with such high hopes. He and his officers, even the viceroy, had staked fortunes on the confidence they'd find vast new encomiendas. In Mexico many had become rich through the Indians' payment of tribute and forced labor. Even the rank-and-file had invested hundreds of thousands of pesos in the expedition. They hoped for encomiendas for themselves, or land to settle in, or at least the king's recognition for bravery that could lead to wealth and honors.

Coronado poked at the fireplace wood, making the flames flare. He sat forward in his chair, his head in his hands. They could have knocked Moho's walls down with ease if he'd brought larger cannons. He shook his head slowly.

Beatríz, his lovely young Beatríz, who was just seventeen. What would she think? He'd convinced her to put up much of her inherited wealth from her Mexican encomiendas and estates. He'd even taken a leave of his position as governor of New Galacia. All so he could lead this expedition into the unknown north.

It's all the fault of that lying monk, Friar Marcos, he thought. Marcos had reported great Indian cities at Cíbola, filled with gold and people rich in material things. Nothing Marcos had said had been true. Coronado worried that he would be blamed for not finding the wealth that had to be toward the north, just as it had been in Peru to the south.

There was still a chance. Soon, after it was warmer and the men's wounds were on their way to being healed, they would leave for Quivira. Friar Padilla was convinced that Quivira might be the Seven Cities of Antilia. The Plains Indian, Turk, still insisted Quivira was where they would find great amounts of gold. There, everything might be justified. Coronado kept to himself his growing worry that Turk's descriptions of Quivira gold were exaggerated.

His men were not used to the idea of Indians resisting Spanish arms so effectively. Maybe Turk was telling the truth. Maybe the men's complaints would cease when they saw Quivira.

Coronado had given up finding anything of value in the Tiguex Province. Other than corn and perhaps buffalo hides from the plains, Coronado doubted the Puebloans could provide much else in tribute payments. They seemed only able to meet their own needs. There were not enough of them to provide encomiendas for more than a couple of his officers. And such pueblo encomiendas would be poor and undesirable compared with the encomiendas of Mexico.

He threw more wood into his fireplace. The flames leaped up and poured heat into his room. Tiguex is so cold, he thought. He dreaded the thought of spending a second winter here with so little firewood and clothing to protect them from the cold. The clothes they had requisitioned in Tiguex consisted of some hides and a few cotton blankets. Those already were worn out.

He put his hope in what they might find in Quivira. He could not return to Mexico now. How could he face Viceroy Antonio de Mendoza, let alone Beatríz, with nothing but failure to report?

He picked up several sheets of paper from the camp table beside him.

Pero Méndez de Sotomayor had come with the expedition as its official chronicler. Coronado had read the pages for events up to the present. They made him depressed and uncertain.

The scribe had tried to write everything in the best possible light for the expeditionaries. Still, Coronado saw ammunition for his rivals to use against him. Even worse, for several years Cortés had been trying to have Viceroy Mendoza recalled. So a failed expedition that Mendoza helped finance could ruin Mendoza. Coronado had come to think that the less said about the expedition, the better, for both him and Mendoza.

He fed the first page of the scribe's report into the fire, watching as the flames curled and blackened the edges before consuming it. Then he tossed in another incriminating page, and another, until all were gone. He would keep asking for regular reports, all of which he would destroy. He could say he'd lost Méndez de Sotomayor's report. Perhaps the man would rewrite it after they returned, but that would be Mendoza's problem. If the expedition could find gold at Quivira, none of this would be a concern.

He expected some officers might write their own personal accounts. But that would be acceptable. They could not criticize him without casting their own actions into doubt.

He thought there would be no one else. There was a horseman, Pedro de Castañeda de Nájera, who asked questions of everyone. He was renowned for his phenomenal memory, regaling the men with stories of the conquest filled with detail from ten or more years ago. However, Castañeda was just a common horseman. Surely no one would pay attention to him even if he did write something about the expedition. Besides, Castañeda had no reason to write anything.

Coronado realized he'd made a mistake in thinking the Puebloans were just farmers. Instead he'd found them to be formidable opponents.

He had already omitted events in his reports back to the viceroy that might show he'd ignored orders to treat Indians well or that he'd failed to pacify them quickly. He vowed he would continue to eliminate anything that might lead to criticism of him or the expedition.

## 48

In the middle of the night a moon later, Poquis woke to a mountain lion's huffing growl of protest as it investigated the encampment of the only other predators it respected.

"You should be used to us by now in your hunting territory, mountain king," Poquis murmured. He looked toward Panpahlu, whose face the campfire brightened. She opened her eyes and smiled at him over the edge of a buffalo robe.

A breeze rustled through the tall pines at the sentry camp. They were behind the first ridge of the mountains, high above the valley floor but low enough to be free of winter's most severe grip. The main camps on the mountain summit were still in knee-deep snow.

"Dawn is coming," Panpahlu said. "I want to see our country again when Sun Father casts his first light across it."

The five warriors with them gathered around. Everyone ate cold corn patties as faint light dissolved the darkness. They climbed to the top of the first ridge and looked over the valley. Water sparkled in the distance where Big River curved through the landscape like a serpent. Treeless except for separated groves of cottonwoods along both banks of the river, the desert grasses shone golden as Sun Father rose higher and poured light across the valley. Scattered along the river were clumps of abandoned villages, looking broken even from this distance.

They could not see the largest pueblo of all, the one far to the south. The strangers called it *Piedras Marcadas*, which Poquis had learned meant "Marked Rocks." The Spaniards named it after the nearby sacred drawings etched on the black boulders near the cones of burned rock where Poquis had been wounded months earlier. That pueblo had not been attacked because it was so far south of Ghufoor. It had been abandoned anyway during the war.

Poquis and the others could see herds of sheep and horses clustered around Watche. Some strangers had moved into that village to guard the animals on the river's east side.

The largest splash on the landscape was on the opposite side of the river, across from Watche. There their one-time home of Ghufoor still stood untouched and crowded on three sides by large striped tents and brush shelters. There were herds of horses there, too. Poquis could see bright pricks of cooking fires even at this distance.

Poquis stared, trying to figure how he could obtain more of the strangers' weapons. Three women had smuggled the maquahuitls Poquis had retrieved from the Ghufoor battlefield. They carried them out beneath their blankets. Poquis wanted more. He had sent men to Xauían's stronghold, hoping to find Spanish weapons they could use. All they'd found were clubs, bows, and arrows strewn around the bodies of Tiwa warriors.

Lines of horsemen leaving Ghufoor caught everyone's attention. "Here they come again," Poquis said.

They watched horsemen wading across the river to their side. Other horsemen headed south along the riverbank on the west side. Every day for a week the lancers had ridden up and down the valley with contingents of Aztecs and Tarascans, destroying and burning the Tiguex Province villages. Two hours later, smoke poured out of Tuf Sheur Teui as more wooden ceilings were set afire.

"I am sorry, Shiw-tu," Poquis said, looking over at the man's anguished face as his village burned.

"It is the men they call Rodrigo de Maldonado and Hernando de Alvarado," Shiw-tu said between clenched teeth. "They come through every day. Soon there will be nothing left."

"That is what they intend." Poquis looked sideways at Shiw-tu. "First they tore out the beams and many of the wood ceilings for their firewood. Now they are after what is left."

Panpahlu reached out to touch Poquis's arm and looked up into his eyes. There was a desperate tone to her voice as she asked him, "Why have they come to make war on us?"

Poquis looked out over the valley. "Our corn and land are like nectar in the flowers that attract insects. They want to take over our corn and land and rule over us."

Panpahlu sobbed. "When will they leave us alone?"

His gaze remained on the valley. Desert grasses and bushes swayed around them with the onset of spring's strong winds. "The matriarch sends word from Ghufoor that the strangers plan to go to the buffalo grasslands," he told Panpahlu. "That is why they are destroying our villages before they depart."

—

Panpahlu sat by the fire mending a knee-length moccasin legging. They had spent much of the day climbing the narrow mountain trail to one of the main camps atop the mountains. They had built lean-tos and lashed branches between tree trunks in the pine forest as protection from the snow, wind, and frigid temperatures. Poquis had stopped the men from trying to build a rock or adobe village complex. He said it would become a target for the strangers to attack. He insisted they remain as mobile as possible. He moved his camp each time after sending men out as runners or scouts. If they were captured and tortured, they would be able to divulge only where Poquis's forces used to be.

Men were left as sentries at each of the passes into the mountains. They acted as guards to alert Poquis to any strangers. They also guided to the camps any runners bringing supplies from nearby villages.

Men from Zia prepared to descend the trail with pottery canteens while it was still light. They had dropped off blankets and corn meal. Now they faced a trip cloaked in darkness to return to their village.

"The Castilians are not like us," Poquis told Panpahlu as he sat beside her in the protected grove of towering pines. "These strangers don't grow their own food. They take food from others. They take blankets, buffalo robes, and feather cloaks from others to keep warm. They use their weapons and horses to seize whatever they want. We gave them as much as we could. But they always wanted more. They order us to worship their God, whom we have never known, and obey their leader, whom we have never seen."

"When does the matriarch with the captives at Ghufoor say these strangers will leave?"

"Soon. Bigotes once told me that the Pawnee the strangers call 'The Turk' will take them out onto the buffalo plains. There they might lose their way and disappear."

"Do you think that will happen?"

"There is a good chance. Those grasslands are large beyond imagining. No one has ever traveled so far except the strongest traders who know the way. And even many of them never return."

"If they leave, then we can rebuild our lives."

Poquis leaned down and stoked the fire, inhaling the burned wood scent with calming pleasure. "Yes," he said.

Panpahlu leaned forward, beaming. "Then I will tell you wonderful news as we build our new life together."

Poquis gave her a bewildered look. "That is a strange phrase to use in this time."

She jumped up and embraced him. "I am pregnant, Poquis. Yes, we will have a new life when the strangers leave."

# 49

Coronado worried about leaving hostile Indians to the expedition's rear. He listened to Juan Troyano and Velasco de Barrionuevo's advice in his room at Coofor.

Barrionuevo again brought up the specter of Enriquillo's insurrection in Hispaniola's mountains seven years earlier.

"These rebels might have a few horses, and the mountains where they would lead us to fight are still heavy with snow. Please remember the barbarian rebel Enriquillo, my general. With horses and Spanish weapons, he was able to fight for fourteen years. And his mountains were not covered in snow. These Tiwas might have eaten any horses they stole. But if not, and if these Tiwas have a leader with half the cunning as Enriquillo, we could be fighting them for a long time. Forget them and let us be on our way."

Troyano agreed. "Fighting them in the mountains will delay our trip to Quivira," he said. "Their villages are so destroyed that they will not challenge us again. So many of their fighting men are dead that they are no longer a threat. Let us go and seize the riches of Quivira instead."

And so the decision was made.

A month after the fall of Moho, on April 23, 1541, the entire expedition filed out of the Tiguex Province. They skirted the northern edge of the mountains. They angled northeast toward Pecos as the rising sun colored storm clouds purple and red. They left no one behind. Even the captive Tiwa women and children were taken along. The expedition had been so successful living off Pueblo provisions that they still had thousands of sheep to drive along with them.

The people of Pecos welcomed Coronado when he returned Bigotes. Once inside the walls, however, Bigotes refused to come back out or go any farther with the expedition. Instead, he sent Turk, Ysopete, and another plains captive named Xabe. They would guide the expedition onto the buffalo plains.

—

Many weeks later Coronado learned that Bigotes and Turk had agreed on a plot while sharing captivity. The best way to get rid of the strangers, the Pecos people had decided, was to wish them well as Turk led them out onto the plains. Then the expedition could become swallowed in the grassy vastness.

After seventy-seven days crossing the plains, after Coronado had sent most of the expedition back for fear of starvation and thirst, after Turk had been put in chains and Ysopete had turned them straight north from Turk's eastward bearing, after Coronado's advance party of thirty horsemen and numerous Mexican Indian allies had reached Kansas, after they found Wichita villages of grass lodges and no gold—after all that, Spanish frustration peaked.

Coronado had Turk tortured. The Pawnee took some satisfaction in confessing why he'd led them so far out of their way.

Pedro de Castañeda reported Turk's explanation. "He said that his country was in that direction and that, besides this, the people at Pecos had asked him to lead [the strangers] off on to the plains and lose them, so that the horses would die when their provisions gave out, and they would be so weak if they ever returned that they would be killed without any trouble, and thus they could take revenge for what had been done to them. This was the reason why he had led them astray, supposing that they did not know how to hunt or to live without corn. While as for the gold, he did not know where there was any of it."

Expeditionary Gaspar de Saldaña would later say what all expeditionaries knew. "The Turk had wanted to lead them lost by that route," he said, "so that they would not go to his land to subjugate his parents, relatives, and forebears. That was because it was a worthier thing for him to die so that his relatives would not be subjects of the Christians."

The expeditionaries became enraged. They accused Turk of lying and leading them astray across the prairie where they were in danger of perishing. It was rumored he'd also tried to convince the Quivira Indians to attack the expedition.

Worst of all, a Spaniard named Diego de Cervatos told a chilling story. During the siege of Moho, Cervatos said, he'd checked on Turk, still in chains. Turk had asked him how many Spaniards had been killed at Moho. Cervatos told him none, but Turk said, "You are lying, because five Christians and one captain have died." Turk was correct at that time. So Cervatos had watched him afterward to see where the Pawnee had learned of the casualties. That was when, Cervatos swore to the others, he'd seen Turk talking to the devil in a jug of water.

The Spaniards had enough. They called Turk a heathen spellbinder in alliance with the devil.

Coronado ordered Turk's execution. With Diego López and Juan de Zaldívar in attendance, an expeditionary garroted Turk. The Pawnee remained defiant to the end.

# PART VI – NEVER GIVE UP
## April 1541 to April 1542
### 50

Poquis led the Tiwas down from the mountains after the strangers had left for the buffalo prairie. They divided back to their original villages. They began replanting their cornfields and repairing their villages. Ghufoor residents were fortunate. Their village was the one left intact.

In a field watered by shallow canals dug from nearby Big River, Poquis kneeled by a mound of clay soil, planting corn, squash, and bean seeds. His back aching from long periods of being bent over, he stood with hands on his hips until the pain eased. He looked toward the top of the cliff where Ghufoor's adobe walls glowed in sunlight. He tried to pick out Panpahlu from the many women bustling about repairing the walls. Young girls carried pots of water on their heads up the cliff's steep side. Older women mixed the water with clay, stones, grass, and ashes. After shaping and drying the puddled mud into irregular balls, they filled in the doorways that the expeditionaries had cut into the walls. Rooftop entrances were opened again.

Poquis looked around at other men planting the crops. When Banqín noticed Poquis watching him, he stood, stretched, and walked over to Poquis.

"You are not working hard enough," Poquis told him, grinning. He motioned toward the sword. "Perhaps you could plant as much as the rest of us if you would quit dragging around that weapon you captured."

Banqín gripped the sword's handle. Over the winter he had fashioned a holder for the sword to replace the Spanish sheath he'd lost in the river in his escape from the stronghold. Flattening two straight pieces of wood, he then carved a cavity for the length of both. The sword fit inside when the two wood strips were bound together by strips of deer hide. It dangled at his side from a cloth belt.

"This is a powerful weapon," Banqín said. "More powerful than your club or even your bow and arrow. I keep it with me always. It has already killed two of the strangers. It will kill more if they return."

"The metal people will not come back." Poquis's smile faded. "But it is a great sadness that so many of our women, children, and elders will be lost and die as captives on the buffalo grasslands with them."

They stood in silence, comforted by the spring birds' songs in the cottonwood trees along the riverbank.

Banqín was the first to speak. "Some are angry with you, Poquis, for giving permission for Keres people from Zia to move into our country above the two rivers that come together. But many of us are glad that you traded the land for seeds, food, and clothing. The Keres and other tribes helped us when we were desperate in the mountains. We could not ask them for even more. Your trade preserved our honor."

"We had eaten all our seeds, and our clothes were rags," said Poquis, more to himself than to Banqín.

"Soon our villages will be repaired and our fields planted," Banqín said. "We will send hunters to the buffalo prairie to bring back meat and hides. Perhaps some of our people escaped from the strangers, and we will find them."

Poquis looked into Banqín's eyes. "That is my hope."

—

It surprised Panpahlu how the other women, once so critical of her and Poquis, now treated her kindly. They vied for the honor of working with her in repairing Ghufoor's walls. They trusted her judgment. And now they praised Poquis on how he'd organized everyone during their time in the mountains. He had obtained food from other tribes that had been rivals and even occasional enemies in the past.

"They respect you," she told Poquis one night in their compartment. The Night People sparkled in the square of dark sky seen through their ceiling entrance. Their cooking fire floated a smoky scent through the room. "Everyone at Ghufoor thinks you have become a valued leader. She poked him in the arm. "Even though you are young. And even though you are from Puaray."

Poquis laughed lightly. Moments of humor had been rare during the months the strangers had been present. Delight had returned.

"Your repairs have made Ghufoor like new."

His compliment brightened her face. "Yes. Now I have asked the women to help in the other villages. Many will leave in the morning to help repair villages damaged so much worse. Now the planting is finished. Have you heard from the men you sent to the mountains to cut trees for new beams and branches for ceilings?"

Poquis nodded. "Some have already joined teams from other villages and delivered much of the needed wood. I fear this will take all summer. Some villages were leveled to the ground."

For three full moons, the work continued. The Tiguex country had never seen so much construction taking place at once. The surviving elders met frequently in Ghufoor's subterranean kivas. There was so much to do, to discuss, and to plan. More and more the elders relied on Poquis to carry out their instructions. He was too young to be a Katsina priest, but even the priests and older men seemed to defer to Poquis. Corn, beans, squash, and cotton rose out of Mother Earth, turning the irrigated fields into green patches in the desert. Sun Father blessed the summer. Big River flowed its life-giving water through Tiguex.

It was the mid-summer month of the Sun House Moon when a Pecos man ran into Ghufoor. He said many metal people and Mexican Indians were returning. He ran from village to village to pass the alarm.

Summoned to the painted kiva, Poquis sat in silence as the youngest man. Elders discussed for hours the return of the strangers. They strived for a common understanding.

*We thought they had gone forever, but the metal people and their many allies from the land of macaws are coming back. The war captain they call Arellano is leading them. Our runners say that Coronado and thirty horseman are pushing on across the buffalo prairie. But they will surely return too. Soon the strangers will be all across our valley again. Our villages must once more give up their independence and combine in common action in this crisis. But who can speak for us all now that Xauian is dead? What shall we do? We cannot stay in our homes, exposed to the cruelties and demands of the strangers, starving and unable to protect our women. We have lost so many of our warriors. The sun priest of Ghufoor thinks the best leader now is Poquis, but he is only twenty-one cycles of seasons. And yet, he is a proven member of the Warrior Society. He still does not follow many of our ways. However, the sun priest is at peace with him, saying that the unusual way Poquis thinks will help him understand how to fight the strangers better than anyone else. His mate, Panpahlu, will have their first baby this winter, so he will fight even harder now to protect them. What choice do we have?*

Finally, the sun priest stood. His dark eyes were piercing from within wrinkles that creased his round face. He walked to Poquis.

"You are young," he said, "but the men of the Warrior Society trust you and follow you. You are young, but you understand these strangers better than anyone else. You are young, but I have faith in you. All of us now say, 'Unite behind Poquis.' You have asked us to pick another. But elders of all the villages want you as the war captain for us all. For we trusted Xauían, and we share the confidence he had in you. You have a gift we do not understand for knowing new ways to fight these invaders."

Poquis looked around at the fire-lit painted figures of katsinas in the dim chamber. Their strength of the ancestors was what he most needed now. A reply was not necessary. Silence would be his assent.

The old man pulled his red and yellow blanket tighter around his shoulders. "The elders believe our enemies will kill us or turn us into slaves when they return, as they did to our brothers and sisters. So we must return to the mountains. What does Poquis say to this?"

"Let us leave, grandfather. But we must destroy the crops so the strangers find nothing to eat here."

"It is decided," the sun priest said. "The Creator knows and will help us."

The Tiwas of all the villages fled to the mountains again. When Coronado's new field master, Tristán de Luna y Arellano, arrived with his force, livestock, and captives, he found a Tiguex Province of ghost towns.

# 51

Poquis's warriors had wanted to fight as soon as Arellano's force returned, but Poquis held them back that summer and autumn. "Stay out of sight and have nothing to do with the strangers," Poquis had said. "For then they will ignore us and demand clothes and food from other villages." Just as Poquis had predicted, the metal people and their Mexican Native allies had gone up and down the valley. They resupplied themselves from the Keres, Towa, and Tewa villages.

Out of the strangers' sight, Poquis drilled his men throughout the warm days on the tactics of ambush. It was a mostly unfamiliar kind of warfare for them. It recognized that their enemies used horses, armor, arquebuses, crossbows, swords, lances, and war dogs.

"Always face the enemy with the wind in your face," Poquis had told them, "so the dogs and horses cannot smell you." They trained on what they should do if they were going up against one Spaniard on horse or on foot, more than one Spaniard, one or more of the expedition's Indian allies, an arquebus or a crossbow, at night or in daylight. When to engage the enemy was the most important lesson of all. Poquis could not afford to lose men in suicidal fighting.

There was little cover in the desert landscape of grass and small shrubs nearest the villages. But they practiced hiding even there. Better opportunities for surprise attacks existed between villages, where bushy evergreen junipers grew as high as two or three men. They focused their practice along the river with its groves of thick cottonwood trees, near deep and steep-banked ravines horses couldn't cross, and among the forests and boulders of the mountains.

The Tiwas learned camouflage techniques and practiced nighttime attacks. They perfected ways to lure enemies into traps by having a few men fire arrows from a juniper or other cover nearest the target. In their retreat, they would lead pursuers to other junipers or a ravine where far more warriors were waiting.

Their most important tactic was neutralizing the expeditionaries' horses. They rehearsed how to attack from slopes too steep for horses to climb and from the opposite side of ravines too deep for horses to cross.

Because most operations would be at night, the warriors practiced shooting their arrows at targets in the dark. They had never spent effort on that skill before. In the mountains, they climbed steep slopes to learn the trajectory their arrows needed to hit preselected ambush sites along trails below. Boulders were piled atop slopes overlooking other sites so they could be rolled down on any invaders.

Wary of Castilian swords and lances, which they'd seen kill so many, the warriors often wanted to attack from too far away. But Poquis taught them to get in close. "Do not shoot your arrow until the enemy is almost upon you," Poquis told them. "If there is a dog present, shoot it first, and then the horse. Once a Castilian is on foot, you can outrun him if you need to, but you cannot outrun a dog or a horse." With drawings in the sand, they studied where their arrows should hit animals and men alike.

Poquis would tell them repeatedly: "Our bows are too weak. Do not waste shots at their metal armor, heavy leather, or quilted jackets. Aim at their faces, arms, and legs."

He urged warriors to capture the strangers' weapons whenever possible.

"Fight the strangers where they are the weakest," Poquis kept reminding his warriors. "Fight them only when you are sure of winning. We will never give up."

# 52

Tristán de Luna y Arellano sent horsemen up the river to all the occupied pueblos. They went to Zia and Jemez to the west and up through the Rio Grande pueblos all the way to Taos. Arellano's men had brought back quantities of tanned buffalo hides to protect them from the coming winter, but other supplies were needed. Other Puebloans knew the example of the conquered Tiwa villages, so the appearance at their walls of armed expeditionaries motivated gifts of food and blankets. The expeditionaries built rafts and floated piles of food and clothing down the river to Coofor—or Alcanfor, as some expeditionaries called the Indian pueblo.

By September, worried about Coronado's failure to return when expected, Arellano led forty horsemen and hundreds of Indian allies back to Pecos. The Pecos people had seemed so willing to help the expedition embark on the plains. But now they attacked. Arellano counter-attacked. With horses, swords, lances, guns, and Mexican Indian allies, he was able to force the Pecos warriors back inside their pueblo after four days of fighting. Arellano's men camped outside Pecos and waited for the general.

Coronado appeared days later, dispirited and empty-handed. The Pecos Indians rejected all demands for food and supplies. Instead they shouted curses and threats from their fortified walls on the ridge top. They accented their anger by firing arrows at any European, Aztec, or Tarascan who came within range.

Pecos was too strong even for a siege. It had its own spring providing water inside and enough stored food to last for years. Its five hundred warriors were more than twice as many as any pueblo yet encountered.

Besides, Coronado had become too weary for another major battle. He told his men they should return to their winter quarters. It was October 2, 1541, when Coronado reached Coofor. Most days and nights were cold, and snow had begun whitening the mountain slopes.

As for Friar Padilla, at every Mass he gave in Coofor he spoke for those who wanted to return to Quivira.

"The Seven Cities must lie beyond Quivira, on the other side of the buffalo prairie," the friar said. "All of you have seen the ancient stone-walled ruins west of us, like the ones we know in Castile. You know they had to have been cities built long ago by Europeans, not by the wretches living here now. The Seven Cities and their Portuguese descendants must be a little farther from where we stopped. At Quivira we met a cacique named Tatarrax with a large copper pendant, which he prized. Beyond Quivira must be all the population and riches of Asia and the Orient, but we did not have time to look. In the spring, we will go back. There is a harvest in souls and riches beyond Quivira."

On their knees, expeditionaries cheered.

Coronado did not share the priest's optimism. On October 20th, in his room at Coofor, Coronado vented his frustration in a letter to the king to be sent by courier to Mexico City. From there, it would go by ship to Spain.

"In this province of Quivira I spent twenty-five days," Coronado wrote, "both to see and ride about the land and to obtain a report as to whether there was anything farther on which might be of service to Your Majesty ... The report I was able to obtain is that there was no gold or other metal in that whole land ... I have done everything I possibly could to serve Your Majesty and to find a land where God, Our Lord, might be served and Your Majesty's royal patrimony might be enlarged."

Coronado said the Tiguex Province with its numerous pueblos remained the best place he had found. Regardless, he said, not even Tiguex was suitable for settlement because it was too cold during winter.

It seemed everything was going wrong.

The man he depended on the most, Field Master Cárdenas, had broken his left arm when his horse fell on him on the buffalo plains. Then Cárdenas had left the expedition to return to Spain because he received news of his oldest brother's death. Every disinherited hidalgo dreamed of somehow claiming the family fortune as the next-born son. Coronado released Cárdenas so he could return to do so.

Adding to Coronado's problems, the Pecos tribe, the most powerful in the region, had become a sworn enemy.

And despite Troyano's earlier prediction that Tiwas would be too afraid to fight any more, the Indians had changed their tactics. No longer fighting from fortified pueblos, their warriors now harassed expeditionaries in hit-and-run guerilla raids. After an attack, they'd retreat to their mountain sanctuaries. The attacks had caused Europeans and Mexican Indian allies to stop venturing into the countryside except in large groups.

Coronado had been forced to lodge a garrison in a rebuilt pueblo on the east side of the river to deter movement of Tiwa rebels on that side. Coofor guarded the west side. Coronado also moved most Mexican Indian allies into pueblos the Tiwas had rebuilt during the summer. His tropical allies needed the re-abandoned villages to protect them from a second winter, which looked as if it were going to be as severe as the first.

Most worrisome were the Towa, Keres, and Tewa pueblos. Seeing the strangers facing a guerilla war in Tiguex and in a weakened condition, they'd stopped or reduced supplies to the expedition despite demands and threats. Even though the various Pueblo tribes often were rivals, Coronado now realized several villages were aligning against him as the common enemy. Coronado suspected they had taken in Tiwa refugees and were supplying the remaining Tiwas in the mountains with provisions they refused to Coronado.

His men said they did not have enough to keep warm. Much of the clothing and blankets they had taken from pueblos the previous winter had worn out or been lost. Food was being rationed. Even officers were complaining.

Several rebuilt pueblos were plundered and dismantled again at the start of the second winter. Horseman Cristóbal de Escobar would later explain why. "Some of the same pueblos that we had burned and laid waste to had been repaired, and we gutted them again, both to make use of the wood and to get the corn and other supplies [the Tiwas] had left buried there ... The company had need of supplies and firewood since we would have died of cold and hunger if it had not been for the supplies and wood that they got from the pueblos repaired and rebuilt."

It seemed everything now depended on destroying the rebels. But winter already had returned, with snow falling again at Coofor. Coronado looked out his doorway toward the mountains. A sheet of snow whitened the air, hiding the mountains from view.

Coronado had not dared to go after the rebels hiding in the mountains for fear of the snow, cold, and enemy's advantages there. Ashamed of his fear, he'd relented. And now he regretted it. An Aztec scouting party Coronado had sent to locate the Tiwa mountain hide-outs had become long overdue in its return.

# 53

As winter intensified with colder temperatures and wind-driven snow in the mountains, Panpahlu's belly swelled with her child. Warmed at their snow-encircled campfire, Poquis and Panpahlu agreed she must leave for the Tompiro villages for the birth, where other women could help her.

They glanced at two warriors crouched in front of a boulder, a high ridge of the mountain rising in pines and snow behind them. "They will take you there in safety," Poquis said.

"And you? Will you remain safe, Poquis, now that the fighting has started again?" The whole camp knew how Poquis had led warriors in a battle with an Aztec scouting party lower in the mountains. Two of the Aztecs had escaped, but eighteen others were killed.

"There will be no more large battles," he said. "We would not have attacked the Aztecs in the mountain meadow if there had been metal people on horses with them. The matriarch sent word they were coming. But from now on, it will be little fights, between very few men. We cannot afford to lose warriors."

"Move the camp after we leave," she said, looking into his eyes. "Then, if any of us is captured, they will not find you no matter how much they torture us."

"You know I will."

"I will miss you," she said. Then, caressing her belly, she added, "*We* will miss you."

Poquis rose and lifted her to her feet. Standing, they embraced. He held her with his hands on her shoulders at arm's length. "You will see," he said. "When you are warm and safe in the village, away from these hardships, your pregnancy will not be so hard for you."

A gust scooped up a cloud of snow and blew it over and around them. It coated them with snow. He held her until she stopped quivering and crying.

—

Poquis looked around at the six men seated in a semicircle before him. The sun priest also sat with them in a sheltered area beneath thick pines. All were older, most of them many years older. He understood the break with tradition it had taken for them to follow him. Yet follow him they had, since that first winter in the mountains. All had been concerned then with caring for their families and finding food and shelter. The sun priest had assigned these men to be his captains. What he had taught them since mid-summer, they had been passing on to their warriors.

There was Shiw-tu, his longtime friend from Tuf Sheur Teui and the closest to his own age. And Banqín from Ghufoor, who had killed two Castilians at Moho. With the sword he brought back, he'd also killed an Aztec leader at the recent mountain meadow fight. The others from different villages were older men and proven leaders of warriors: Huipi, Nahchu-Rúchu, Chiwtamanin, and Parraga.

The sun priest sat cocooned inside a buffalo robe. He watched the men but remained silent. Poquis and he now shared each other's thoughts.

Xauían's defenders of the mesa-top fortresses had tied down Coronado's expedition with their resistance. They had kept Poquis's Tiwas safe from attack in the mountains for the first winter. But now Xauían was dead, and the battle in the meadow made it clear the strangers might come after them in the mountains this winter. Poquis prayed every day for the Creator and Twin Warriors to make him equal to the challenge.

Over the last few weeks, warriors had begun filing down from the mountains in small groups to find opportunities for ambushes. Now the large victory against the twenty Aztecs charged the air with excitement like lightning flashes.

"Remember what we did at the meadow," Poquis told his captains. "Release any warriors of the Christians or metal people who surrender. Once they know they are safe in surrender, they will stop fighting when they are in trouble. Strip them of their weapons and let them go."

Poquis turned to Huipi. "The matriarch and our women at Ghufoor will warn us, as they did when the invaders marched to the meadow. Your men must protect any runner who comes out of the village. Knowing the plans of our enemy is essential."

Mention of the women at Ghufoor reminded him of Panpahlu. Once winter started, most children returned to villages where they had stayed the previous year, but many women had stayed in the mountains with the men to support the resistance with food, shelter, and clothing. Poquis knew he would need women as much as men if he were to succeed. Now Panpahlu had left. In one way, that saddened him, but in another it was a relief because she would be safer in a village for the birth.

They reviewed the success of their tactics so far. They discussed why some failed and others succeeded. Indians from Mexico who guarded the livestock had been careless at first, and Poquis's men were able to kill, wound, or chase off several. They'd gained four sharp-edged maquahuitl weapons before the Christian allies became more cautious.

They had even neutralized the Spaniards' war dogs. As Poquis suspected, once the first dog was wounded, Pedro de Tovar refused to let his dogs go out in the countryside unless they were with large detachments. Poquis was not interested in attacking large groups anyway. As small attacks succeeded, Coronado moved his forces closer to the occupied villages. Best of all, some Keres and Tewa villages had become emboldened by the Tiwas' harassing attacks against the expedition and were refusing to cooperate further with the metal people. The Towa people at Jemez had joined their tribe's people at Pecos in hostility toward the strangers.

Slowly, the expeditionaries were losing their confidence and becoming more miserable in their lice-ridden, freezing frontier outposts.

# 54

Since the previous winter, the young Indian woman named Luisa had been bonding with the Tiwa women captives and learning their language. She was far from her home in Culiacán in northwestern Mexico and had joined the expedition as an interpreter.

More than a hundred Tiwa women were captured in the fall of the two mesa-top fortresses. Luisa had been appointed to supervise the captive women's work because she already knew many words in Tiwa. Now, after a year among the women, she spoke the Tiwa language well.

She paused at the rooftop hatchway to the corn grinding room. A cold winter wind buffeted her. At the roof-hole entrance, she visited with two Tarascan guards she knew. Like her, they were wrapped in buffalo robes against the weather. Then she descended the ladder into the chilly room's dim light.

Twelve Tiwa women were kneeling, their backs to the walls, leaning over the large trough-shaped stones known as metates. They poured kernels onto the stones and then ground them into a powdery meal with an oblong, double-hand-sized stone called a mano. These women and others spent every day grinding corn to feed the expedition's people. An old man sat cross-legged in one corner of the grinding room playing a bird-bone flute for the women as they worked to the music. Children shucked ears of corn from piles in the plaza. Women carried the kernels into the grinding room in large bowls balanced upon braided yucca coils on their heads. Other women carried out the corn meal the same way to be mixed with water and cooked into Puebloan cornbread. Still other Tiwa women and child captives worked to make pottery and clothing. Others accompanied expedition members scouring the abandoned pueblos for firewood and any food they could find.

Sunlight angled into the room from the overhead entrance. Motes of corn dust sparkled as they twirled in the light. The room was cool, but the thickness of the walls held back winter's freeze outside. The stone-on-stone grinding of the corn thrummed as Luisa descended into the room.

The matriarch smiled at Luisa from where she sat on a ledge along one wall. A Spaniard had assigned the old woman to grind corn, hoping to wear her down. It didn't work. The other women ground their share and hers too. They asked the matriarch to sit on the ledge and tell them stories of the ancestors as they worked. She would move to the stone grinders when a Spaniard descended into the room. When Luisa had allowed the old woman's exemption, she gained everyone's trust. The matriarch was a heavy-set woman, her hair grayed by age and her face crisscrossed with deep wrinkles like eroded ravines. Her eyes saw everything. She had never been known to complain. She sat on the ledge, telling stories of the Tiwa people in her brittle voice.

—

The next morning, an hour before the sun could burn the eastern sky into hues of orange and red, Luisa crouched beside a wall, a buffalo robe pulled around her for warmth. She gazed down the steep bank to the river and cottonwood trees along its edges. Was there a movement by the trees? Winter-bare tree branches clicked together in a morning wind. She watched as several boys emerged from the rough shelters of the Tiwa captives' camp. The boys walked along the top of the high bank above the river. They crowded together and pulled apart. Because she'd counted the boys, Luisa realized another small shadow had materialized among them. The boys returned to the camp, and the small shadow left the group and entered the matriarch's brush shelter.

The new day's light brightened the corners of Coofor and the camps of the other Mexican Indians and the Tiwa captives. Luisa still sat beside the wall watching the area come alive. The women filed off to jobs assigned to them each day in the pueblo and surrounding fields. The children poured out sullen. Some were assigned to work while the youngest ones ran about. The boy who had been a small shadow an hour earlier pushed aside the mat of sticks and grass making up the door to the matriarch's brush shelter. Luisa could see him better now. She studied him. He appeared to be eight or nine, but she knew he was at least twelve. He looked so young because he was skinny and short. Small enough for the Castilians to ignore him. He joined other boys as they walked to the fields to glean anything they could find in the crop fields. She rose and followed the boys, listening to them. She remembered how other boys had once ignored the shadow-boy because he was so small. Now they treated him like a hero. Why? She learned his name consisted of Tiwa words meaning Runs Between Legs. What kind of name was that?

She smiled with tightened lips. She thought she knew the shadow-boy's secret.

For the next few days, whenever one of the women lamented about the miseries of the mountain fugitives, Luisa would ask how they knew. She received silence in reply. She asked about Runs Between Legs. His mother and father were killed at Xauían's stronghold, they told her. The matriarch cares for him now. Luisa continued watching the boy every chance she got. She listened to the women talk without seeming to overhear them. Coofor buzzed with rumors that the first Spanish scouting party to the mountains had been ambushed. It was said that another scouting party would be sent out to learn what happened.

It was late on the second night after the boy had returned that two Spaniards, each armed with a sword, admitted Luisa through the gate cut into Coofor's walls. She made her way through the moonlit and snow-covered plaza to a ladder leaning against an interior wall to a second-story rooftop. She paused at the ladder's top when she heard an owl softly hooting. An owl was always a bad omen. Advancing toward a doorway cut into one of the second-story rooms, another Spanish sentry stopped her. The man was hard to see against the wall in the darkness. The sentry pushed aside a crude door and spoke to someone inside. He shut the door and told her to wait.

She shivered against the freezing night-time of the advancing winter. It seemed a long time until she heard an order from inside to the sentry. The guard pushed the door aside again and told her to enter.

As her eyes adjusted to the brighter room with its Spanish fireplace, the occupant came into focus. A tall, thin man stood to meet her, his full beard so black that most of his face seemed to disappear at night. Field Master Tristán de Luna y Arellano, who had succeeded Cárdenas. He motioned to her to sit by the fire. He remained standing, looking down at her.

"Luisa, you are right on time," he said to her in Spanish. "What are the Tiwa women talking about these days?"

Luisa was as comfortable in Spanish as she was in the Tarascan, Nahuatl, and Tiwa languages. It still took her a second to switch her mind to Spanish from the thoughts she had been thinking in Tarascan as she entered.

"They know about the ambush in the mountains," she replied. "They say it was executed by the young warrior Poquis. The one who was learning Spanish from the youth Alonso Álvarez, who used to be the general's standard-bearer. Poquis is the one who went with Hernando de Alvarado to Taos and Pecos and then deserted."

Arellano slammed one fist into the other palm. "I had heard this Poquis was the leader," he said. "I talked to young Álvarez about what kind of man this Poquis is. He said he did not know the Indian very well except to teach him some Spanish. I wanted to question the youth under torture to find out if he could tell me more. But the captain-general would not let me." Arellano shook his head in disgust.

"Somehow they send information back and forth to the mountains. You were right about that."

"I tell you it is that witch, the one they call the matriarch. I would torture her for some answers, but I doubt the old gristle would tell me anything except lies. She's a hard old woman. Killing her would not do us any good either. The other women would just find someone else to spy on us. It would be better to find out how she communicates with this Poquis. That is your job."

"I am trying to find out. They do not trust me and tell me very little."

"Do you think it is the matriarch?"

She paused, as if in thought. "I do not think so. Someone else, I think."

Arellano scoffed. "You are wrong. We are sending another patrol out tomorrow morning, this time with many more horsemen and our Indian allies. We will find this rebel and hang him."

"The mountains are very large. How can you find him?"

Arellano chuckled. "Some of our Indian allies survived an attack in the mountains. I just learned they have returned. You should have been able to find that out for me, but someone else told me. Perhaps, Luisa, your belly has become too full with the extra food I give you. Perhaps I should find someone whose belly growls with hunger to keep me informed. Someone who wants to eat this winter. Think about that. In any case, they will lead a patrol back to the site of the ambush. We'll spread out from there."

"I will try to discover if the matriarch is the spy."

"Yes, you do that, or I will find someone else who will." He picked up a leather sack of dried buffalo meat from the floor and tossed it at her. "Now leave. I am starting to think you are worthless."

Luisa rose and walked out of the room, past the sentry. Her face dropped from view as she descended the ladder. No one could see her grim expression in the dark. She wondered if Arellano would ever realize she told him only what he already knew. Or, sometimes, what she had been instructed to say to him. His predecessor Cárdenas had never seemed to realize what she was up to when he was field master.

She bared her teeth as she remembered. Many warriors on the expedition were Aztecs, long-time enemy of her Cáhita people. And then there were the Castilians, who had killed so many of her people and treated her generation like animals. She had taken a Tarascan warrior for her mate. He soon volunteered for the Coronado expedition. Serving as mercenaries in the Spaniards' wars against other tribes had become the way for Tarascan men to feel worthy in their warrior culture. That cost her husband his life. When water became nonexistent between New Spain and Cíbola, her husband had given what little water he had to her. The Europeans had filed by ignoring her pleas while her husband lay dying of thirst and poisoned by a plant he'd eaten after all food was gone. Later, as she'd mounded sand over the shallow grave of the man she'd loved, her resentment of the bearded men turned into hatred.

Within an hour, the matriarch gave Luisa's information about a new patrol to the mountains to Runs Between Legs. Minutes later, the little shadow-boy slipped between the cottonwood trees along the river and disappeared into the darkness.

—

The small boy looked up at Poquis with a toothy grin. Snow fell in a silent cascade, already filling the boy's tracks along the trail he had climbed to the mountain hideaway. "They are going to the meadow again," he said breathlessly. "Tomorrow. This time with many Castilians on horses. Many of their allies from the south."

Poquis thanked Runs Between Legs and handed him a pottery canteen of water and some thick cornbread. The boy grabbed at the canteen and food with an even bigger grin. Poquis had wondered how long it would take for the Aztecs he'd released to lead the metal people back to the battle site. He thought the metal people would be surprised by what they would find. Perhaps even frightened.

He wondered if Alonso Álvarez would be in the patrol now that he was a militiaman on foot and no longer a standard-bearer on a borrowed horse. Poquis had heard months ago from the captive women that Coronado had replaced Alonso as standard-bearer. They said Coronado became angry over Alonso's refusal to burn Xauían's stronghold and the people in it.

Poquis would like to talk with Alonso again. He regretted that was impossible.

## 55

Alonso Álvarez moved his arquebus's weight from his right shoulder to his left. He looked up at Juan Pastor astride a horse beside him, his lance pointed skyward. Then Alonso looked again at the mountain meadow before them. It lay beneath more than three feet of snow. Twenty lancers on horses, thirty men on foot, and a hundred Aztecs trampled all over the meadow. There were no bodies of men, no dropped weapons.

"Only their ghosts are here," said Juan, shifting in his saddle. He touched his forehead, chest and both shoulders with the sign of the cross.

"Strange," Alonso replied. "Why would the Indians hide all evidence of their victory?"

Several militia men aimed their crossbows and arquebuses up at the boulders strewn over the steep hillside. They whispered to each other.

The scouting party could not go farther. The snow had become so deep that horses and men alike struggled to get through it. Bitter winds numbed the men's faces, hands, and feet. Frostbite threatened everyone. Finally, they turned around, never taking their eyes off the trees around them. Wilderness silence enveloped them.

"Where are you, Poquis?" muttered Alonso as they retraced their steps through the pine forests and along the cliffs.

—

Upon the second scouting party's return, Coronado stood up from his room's camp table and paced back and forth. Captain Barrionuevo stayed behind at Coronado's request after the other officers left.

Coronado stopped and jerked his head up. "The first patrol was supposed to find the rebels, not fight them. Give thanks to God that our friendly Indians said the rebels have just two horses."

Barrionuevo looked worried. "My general, please do not report that."

"Do not worry. There will be nothing about horses in my report. I have told the officers to say nothing. I want a heavy guard on our horses. Keep the men close to camp. I cannot send men to the mountains in the snowstorms, as much as I want to. If we stay together here in Coofor and also in the pueblo across the river, the rebels will be no threat to us."

Barrionuevo shifted from one foot to the other. "But we have a more serious problem in supplies. The other pueblos defy us, saying they cannot spare any more blankets or food. There's no way we can keep that secret, not even from the rebels. Our men satisfy their lust with the Indian women, but at what cost? Our camp is infested with women spies and saboteurs. An ingot of copper for more crossbow points is missing. The Tiwa women captives must have stolen it."

Coronado rubbed his face with both hands. "It's almost December. We can live off our sheep. Repair the clothes and blankets as well as possible. Our immediate need is wood for fires to keep warm. Our axes have brought down the closest cottonwood trees, so Maldonado and Alvarado have been leading their cavalry out to pull beams from the rebuilt pueblos. Each week they need to keep going farther for wood. Two days ago I ordered Captain Maldonado to take his horsemen all the way to Piedras Marcadas Pueblo to drag back wood beams. Now I hear he needs reinforcements because Indians have returned to that pueblo. Perhaps a battle will again energize men who are too discouraged to care any more."

"And the Keres and Tewa tribes who now refuse to aid us?"

"They stay behind their walls, and our threats just embarrass ourselves. Our men become more miserable every day from the cold, the cursed lice, and hardships. Doctor Ramos says many are sick. Our horses are weak from lack of corn and grass. Our men's clothes are rags. Damn your protests, captain, we are in a difficult position here. We need to hang on until spring."

"And then we will return to Quivira?"

Coronado stared at Barrionuevo. "If God wills that winter ever ends. That is when I will decide."

—

Chiwtamanin and Parraga looked down from a third-story tower at the lancers trotting their horses around the village in the dawn's light and staying out of arrow range.

"You were right," Chiwtamanin said as he turned toward his companion. "We should have had men outside each night watching for the metal people. Now they are at our walls without warning."

Parraga growled between gnashed teeth. "Nowhere is safe except the mountains, where these killers do not dare go any more. Poquis feared it would come to this, even so far from

Ghufoor. He told us not to fight from our village walls any more. We came here anyway, and now we are trapped." He looked down into the rectangular open space inside the walls where women and children, who had been freezing in the mountains, now mingled in worried chatter.

"There are not many of them," Chiwtamanin observed. "Perhaps they will leave now that they know we have reoccupied the village. When they go back for reinforcements, we can escape."

Parraga laughed. "You are foolish, Chiwtamanin. They will send someone back alone to bring reinforcements. We will need to fight."

Chiwtamanin's eyes swept around the village from his high vantage point, counting the warriors crouching and laying on the rooftops watching the horsemen. "We do not have enough warriors."

"To win, no. But we have enough to fight."

Chiwtamanin thought aloud, saying they would have one more night behind the walls and then the strangers would have their reinforcements in place. "Escape now is impossible. If we try to run to the river they will run us down and kill us, just as they did to Xauían's people."

Parraga nodded. "And if we surrender, they will burn us at stakes, just as they did to Ishpanyan and the others. Poquis said if we cannot escape, it is better to die fighting."

"They are after the wood beams and ceilings for firewood and for any food that might still be here."

Parraga's hatred darkened his face and burned from his eyes. "And to make slaves of the women and children."

"We will pray tonight to purify ourselves," Chiwtamanin said, as he turned toward the ladder to descend to the roofs and talk to the warriors.

As Parraga had predicted, the next morning there were hundreds of attackers—arquebusiers, crossbowmen, swordsmen, and Mexican Indian allies. The attacking force had moved during the night behind the cover of the ruined walls of a long-abandoned and deteriorating village complex a short distance to the south. At first light arquebus muskets and crossbows began being fired at every Tiwa seen on the rooftops.

Chiwtamanin and Parraga left a handful of men to watch the other sides, but moved most of the defenders to the rooftops and firing loopholes on the south.

"They are planning to attack in one mad rush against the south wall," Chiwtamanin said. "We do not have Xauían's defenses or manpower. We cannot stop them."

Expeditionaries on horseback and on foot along with hundreds of their Mexican Indian allies swarmed from behind the walls of the old village. They raced toward the south wall. The Spanish war cry of "Santiago" echoed through an air ripped with arrows, musket balls, and crossbow bolts. Ladders banged against the wall as sword-wielding expeditionaries and Aztecs with maquahuitls leapt up the rungs. Tiwas ran to the front of the rooftops and pushed ladders aside, sending columns of attackers to the ground. But expeditionaries firing crossbows and arquebuses killed so many that soon there were not enough warriors for all the ladders.

The expeditionaries and their Indian allies gained the rooftops. Tiwa defenders rushed forward. The two forces clashed in a furious turmoil of hand-to-hand combat. Men were clubbed, slashed, and stabbed from all sides as they whirled together. Stone clubs were no match for swords and maquahuitls. Tiwa warriors went down fighting.

The women and children hid themselves in the rooms as the battle spilled into the open area of the village's interior. Parraga died on the rooftop trying to stop the first onslaught. Chiwtamanin and some Tiwa warriors made their last stand in the northwest corner. Not a single man survived.

The women and children were dragged from their hiding places. Standing together, sobbing among the bloody remains of their men, they watched as the strangers dismantled the pueblo. The horses dragged the ceiling beams through freshly fallen snow. Loads of wood branches from the ceilings were piled on the bent backs of the women and children. They were force-marched back to Coronado's headquarters thirteen miles away.

As the expedition grew more desperate for food, clothing, and firewood in a worsening winter, morale became a serious problem. Efforts to obtain food and clothing from other pueblos were becoming less effective while men became sick. Everyone became miserable from lice, the cold, and declining provisions.

Even twenty years later, Castañeda had a vivid memory of the grim circumstances, recalling:

"Necessity knows no law, and the captains who collected the cloth [from pueblos] divided it badly, taking the best for themselves and their friends ... and so there began to be some angry murmuring on this account. Others also complained because they noticed that some favored ones were spared in the work and in the watches and received better portions of what was divided, both of cloth and food. On this account, it is thought that they began to say that there was nothing in the land of Quivira which was worth returning for."

# 56

It was a strange world, Poquis thought, where the stronghold of former enemies was now the safest place to be. He'd returned to Pecos at Bigotes's request. Poquis stood on the roof of the first terrace overlooking the bustling Middle-Heart Place, which he'd learned the Spaniards called a plaza. The rooms and walls of another level rose behind him. On the interior, the rooms had mica windows with doorways opening onto the roof above ground-level rooms. A person could walk all around the village's inside on the roof at the second-story level. Men and women sat along the way, working in sun-warmed areas. They cut hides, chipped obsidian and stones into tools, and painted pottery. Similar activities were taking place in the Middle-Heart Place, where turkeys, small dogs, and children mingled. A winter wind gusted against the outside walls, but Sun Father warmed the protected interior.

"Welcome," Bigotes said, as he climbed a ladder to the roof. He was dressed in a deerskin shirt, leggings, and moccasins with a multi-colored blanket over his shoulders. "I am glad you could come. While your men are obtaining corn meal to take back, we can talk."

Bigotes led Poquis into a room. After he placed more wood on the fire, the flames flared and sent a wave of warmth across them. It was late in the Corn Ripe Moon. Winter already had locked the high country of Pecos in ice and snow, as it also had done in the Tiwas' mountains and the Tiguex country.

They sat on buffalo hides on the floor, facing each other across the fire. Bigotes congratulated Poquis on the baby that Panpahlu was expecting.

"Thank you. We are both excited, for the baby will come soon. Panpahlu had been bothered by pain and cramps. She left the mountains and went to the Tompiro villages. I have not seen her for many suns."

"It will all be well," Bigotes assured him.

Eventually, as always everywhere, the conversation turned to the strangers.

Poquis explained how Alonso Álvarez, when he was still Coronado's standard-bearer and teaching Spanish to Poquis, had talked about the land of the metal people.

"He told me the world is shaped like a ball, as we have believed, and that the metal people live on the opposite side. He said they have metal for many things, not just weapons, so we have named them well. Even if we set many trees one upon another into the sky, the strangers have stone buildings built even higher." Both men's eyes widened at the thought of such architecture. "They worship their God in some of these large buildings. They fight from others. Their entire country is filled with villages much larger than ours. One family lives in each house. They have crop fields everywhere. Their crops are different from ours. They make clothes from cotton and the hair of white animals. They have great herds of the bizarre animals they brought here. They fight many wars with their horses and metal weapons and conquer everyone."

"It is not easy to understand this," Bigotes said. "We thought this was the whole world." He motioned with both arms outstretched. "The strangers seemed to have come from nowhere with their horses, weapons, and large dogs. Their Gray Robes— they are like our priests but with a different God? Why do they put up crosses everywhere they go?"

"Alonso told me the crosses are to talk to their God, who was hung on such a cross in ancient times. But like our Creator, he could not be killed. They talk to their God at the crosses. They do not dance, however, which seems odd to me. Why don't they honor their God and the memory of their ancestors by putting on masks and dancing?"

Bigotes shrugged. "It is a strange religion."

"The old Gray Robe named Luis told me that they believe in one great creator, just like us. Not three like you once told me. But he said their God is three deities in one. I did not understand it."

"But they have many other supernaturals," Bigotes said in an irritated tone, defending his earlier description of the metal people's religion. "They are like our katsinas, although they call theirs saints."

"It seems so," Poquis said. "Some of our women living with them at Ghufoor say they find the new religion interesting. Some are starting to worship the metal people's God."

Bigotes clenched both fists in front of his chest. "We must make the strangers leave if we are ever to have peace. They take our women, mock our religion, and want to destroy us so they can seize our country."

"That is why we need your help in Tiguex."

"What can you do against their horses and metal weapons? Some cover themselves with metal that our arrows break against. Others wear leather and other jackets our arrows cannot penetrate. Their swords and lances prevent our warriors from getting close enough to fight with our clubs. These strangers are cowards."

"No, they are brave men. Think of the hardships and courage it took for them to come so far to find us. To fight them, we must use new tactics. The old ways do not work against enemies such as these."

Bigotes curled his lips. "I heard how you are fighting the strangers from your mountain hideaway. But you are ambushing just small groups, asking other villages to deny them supplies, and depending on your women inside Ghufoor to steal and hide what they can. You are foolish to use such timid measures."

Poquis smiled. "What do you suggest? Should I send my warriors against them in force? Our weapons are inferior and we are outnumbered."

"Without courage, a man's life is not worth living." Bigotes sat erect, his face obscured by the flames and smoke of the fire between them. "We should choose to die like the mountain-king lion in combat. Fierce and unafraid. That is better than sneaking around like Grandfather Coyote just to catch an occasional rabbit."

Poquis raised his chin. "But when many of the metal people came here to wait for their leader called Coronado, what did the brave warriors of Pecos accomplish when they fought like the mountain king?"

Bigotes pulled one end of his long mustache between the forefinger and thumb of one hand and then the other. His eyes narrowed.

"We killed some warriors of the Christians," Bigotes said in a low, menacing tone. "And we wounded some of the metal people. Now they know that fighting men occupy Pecos."

Poquis knew the details. The Pecos men had attacked Arellano's force in the pine and piñon forest around Pecos. He knew how the Pecos buffalo-hide shields proved all but useless against Spanish weapons. The arquebus metal balls, the copper points from crossbows, the horsemen's lances, and the double-edged swords—all of them pierced the shields and killed Pecos warriors. In combat against individual Aztecs, the Pecos men had not fared much better. Even the enemy Indians' maquahuitls were superior to Pecos clubs. Many Pecos warriors and two Pecos war captains had died before the rest retreated to the safety of the village's walls.

Poquis let silence settle into the room as he searched for words. What would persuade Bigotes that wouldn't offend him?

"We cannot fight these strangers as though we are matched," Poquis said. "Even the five hundred warriors of Pecos, more numerous than any other village, still were outnumbered. The warriors of Pecos, brave as they are, found that their arrows, clubs, and spears were no better than sticks and stones against the horrible metal weapons of the strangers."

Bigotes glared at the younger man.

"You have been able to defend your village while all of ours have fallen," Poquis said. "For this, we honor the courage and fighting ability of the Pecos men. For this, we praise you for building such a strong fortress. And for this, we thank you for being able and willing to help us with food and clothing."

Bigotes nodded, unclenching his fists.

Poquis spoke with a firm voice. "Once we were many. We fought the strangers with all our strength from different villages while everyone else watched. Look what happened to us. Now we are reduced to a small band of warriors surviving in the mountains. Many of our people are captives. Many of our remaining women and children are refugees in foreign villages. Yes, it is true we fight like a cornered coyote and not a mountain lion. What choice do we have? But every day the strangers grow weaker. Every day we conserve our strength. The metal people and their Christian warriors still have the most power. But we have the most time."

# 57

Coronado expressed his doubts to Tristán de Luna y Arellano in December 1541.

They had walked together to the edge of the cliff overlooking the river, where no one could hear them talking. Each was wrapped in a buffalo robe against the icy wind that blew across the river at them. The wind whistled as it blew through Ghufoor's open entrance.

"I tell you, Don Tristán, I think it best if we just return to Mexico City in the spring. There is no gold in Quivira. It is more wretched and poor than even Tiguex. The men have lost their spirit. Many want to go home. I think we should leave."

Arellano stared, a look of disbelief on his face. "We have suffered so much," he said carefully, "and some have died. Most of us have gone into debt to invest in this expedition. Unless we find riches or a place with enough Indians to work in encomiendas, all of us face financial ruin. We cannot give up now. We must look farther. Perhaps in a different direction."

"Open your eyes. Look around you at this country. All desert, mountains, and wasteland. Away from the river, you can walk all day and never find water. There is no gold, too little rain to farm, and no real potential for profitable encomiendas this far north. We need to cut our losses, no matter how painful they may be, and return home. There is nothing here for ourselves or the king."

"Viceroy Mendoza will be upset."

"My mind is all but made up. And I already am making plans on how to deal with the viceroy. Call a meeting tomorrow of my council. I will propose to the officers and king's representatives that we circulate a petition for the men to sign. It will ask that we return to Mexico City. With a petition, it will be everyone's decision to return, so what can the viceroy say? We will announce no decision to the men until after Christmas. Better yet, we will announce nothing until after the new year."

"What if the council does not agree?"

"The priests will object. But I assure you everyone else is as sick of this barren country as I am. I already have talked to many, and now to you. I expect your loyalty as my field master."

"But last winter's war, my general, and the hostilities that continue today. Burning Indians at the stake, cutting off noses and hands of prisoners, taking food and clothing by force, burning the pueblos. Certainly the viceroy will disapprove of those actions, even though the savages started the war and deserved the punishment."

Coronado turned and looked in Arellano's eyes. "I do not know what you speak of. I treated the natives here with the greatest possible benevolence, in compliance with what His Majesty ordered. In no way have they received harm from me or from those who have traveled with us. All my reports make this clear. My reports to the viceroy and to the king have emphasized this. They will continue to emphasize that we have treated the Indians well. We did everything possible to find lands to settle and riches. We did all we could to serve God and the king."

# 58

It was a bright and cold morning during the Night Moon as Poquis received the last group of his men reporting on the previous night's actions. He congratulated twenty warriors for ambushing and chasing five Aztecs back inside the strangers' perimeter. No one had been killed or wounded on either side, but his warriors had succeeded in turning back an Aztec evening patrol. As the warriors left, Poquis spotted a runner from the Tompiro villages. A sentry had left the runner standing beside a tall pine. Poquis stood, but his smile faded as he saw the dark look on the runner's face. The runner stared at the ground as Poquis approached.

"I weep for you, Poquis," the runner said, raising his tear-stained face. "Panpahlu walks with the ancestors now. The women did all they could. Panpahlu and your son both died during the birth."

The news struck Poquis like a club. He fell to his knees in the snow. He felt numb. His vision went blank. He heard a raven screeching in a tree. His thoughts raced. He should have gone with her. He should have been with her. Why should they keep resisting the strangers? Death and suffering had been the result. Ishpanyan had been right. They should have fought sooner, before the strangers became so strong. Ishpanyan was among the first to die. And then Xauían, who had sacrificed himself so other Tiwas could escape. His two best war captains, Parraga and Chiwtamanin, and many warriors had died in action. Eye-Black Leader and many other elders had starved. More than a hundred of their women and children were captives. And now Panpahlu was gone. And their baby. How could he deserve to live when so many others had died?

Poquis staggered to his feet. Turning his back on the camp, he walked farther into the dark and snowy mountains. He would pray at the shrine of the Warrior Twins. But the strength he had found there in the past, he no longer believed was possible.

—

In February 1542, Coronado went horseback riding along the west bank of the river with Rodrigo de Maldonado. They decided to race each other back to Coofor. The horses' hooves roiled puffs of dusty snow behind them as they galloped at full speed along the high cliff over the river. Men watched the approach from Coofor and began cheering the riders as Coronado edged into a small lead. Onward the two men raced, bending over their mounts, shouting and spurring the straining horses.

Suddenly the girth snapped on Coronado's saddle. The general tumbled under the pounding hooves of Maldonado's horse galloping close behind. Men rushed from Coofor and carried their unconscious general on a litter to the pueblo.

An eyewitness reported that Coronado's injuries included a severe blow to his mouth. It resulted in a great swelling that had to be cut open.

After he awoke a day later, still stunned and disoriented on his camp cot, Coronado became tormented by a memory of an astrologer he'd met before the expedition started. The astrologer had predicted Coronado would be injured in a fall from which he would never recover.

A fear seized Coronado's heart and mind that he would never see his family again.

Castañeda would later explain what the men began to think was the real reason for the expedition returning to New Spain. He would write, "This mental image [by the astrologer] of his death gave him the desire to go back to where he had a wife and children to die."

———

A sixteen-year-old who had become a man on the expedition, Alonso Álvarez walked his rounds of guard duty in the freezing night with Juan Galiveer. A glow from the smoldering wick of the matchlock on Alonso's arquebus cast a faint light on his face that night as they tromped around Coofor's walls on top of the packed snow. It was February 16, 1542, and a cold wind numbed their faces. The river lay frozen into stillness at the bottom of the cliff.

As they rounded one corner, a Spaniard came down a ladder and stopped them. He said the horseman Juan Jiménez was sick and dying. He needed another witness for his will.

Leaving Galiveer to continue the watch, Alonso climbed the ladder. He descended through the rooftop opening into the room where Jiménez lay.

The room was cold and dimly lit by candles, whose waxy scent enveloped Alonso after leaving the clear air outside. Jiménez was covered with a buffalo robe and shivering. His hair was greasy and matted and his beard untrimmed. He had been ill for several days. He looked up at Alonso with droopy, red-rimmed eyes.

"Sir," Jiménez said in a raspy voice to Alonso, "you are to serve as witness since there is no royal notary in the camp on this side of the river. Because I feel very ill and think that I will not survive until morning."

A man handed Alonso a sheet of paper and an ink-wet quill. It was Jiménez's will, dictated to one of the other men. The ink on the quill was already starting to freeze, but Alonso managed to sign it.

When Alonso returned to the room just before dawn, Jiménez had died.

On February 18, the expedition's public crier, an African named Pedro, served as auctioneer for the deceased's property. He accepted promissory notes for two half-starved horses, a lance, a sword, two old saddles, and clothes that were little more than rags. In the next few weeks, other members of the expedition died, including another Spaniard, Jorge Báez.

# 59

In March 1542, a guard admitted Arellano. Juan Troyano accompanied him into Coronado's room at Coofor. The guard stepped back outside and closed the door. Coronado lay on his bed against one wall. Six guttering candles stood on a table beside him and lit the room. The stale smell of a sickroom mingled with the scent of melted candle wax.

Coronado turned a gaunt face toward the men at the sound of their arrival. "Who comes?" he asked in a weak voice.

Arellano and Troyano stepped more into the light and identified themselves.

"What do you want?"

"General, the men are worried about you after all this time of your illness." Arellano's face showed his concern. "Some of the officers and men have changed their minds and now want to stay, in spite of the petition they signed to return to New Spain."

There was a long silence before Coronado answered. "How many?"

"Juan Jaramillo influences a few captains, as well as about sixty men. They want to stay until the viceroy can send them reinforcements or until they are recalled. They want the petition voided because they no longer agree with it."

"Damn the insubordination!" Coronado raised his head but collapsed back onto his pillow. "The council decision to return to Mexico City and report to the viceroy still stands. The petition remains in force. I have their signatures. I have hidden the petition. I do not go out of my room, which is guarded at all times. Do you think I am not aware that someone already has tried to steal it? No one stays. We all return together."

"Francisca de Hozes and her fool of a husband want to stay here as settlers with their son. What are we to say to them?"

"I will tell you what to say. Tell Alvarado to rebuild a gallows like the one we had last winter to threaten Bigotes and the cacique. Tell these trouble-makers that the ones who stay will be the ones I hang." Coronado gasped for breath. "Send Captain Jaramillo to me. I will deal with him."

"Friar Padilla and Brother Luis also refuse to return to Mexico City with us. Friar Padilla wants to go back to Quivira. Brother Luis wants to minister to the Indians at Pecos."

"I cannot tell these Franciscans what to do. I am sure they will receive the martyrdom they desire. Give them what companions they need. But everyone else goes back. We all go together. Be mindful that the viceroy ordered me not to take any slaves. So no one can take back any Tiwa women and children captives. I am sick of this Tiguex. We all face financial ruin."

"But general—"

"No more discussion. Leave, for I am not feeling well."

The two men bowed and left. As they walked into Coofor's plaza, Troyano grabbed Arellano's arm and held him back. Troyano scowled. "The general is better fit to govern that room than the expedition."

Arellano's eyes narrowed. "I will forget you said that. This time. Truth, the general is incapacitated. That is why everyone will follow my orders. I will carry them out as I think the general wishes. Anyone who defies me could hang from that same gallows the general wants me to remind Francisca de Hozes about."

"I married a Pueblo woman. She is not my slave, my servant, or my mistress. She is my wife. We love each other. I will not leave her behind."

Arellano sighed. "Tell no one else," he said. "And keep her out of the general's sight for as long as possible. You are the only exception I will make. I warn you, Juan. If you encourage anyone else, then she will stay behind no matter how much I respect you."

"What about the Aztec chieftain, Tlecanen? I hear he has a Tiwa captive. He is probably not the only one secretly taking someone back to Mexico."

Arellano glared at Troyano and looked around to make sure no one else had heard. "I know nothing of what you speak about. Do not speak of it again."

Troyano was not a man easily intimidated. He shrugged and said Arellano faced a rebellion among his own Spaniards. "Juan Jaramillo is not the only dissenter," he said. "Many oppose our abandonment of this country after all we have gone through."

Arellano started to walk away. Then he stopped and turned back to Troyano. "That is why I need men to stand by me. With their swords, if necessary. For this favor I grant with your wife, I expect you to be one of them."

—

Two years later, an expedition member testified to the hardships of that second winter in Tiguex Province, saying: "Some Spaniards fell ill and were dying because of the great cold and many hardships they endured and because they had few medicines and little clothing. And many horses died. Also, the food was running out, without anywhere to get more. Furthermore, Mass was not being said in the camp, nor was there anyone to say it."

Castañeda reported that Coronado "tried" to requisition more blankets from the Keres and Tewa pueblos "because the soldiers were almost naked and poorly clothed, full of lice, which they were unable to get rid of or avoid."

The expedition was dying from within. Men began cursing Coronado's name for having brought them to such God-forsaken country. Many discarded their respect for Coronado as if it were trash. "[The nobles and officers] did not obey the general as had been their habit," Castañeda said. "And he was disliked by them."

Matters continued to deteriorate until Coronado had little authority. He would finish much of his trip back to Mexico ill and traveling with guards.

## 60

Well enough to talk to his officers but still bedridden, Coronado learned of the surprise return of García López de Cárdenas in late March. He summoned Cárdenas to his bedside.

Cárdenas arrived, the left arm he'd injured on the buffalo plains still in a sling. On his way back to claim his family's inheritance, he said, he'd gone as far as San Gerónimo in northern Mexico. There he found the Indians at war. The garrison Coronado had left to hold the rear area was destroyed with its men dead or scattered. The uncle of Coronado's wife, Diego Gutiérrez de las Caballería, was among the dead. Cárdenas feared fighting could spread as far south as the province that Coronado governed. He'd returned as fast as he could to alert Coronado.

Coronado made his decision and struggled to find the words to express it because of his head's pain. He told Cárdenas how he'd convinced his officers and men to sign a petition calling for a return to New Spain. Viceroy Mendoza could not object very much if the entire expedition had asked to return. Besides, it no longer was a question of whether they should continue seeking their fortunes in the north or looking for a passage to Asia. Now they must go home and help put down an Indian rebellion.

Everyone in the expedition rendezvoused at Coofor on April 1, 1542, for the trip home. All faces turned to the west. They would return to Cíbola, the province of their first disappointment, then angle southwest on the exhausting return trip. It would take months, and everyone worried about the horses, weakened from an unknown ailment.

—

Galiveer and Alonso prepared to join the westward line of expeditionaries as they stood outside the walls of Coofor. "Well, boy, we're going home whether we want to or not," Galiveer said.

"Good," Alonso said. "There are no Seven Cities. And even though we are in Asia, it is obvious that China and India are still too far away. We never should have wasted our time coming here."

"I have plenty of time to waste. It is the money I am going to miss. I spent everything I had to equip myself for this expedition. What do I have to show for it now? My clothes are ripped and worn. All I have left is my sword."

"Is that why you wanted to stay?"

"Truth. Here I might still have a chance. In Mexico City I will be in poverty."

Alonso turned to look behind them at the river and mountains. The ducks, cranes, and geese had flown north. Now there were flocks of small birds chirping and pecking where corn meal had spilled on the ground between clumps of melting snow. The wind felt balmy on his face. He had even seen a butterfly, brown with a yellow stripe along the trailing edge of its wings, fluttering between the still bare branches of cottonwood trees the previous day.

Alonso turned back to Galiveer. "The general is not allowing anyone to stay here except some Indians going with the Franciscans. I heard you volunteered to stay behind with either Friar Padilla or Brother Luis." Alonso grinned. "I did not know you were so interested in converting the Indians."

"Hah! Even that would be better than going back to New Spain a debtor. But Brother Luis prefers being by himself at Pecos. He says he goes to bring the peace and love of Jesus to the Indians. As for Father Padilla, he is returning to Quivira because he wants to keep looking for the Seven Cities."

"Ah, so that is why he is taking the lancer Andrés do Campo and his horse. Campo is Portuguese, and Father Padilla thinks they still will be speaking Portuguese in the Seven Cities."

Galiveer snorted to show his contempt. "The friar is a fool, I tell you. The Seven Cities do not exist—at least not anywhere around here." He turned to Castañeda, who had walked up to them. "Ask him."

Alonso turned to Castañeda. "Yes, what do you think?"

"Our English friend is right," Castañeda replied. "We should have gone northwest. Then we would have found India and China. Instead the general kept leading us to the east. Nothing is there except his mirage of Quivira and a prairie that goes on forever."

"We are all returning bankrupt," Galiveer said. He looked toward a group of expeditionaries who had begun picking up their gear. Others had already started their long walk west in small groups.

"I wish you and I could remain here with the others who want to stay," Castañeda said to Galiveer. "Many of us would rather take our chances here. What can we look forward to now except fighting more Indians in rebellion back home? Well, we will do what we must." Castañeda left to mount his horse.

Alonso hoisted his arquebus off his shoulder and settled the gun's stock on the ground. "Here comes the general now," he said, pointing toward Coofor.

Four Aztecs came around a corner of the pueblo carrying Coronado on a litter made of a buffalo robe stretched between two poles. García López de Cárdenas walked on one side of the general and Diego Lopéz on the other.

"Look at our leadership," Galiveer said. "The general lays on a litter. Don García has a crippled arm. And is Diego Lopéz our fourth field master? I am losing count." He shrugged. "The general pretends to be sick to force us to go back. Rich men have weak blood. My mother used to hit me harder than the horse of Don Rodrigo hit him."

Coronado's litter was hoisted and tied between two mules. The animals were linked together by wood stocks so they could neither move apart nor toward each other.

Amid shouts of men leading and riding half-starved and sick horses, the expedition began filing toward the west. Horsemen and hundreds of Mexican Indian allies led the way.

Tiwa women and children, freed from their bondage, lined outside the walls.

Luisa came out of a room where she'd been hiding and stood with them. "I have nothing to return to," she explained to the Tiwa women who'd grown fond of her. "Some of the Aztecs and Tarascans also are planning to desert at Cíbola and stay in this country."

When the last of the expedition began moving westward, some Tiwa women cried. Others scowled or shook their fists. Many women held light-skinned infants in their arms, some with reddish-brown or golden-brown hair. They called their babies "Children of the Moon." Others were pregnant.

Little girls clung to their mothers. Several boys picked up stones and threw them at the backs of the departing metal people.

# 61

Poquis was surprised. The matriarch had not been able to send Runs Between Legs in time to tell Poquis of the expeditionaries' departure. The decision must have been made at the last minute. Perhaps it depended on the weather or Coronado's health. Camp spies had reported Coronado was very sick. In the morning Poquis looked down from the heights and saw the strangers congregating at Ghufoor and departing in a long line westward.

"They are leaving," Shiw-tu declared. "They are finally leaving."

"I cannot believe it," Banqín said. "Our women with them did not think the metal people would leave this soon."

Standing on each side of Poquis, both warriors reached out and slapped Poquis on the back. They laughed. Shiw-tu said it again, wanting to hear it once more. "They are finally leaving."

Banqín gripped the hilt of his sword. "Now they are weak," he said through gritted teeth. "I have talked to warriors from other villages. We are agreed. We can attack them while they are spread in a long line. Fight them all the way back to where they came from."

"No," Poquis said. "The warriors can follow, but only to watch. Our goal is to rid our country of them. Send runners to the Zunis to alert them. Shiw-tu and I will follow them on the horses until we are certain they are leaving and not just relocating."

—

Poquis and Shiw-tu rode the Tiwas' two horses. Warriors from the pueblos stayed hidden on mesas or mountains on each side. Poquis and Shiw-tu followed a trail marked with horse carcasses across the desert. They stopped and mourned each horse they encountered. Their own horses had turned their initial fear of the animals into affection.

"This is the end," Poquis said, as they stood over another dead horse sprawled before them. "Both our horses are males. I do not know how long they live, but when they are gone..."

He left the rest unsaid. They remounted their horses and continued behind the expedition's retreat. They caught up with the expedition at the Zuni towns but stayed out of sight. After a few days, the expedition started again, now angling southwest. Poquis and Shiw-tu watched from a distance as Zuni men walked up to the expedition's rear, urging warriors of the Christians to stay. Whenever one agreed, the Zunis would shout with celebration, lifting the foreign warrior onto their shoulders and carrying him back to their towns. The rest of the expedition plodded onward. No one seemed to care.

Coronado's men trudged through the mountain pass where two years earlier they'd chased away several Zunis. Then they descended onto a rolling desert terrain with small hills that led to mountains. Poquis and Shiw-tu urged their horses into a gallop, riding along the expedition's route while remaining concealed behind the hills. When they stopped, they could hear the expedition's clomp of men's feet and horses' hooves. Clouds of dust rose over a hill.

"Hold the horses in case the metal people try to come after us," Poquis told Shiw-tu. "I want to see them leave forever."

Poquis climbed to the hill's top. There he stood and watched the expedition passing. He was just close enough to pick out Alonso Álvarez walking with two other men, all of them carrying arquebuses over their shoulders. Somehow Alonso must have sensed Poquis's presence. He stopped and looked at Poquis, who stood silhouetted against the sky.

The two other arquebusiers saw Poquis too. They propped their guns onto their forked support poles, aimed them at Poquis, and scrambled to light their matchlock fuses. Alonso lowered his arquebus stock to the ground. Poquis could hear him arguing with the other two men. Those men lowered their guns, cursed at Alonso, and stalked off. For a long minute, Alonso and Poquis looked at each other while other metal people rode their horses or walked around the teenaged Castilian.

Then Alonso turned to follow the rest, a gray figure in a haze of dust, heading for the horizon. Poquis turned and descended the hill back to Shiw-tu.

———

Tiwas came down from the mountains. Others returned from the outlying villages that had been their winter sanctuary. They gathered in and around the ruins of a dozen villages. Many Tiwas, young and old, had died. The children were hungry. Great sacrifices had been made, and the women wept every night.

At his home of Ghufoor, Poquis held his grief close to his heart for Panpahlu and the son he would never know. The sun priest, wearing a tattered turkey-feather robe with missing feathers, walked toward Poquis. He clasped his wrinkled, browned hands on Poquis' shoulders. They would rebuild. They would replant. The katsinas would return now.

They would not see another Spaniard for nearly forty years.

# PART VII – CHARGES OF WAR CRIMES
## 1544 – 1546

## 62

No Tiwa survivors would ever learn of it. However, in the 1540s the Spanish legal system filed charges of war crimes against Francisco Vázquez de Coronado and his field master, García López de Cárdenas.

The charges came out of tireless efforts by Dominican Friar Bartolomé de las Casas. His eloquence against Spanish brutalities led to Spain adopting "The New Laws of the Indies for the Good Treatment and Preservation of the Indians" in 1542. The New Laws required the courts to "inquire continuously into the excesses and ill treatment which are or shall be done [to Indians] by governors or private persons."

At about that same time, the Coronado Expedition returned with tales of warfare against natives they'd encountered. It must have seemed a direct challenge to the New Laws' moral authority.

The Spanish monarch Carlos appointed Lorenzo de Tejada to investigate complaints about crimes committed by the Coronado expedition. Tejada was a judge with the royal *Audiencia of Nueva España*. It exercised legislative and judicial authority in Mexico City. Tejada's commission stated that "in the expedition which Francisco Vázquez de Coronado made to the province of Cíbola, he and the Spaniards who went with him committed, both going and returning, great cruelties upon the natives of the land through which they passed."

Tejada began his forty-day investigation of the expedition's conduct in mid-1544, about two years after Coronado returned.

Tejada accused Coronado of ordering the wanton execution of Indians in Mexico where Lope de Samaniego had been killed, using poor judgment that cost many Spaniards their lives in the Mixtón War that erupted in Mexico while he was gone, attacking Hawikku without military justification, setting dogs on Bigotes and other Indians, ordering Turk executed in secret, and abandoning Tiguex Province with the Indians still at war.

Underscoring everything was the belief that Coronado had wasted his investors' money. Resentment simmered about the expedition's failure to find riches.

In regard to the Tiguex War, the Audiencia charge read:

"He [Coronado] reached the province of Tiguex, which was heavily settled and had much food and many structures built like those in Spain. The people came forth in peace, rendered obedience to His Majesty, and fed everyone in the army corn, poultry, and other foodstuffs. When they were at peace and without legitimate cause the general and his captains, by his order, set dogs on the leaders of that pueblo and its neighbors...

"Because of this, the leaders and people of those pueblos rebelled and rose up in arms. In waging war again, the Spaniards destroyed and burned many pueblos. In others, the Indians fortified themselves, as they do in that province. Though they had been at peace, they returned to war and are so to this day. In response, the Indians killed many Spaniards and everyone was on the verge of being lost."

Coronado fought back by generally denying everything. He was protected by friends in Mexico City and by Viceroy Antonio de Mendoza, whose own office could be at stake if his general were convicted.

Nevertheless, testimonies from several expedition members contradicted Coronado's version of events. Among those who provided incriminating testimony against Coronado were some of the men closest to him. They included his personal aide, Pedro de Ledesma; his head groom, Juan de Contreras; and some officers.

Alonso Álvarez, who had been Coronado's standard-bearer as a teenager and also a former member of Coronado's household staff, provided the most damming testimony at odds with the general's account.

Alonso appeared before the Audiencia in September 1544. He testified that he was certain Coronado ordered the dogs set on Bigotes; it was public knowledge Villegas had raped the Pueblo woman and so Coronado must have known as well; Alonso had heard Coronado order all abandoned pueblos be destroyed; he knew Coronado ordered Cárdenas to burn the Arenal captives alive at the stake; and he was certain Coronado ordered dogs set upon some Indians captured at Moho and to have the hands and noses cut off others.

Just two days earlier, Coronado had denied such atrocities. He'd also denied other expedition members' accounts of events. He claimed his officers did not keep him informed. He sometimes declared he could not remember details.

After testimony by Alonso and others, the court placed Coronado under house arrest in February 1545. He remained confined to his house for the year of the investigation.

In the end, however, Coronado's word carried the day. Viceroy Mendoza was among the five legislator judges of the Audiencia who absolved Coronado of all charges in February 1546.

Cárdenas, charged in Spain with war crimes, would be judged more harshly than Coronado was in a more sympathetic Mexico City.

Even before Coronado's case ended, the Audiencia's prosecutor forwarded the investigatory file with testimonies to Spain. He maintained that, as second in command to Coronado, Field Master Cárdenas also was culpable. Juan de Villalobos, the prosecutor for the king's Council of the Indies, ordered Cárdenas arrested in January 1546. He imprisoned Cárdenas in the fortress of Pinto, south of Madrid.

By then a noble of high privilege and wealth upon inheriting his father's estate, Cárdenas spent the next three months in prison until being transferred to a rigidly enforced house arrest that April. The case, drawn out with appeals by Cárdenas, would not be concluded for five and a half years.

The charges were more detailed against Cárdenas than they had been against Coronado. That was because of new information acquired through other expeditionaries' testimonies in Coronado's case.

The Council of the Indies accusation against Cárdenas regarding the Tiguex War read, in part:

"On this journey, both on the way forth and back, the said defendant and the Spaniards whom he took in his company perpetrated robberies, burnings, cruelties, and many other offenses against the native Indians of the lands through which they passed, killing a large number of them, taking their women by force and against their will and that of their husbands and parents, lying with them carnally. He apprehended other Indians, unleashing vicious dogs to attack them, taking by force the food and clothing they had to maintain their lives. He drove the Indians from their homes when they had received him peacefully and had given him willing of what they had. They inflicted upon the said Indians much bad treatment, wherefore by necessity, in order to defend themselves against them, the Indians revolted. The defendant and the Spaniards and soldiers that he brought with him besieged the said Indians and attacked and fought them by fire and sword. In this war the Spaniards burned twelve or thirteen pueblos belonging to the said Indians...

"This was all through greed of getting gold and silver ... The said defendant caused and perpetrated many other bad abuses, injuries and cruelties against the Indians. For this reason the said Indians rebelled and ceased to be friendly and peaceful, and the discovery, pacification, and settling of the land was abandoned, and the propagation of our holy Catholic faith hindered, whereby God, our Lord, and your Highness were very poorly served."

In 1549, the Council of the Indies convicted Cárdenas of brutalities against the Indians, including the burning of Arenal's defenders at the stake. Cárdenas appealed, still under house arrest. The Council reaffirmed its finding in 1551. The Council fined Cárdenas and sentenced him to a year in the king's service without pay at Vélez-Málaga near the Mediterranean coast.

Cárdenas would be the only person convicted and punished for the expedition's conduct.

Hernando de Alvarado was almost swept up in the investigation. He had taken Bigotes and the cacique by force from Pecos Pueblo, had sicced one or more dogs onto Bigotes, and been in the vanguard of other abuses. In February 1545, when Coronado was placed under house arrest, Tejada summoned Alvarado to appear before the Audiencia, saying charges should be brought against Alvarado too. But Alvarado was never prosecuted.

Despite Coronado's acquittal, his expedition was considered a failure. The Mexican historian and jurist Matías de la Mota y Padilla observed two hundred years later in a report to the king: "It must have been the punishment of God that they did not find ... riches on this expedition, because this ought to have been the secondary object of that journey and the first the conversion of all those heathen. But they pushed aside the first and coveted the second."

In 1554, eight and a half years after his acquittal, Coronado died of a contagious disease in Mexico City. He was forty-three. Alvarado, who was almost charged with war crimes, had died four years earlier at age thirty-two. Cárdenas died nine years after Coronado, at age fifty.

Alonso Álvarez, who had been fifteen when the expedition started and was barely twenty when he testified against Coronado, settled in western Mexico. By 1576 he had become a leading citizen of San Sebastián, now known as Concordia. He never returned to New Mexico's Pueblo country.

The numerous contingents of Mexican Indian allies who accompanied the expedition suffered casualty rates of 30 percent or more as they bore the brunt of hardships and assisted

Spaniards in the fighting. Some also deserted to return on their own or stay at the pueblos.

Today, almost five centuries after Coronado, the Tiwas still remain on parts of their original homelands in the pueblos of Taos, Picuris, Sandia, and Isleta. They and fifteen other pueblos of the Hopi, Zuni, Keres, Towa, and Tewa nations still remain on or near where Coronado's expedition found them. Another, San Felipe Pueblo, did not exist in 1540.

Four Spanish-led expeditions of a few men each would briefly revisit Pueblo country starting in 1581. It would be fifty-six years after Coronado's withdrawal before the Spaniards would come to stay. When that happened in 1598, Juan de Oñate y Salazar brought men and women settlers more in line with Alonso Álvarez's temperament.

That year, Oñate met with only one Tiwa leader—a respected elder named Poquis.

# ACKNOWLEDGMENTS

As historical narrative, this book is based on fact and on plausible scenarios to fill in the historical gaps. It would not have been possible without standing on the shoulders, as it were, of research giants in the fields of archaeology, anthropology, ethnography, and history.

Readers who are interested in sources and more historical background can download the book's historical notes at http://tinyurl.com/d7wfb69.

I am grateful for a research grant in the early stages of writing the book from the Institute for American Indian Research.

It struck me in my research how different our traditional history would be if, over the last five centuries, native people of the Americas had written it instead of their conquerors.

A history written by Indians would elevate Xauían, Bigotes, and Turk to a pantheon of heroes. As an example, an exhibit at the Indian Pueblo Cultural Center in Albuquerque refers to Turk in the following way: "We [Puebloans] were able to find a man to steer [Coronado's expeditionaries] to Kansas to search for gold and riches, but they soon realized that these could not be found, so they killed our friend."

Instead of being heroes, all three of these Native patriots have been depicted in Spanish records and American history books as treacherous villains.

No one knows the real names of Bigotes and Turk. As for Xauían, when he is remembered at all, he's almost always referred to by the incongruous nickname the Spanish gave him of Juan Alemán, which meant "John the German." Anonymity remains for most other native leaders during the first century of the conquest.

The efforts of Xauían, the Tiwa from the pueblo known as Ghufoor; Bigotes, a leader of Pecos; and Turk, a captive Pawnee from the Great Plains, are three major reasons the Coronado expedition failed to establish a foothold in the American Southwest. Those men, and the Indian resistance leaders personified by Poquis, frustrated the Spanish effort.

Pablo Abeita, an Isleta Pueblo leader, summed up the Puebloans' eventual plight in 1916, stating: "The white people came into this country without our invitation. We admired them, we feared them, we had reason to be afraid of them. They were big men, had big things. They appropriated our land without asking for it. We did not know what to do. We protested against them, but they were stronger and much more in number. They rounded us up, they settled around us, took our land, our hunting ground, our water, and all they could lay hands on."

Pueblo Indians have survived rule by the Spaniards, the Mexicans, and the Americans. They live in many of the pueblos where their ancestors encountered Coronado, still performing traditional dances, holding on to their ancient religion in syncretism with Christianity, selling their arts, and exerting a major influence on New Mexico culture, tourism, and architecture.

Quoting again from the Indian Pueblo Cultural Center in Albuquerque: "Our firm Pueblo beliefs and traditions have enabled us to keep our cultural heritage while many of the world's native peoples have lost theirs to the dominant culture of their conquerors."

For this book, a special note of appreciation is due to Coronado expedition scholars Richard Flint and Shirley Cushing Flint. Their research has discovered many previously missing documents. They have clarified the history that's often been distorted by nearly five hundred years of retelling only the sixteenth-century conquistador point of view. They have written several books on the Coronado expedition, all of which this author relied on extensively in writing this book. This book would not have been possible without their research, documentation, translations, and advice.

Also invaluable were the writings on the expedition and its time by ethnohistorian Carroll L. Riley. A retired Midwestern professor, he is a pre-eminent scholar on sixteenth-century New Mexico.

Several people encouraged me over the years to tell the previously unwritten Puebloan viewpoint of the Coronado expedition. They read early drafts of chapters or the entire manuscript, gave me advice, or provided exceptional encouragement. Such people included my writers group of Fred Bales, Jim Belshaw, Bob Gassaway, and Margaret Parks, and my immediate family of Michael Herrick, Jennifer Gage, Alec Laughlin, and Michael Howard.

Others included artist Persingula Tafoya of Kewa Pueblo, Susan M. Boe, Stanley Robb, Ken and Gail Boring, John Byram, Roger Van Noord, Richard Schaefer, Ilia Rodríguez, David E. Stuart, Dick Pfaff, Jane Lindskold, James L. Moore, Christopher

Sanchez, Elizabeth Belshaw, Kathleen Phelan, Tony Catalanotto, Brian and Carolyn Gilmore, Jack and Deborah Ellis, Karolyn Cannata-Winge, Todd Winge, Jim Du Bruille, H. Bert Jenson and too many others to count.

Special thanks are owed to a renowned Puebloan historian, the late Joe S. Sando of Jemez Pueblo. He graciously read this book's early draft and encouraged me to continue.

Any errors or misconceptions despite their advice and my years of research are my fault alone.

This book would not have been possible without many others, including Lawrence Knorr, owner and editor of Sunbury Press, copy editor Allyson Gard, as well as Amy G. Johnson and Marth Becktell of the Indian Pueblo Cultural Center in Albuquerque.

Most especially for her patience and support, I thank my wife Beatrice.

Made in the USA
Charleston, SC
05 March 2014